Heartwood
(Book 7)

By Lea Carter

ISBN 978-0-9989678-4-4

Cover photo by Michael Jastremski
(https://openphoto.net/gallery/image/view/5238)
Photo has been altered per project specifications.
Cover illustrations and design by Daniel Manfredini

Learn more about the author at
leacarterwrites.wixsite.com/wholesomefantasy

"Same old same old," Prince Isaac mused as the windship *Zelkova* entered the Mists. He exhaled sharply to clear his nostrils of the smoke and ash that filled the air around him and tugged the kerchief tied around his neck up and over his nose. Slipping on a pair of goggles, he grinned at what he could still see of his old friend Sir Stuart. "The Wood Fairy Tribe, keeping Fairydom safe from danger."

"With a little help from the three other fairy tribes," Stuart remarked, smacking him lightly on the shoulder. This was the first time in recorded history that the four tribes had all come together to fight against the pirates.

"Can't leave them out when they're the ones who figured out the pirate build-up in the first place." Isaac folded his arms across his chest, trying to ignore the way the gray and white nothingness was making even the mainmast he was leaning against difficult to see. "Awaiting your orders, Captain!" Isaac shouted over the rapidly increasing roar of the Mists. Nobody really knew the source of the Mists, and he idly wondered if that mystery would be solved on this mission. He jerked with surprise when the captain responded from right beside his elbow.

"I wish you would reconsider going, Your Highness. The visibility couldn't possibly be worse, not if I put a bag over your head. And my own gun crews can't hear their gun captains over this infernal roaring." Thank goodness they all had their safety lines secured before they entered the Mists. Going overboard in this mess would be a death sentence.

"The pirates will never know what hit them." Isaac clapped the captain on what he thought was his shoulder. The captain promptly crumpled to the deck. "Captain?"

"Look out!" Stuart jerked Isaac away from the mainmast a heartbeat before something struck it with a sickening thud.

"Pirates on deck!" Isaac shouted at the top of his lungs. Stuart had already found a "dancing" partner, so Isaac jerked his belt knife free and cried, "Down with pirates!"

As expected, a shadowy figure appeared before him. Parrying on instinct alone, Isaac felt the blade of his knife shoving another weapon aside. Stepping into the gap between them, he swung his left hand at just above shoulder level, so that it connected solidly with his opponent's head. A terrible scream followed the moment of silence and Isaac shuddered. Giving his own safety line a sharp tug to make sure it was securely attached, he shouted again.

"Down with pirates!" The cry was coming from all over the main deck now, their rallying cry, the very way they had intended to keep from fighting with each other after transferring to a pirate windship. Except somehow they'd never expected the pirates to get the jump on them.

"Down wid landlubbers!" a deep voice roared from Isaac's right.

Again Isaac moved on instinct, the hairs on the back of his neck rising as most of a full-length sword slid along his knife, both blades noisily protesting. He took a fist in the gut next, and dropped as silently as he could to the deck, rolling sideways too late to avoid the searching swing of his enemy's blade. Isaac felt his hindwing tearing as he completed his maneuver.

The *Zelkova* shuddered beneath him, probably the result of cannonballs bouncing off her exceptionally thick sides. She'd been built for battle and seemed to be shaking with mirth at the pirates' efforts—until Isaac heard something hit the rigging above him.

He looked up, forgetting for a moment that he couldn't see his own fingers at the end of his arm. Ignoring the stabbing pains in his hindwing, he came sharply to his feet. He turned to run…and his safety line stopped him cold. An ominous creak came from the direction of the foremast.

Isaac's arms flew forward as the safety line jerked him backwards. The deck slapped him in the face and he slid the rest of the way belly-down, but he focused what little thought he had time for on the sensations coming from all around him. *The mast bounced.* Reaching behind him, he cut through the safety line with a single swipe, leapt to his feet, and fell in a crumpled heap when he was struck in the spine from behind. A heavy cannon, which must've broken loose somehow, loomed over Isaac like a victorious copper pirate as the mast landed a second time, breaking over the top of the cannon like a straw in a child's hand. Dazed, Isaac lay where he'd fallen.

I...I can't move my legs.

Chapter 1

A brisk fall breeze stirred the last batch of leaves that adorned a stately, old sugar maple in the heart of the Deep Woods. A handful of the leaves surrendered to winter's precursor, languidly floating down from their lofty perch, down through the young, thinner branches and past the thick branches. Some of them brushed against the rough ridges of bark that ran the length of the trunk, catching the attention of the tree's lower-level occupants.

"Stuart, wait." Isaac spoke to his Wrangler buddy, who stopped. Isaac stared out the window at the falling leaves. "The tree is nearly bare of leaves and there is not a snowflake or an icicle in sight," he mused aloud.

"I have heard talk all over Weetu," Sir Stuart responded from his place behind Isaac's wheelchair. "No one can remember winter being so late to arrive."

Isaac nodded, then frowned at the sound the pipes on the wall beside him were making. Copper pipes lined the side of every major corridor in the city of Weetu, busily draining the reservoir into the hundreds of tubs, sinks, buckets, and barrels that dotted the city, just like every morning. To those most familiar with the city, the pipes also acted as landmarks and could be followed to the heart of Weetu: the pump rooms. One pump room supplied Weetu with water; the other with fresh air during the winter.

"Sounds like we had better be on our way," Stuart chuckled as the sound of rushing water increased. He knew that the constant need for water was part of why Isaac, like so many of the windship *Zelkova*'s crew, had chosen to do his physical therapy exercises in the pump rooms. Due to the dangerous nature of animal and insect wrangling, less than a third of Wranglers lived to die of old age. Fully a third ended their careers early due to one debilitating injury or another. They might never fly afterwards, nor wield a weapon, but they could be sure that they were being useful.

As Stuart wheeled him into the pump room, Isaac wondered again if he had made the right choice in agreeing to Stuart's assistance. If not for Stuart's dogged insistence, Isaac would have chosen to rely on Wrangler apprentices for wheelchair drivers, like the rest of the patients. What made this therapy group unique was that all of their injuries were the result of action during the joint-tribal windship battle with the pirates. Everywhere Isaac looked, he saw crew members from the *Zelkova*. He knew them all by name. A few months ago, they all left port together. They returned together. And, as was the custom, the injured crew members of the *Zelkova* were all recuperating together, secure in the knowledge of their shared horrors, each grateful for the trusted companionship during the difficult adaptation period. It was the one place in Weetu that Isaac should have fit in. And he would have, except…

"Your Highness!" A much older man straightened in his wheelchair when he noticed Prince Isaac.

"Now, Bert." Isaac's wheelchair began moving in Bert's direction as if Stuart could read Isaac's mind. "How many times," Isaac made a point of gesturing with his crippled right hand, just as though he was not shocked anew at the damage every time he noticed it, "must I ask you to call me Isaac?"

"I suppose until I get used to it," Bert grinned, relaxing a little in his chair. Something about the way he remained pitched unnaturally forward gave the impression of the willing anticipation that characterized his short—four hundred years—but spectacular military career. He had just been entering his prime when he volunteered for the *Zelkova*'s crew, where he lost one leg and shredded a hindwing. "Shall we join them?" He jerked his head towards where a group of their crewmates had begun the checking-in process.

"After you," Isaac half-bowed, grinning. As soon as Bert was a half a twig away, Isaac beckoned for Sir Stuart to come forward. "That will be all." He held Stuart's gaze a moment longer than absolutely necessary, relying on centuries of comradeship to convey his silent thanks. It was more than duty that kept Sir Stuart at his side. It was the brotherhood common to Wranglers.

Jared, a second-year apprentice, appeared beside Stuart, ready to take over driving Isaac's chair. Jared was a well-muscled lad who had shown the good sense of doing his job without chattering on about nothing. Isaac knew he would miss the lad when his month was up. He also knew they were lucky to have him in the Wranglers. Jared could have chosen to become a woodcutter or signed on with a Master Carpenter. Neither of those occupations required their apprentices to volunteer for long hours in a windowless cavern, lit only by the bioluminescent fungi growing from the ceiling and the professional smiles of the medical staff, Isaac reflected grimly.

"Alright, Filmore," The nurse in charge, a thin, elderly fairy who answered to Rosie, shook a finger at the burly patient she had just finished examining, "the same machine and workout as yesterday. But take it easy. If you go as hard as you did yesterday, you will only slow your recovery down. Understood?"

"Aye, aye," Filmore answered cheerily. Not that he really understood Rosie's figuring, but he did understand that it was an order. And taking orders was bread and butter for a windfairy like him.

"Good morning, Rosie," Isaac smiled as his wheelchair came to a stop in front of her.

"Well now." As Rosie held Filmore's file out to one side, her apprentice promptly exchanged it for Isaac's file. "Back for more, eh?" She pretended to study a non-existent note in Isaac's file while she took stock of his appearance instead. "Getting all of your basking in?" she asked, concerned by how pale he was becoming, a clear indication that he was ignoring the standard order to spend a few hours in the sun every day before winter set in. There were no windows in the water pump room, or in the wind pump room for that matter. Windows were being shut and shuttered all through Weetu to protect them from the harsh winter they were expecting. The forest animals had been showing sign of it for weeks, almost to the point of appearing anxious for it to finally arrive. But it was twice as bad for the fairies. Being cooped up inside was like being deprived of oxygen for a Wood Fairy, especially one as young and athletic as Prince Isaac.

"No, not really," Isaac answered coolly.

"Why not?" Rosie shut his file and folded her arms across her chest.

Isaac shook his head, deliberately tilting his head forward slightly and looking off at nothing, as though remembering something important but confidential.

"It is difficult to find the time. My duties…" He gestured vaguely.

Rosie's eyes narrowed. Her vision might be fading, but she could still see plenty and what she saw here bothered her. It was plain unhealthy for him to avoid the sun like this.

"Well from now on, you will *make* the time," she informed him. "Doctor's orders and no squirming out of it. Understood?" Plucking a pencil from among the many sticking up out of her loose ponytail, she added a note to his file. "I know how busy your royal duties keep you." She lowered her voice a bit for that, sensitive to the fact that he usually tried to downplay that part of his life as far as the other patients were concerned. "But whatever it is that is keeping you so busy, you can just do it on the balcony." She waved her hand at him dismissively. "Get on with you now, there is work to be done. Same exercises as yesterday and mind that you do not strain your back." Spinal injuries were tricky enough. Some healed; some did not, a fact that irritated her greatly. There simply was no reliable treatment for his condition. The most she could do presently was warn him against doing more damage.

Isaac fumed silently while Jared wheeled him over to the nearest unoccupied leg station. *Basking. What good is it? And what is the use of this?* he raged to himself as Jared removed the footrest from his chair and placed his feet on the station's pedals. Isaac's mood soured further when Jared dutifully adjusted the tension on the pedals to the lowest setting. With all of his might, Isaac pushed his left foot down. The pedal barely budged. His effort with his right foot met with the same result. *I will never walk again.* Left foot. *They know it, if they would just admit it.* Right foot. *I know it.* Left foot. *I will never walk again!* His anger made him careless, so that what little movement he achieved quickly became sloppy.

"Hi!" Jared produced a clean white towel and lightly mopped Isaac's damp forehead. "Slow and steady, yeah?" Nodding at the station's miniature sandglass he reminded Isaac, "No need to wear yerself out in the first minute. Save some fer the other nine." He discreetly failed to mention his real concern—that Isaac's movements would get jerkier and jerkier until he really did hurt himself. Back injuries were nothing to fool with; any fool knew that.

Isaac inhaled shakily, embarrassed but still consumed with the apparent futility of the exercise. Fortunately for all concerned, Isaac considered shouting at his subjects to be the lowest form of weakness. Anyway, Jared was too nice a lad to glare at.

"Right," Isaac ground out between clenched teeth. Carefully, he started again. Left foot. Right foot. Again. Smooth, controlled efforts that required all of his concentration.

"Done." Jared grinned at his prince and held out the towel.

Isaac automatically began reaching for the towel with his right hand, then took it with his left. He probably could have hooked the towel with the curled fingers of his right hand, but it was not worth the risk of accidentally dropping it on the floor.

"You moved the marker, you did," Jared informed him, pointing at the machine with his pencil, then jotting down the achievement with a flourish. It was a small increase, as one measured ordinary things—a fingernail's thickness at most. But Jared, in the infinite wisdom of compassionate youth, was beaming with pride in his prince. "Near half a woodgrain up from last time. Have a drink, yeah?"

"Not until I bring a drink's worth of water up from the well," Isaac muttered under his breath. He was no expert on the efficiency of Weetu's water pump systems, but he was confident that he had sweated more moisture than he had pumped as yet.

"Hey?" Jared frowned, one hand on the pitcher of specially treated 'doctor's water.' Every patient was supposed to have a glass after each exercise.

"I say," Isaac pasted on a grin, "none of that doctor's water for me!" He tossed the towel back at Jared only to watch wistfully as the youth caught it easily. "Save it for after the arm workout, when I really need it."

Jared shook his head and bent to trade the pedals for the foot straps. While doctor's water eased aches and pains and was good for rehydrating after a grueling workout, it tasted bitter and woody because of the herbs and potions it was made of. How could he blame Isaac for being reluctant to drink it?

"Come on then." Jared moved the station's marker back to zero and flipped the sandglass over. "The good citizens of Weetu are waiting!"

From somewhere deep inside, Isaac found enough patience to get through the leg lift exercise. Whether he walked or not, he knew his mother would ask at lunch how the exercises had gone. And he had better have the right answers if he did not want her conspiring with Rosie 'for his own good.' At least he had finally convinced his mother to dine with him privately. He had always been reasonably coordinated with his left hand, but he desperately wanted more practice with soups, stews, etc., before winter set in and his options dwindled. He liked soups and stews, appreciated their warmth and nourishment. They just had a habit of slipping out of his spoon before it quite reached his mouth.

Jared, sensing that Isaac was in a less-than-talkative mood, handed him the glass of doctor's water as soon as the sandglass ran out. "A sip, at least, yeah?" he implored—then promptly became absorbed in checking and jotting down the marker's location.

Isaac dutifully placed the glass to his lips, tilted his head back, and pretended to swallow. While he knew Jared was not watching, he never doubted for a moment that Rosie was.

At last they moved on to the arm workouts. Isaac almost looked forward to those. Both of his arms were in good working order, so it was a simple matter to slip his hands into the straps and actually accomplish something. It felt fine to watch Jared adjust the tension on this machine to what Isaac considered a respectable setting before starting the sandglass. Isaac was not even allowed to propel his own wheelchair for fear of damaging his spine further, but at least this machine was an old friend from before the accident. In fact, this was the one machine where Isaac knew exactly how much water he was pumping with each stroke: twelve curls brought up half a drop; pushing forward twelve times brought up the same. At the sandglass' half mark, Jared helped him switch straps so that he could work his other muscles, pushing his arms out to the sides, pulling down so that his elbows touched his knees, and so on.

"Alright, Jared." Rosie patted the lad on the shoulder. "Finish your notes and go find someone to talk to."

Jared obeyed, but only because he knew how much the hand workouts hurt Prince Isaac. Sometimes, when he was working with the patients, he wondered how he would handle his own probable future injury. It was a sobering thought, which he suspected was the point of having the first- and second-year apprentices volunteering there.

"Here," Rosie produced a soft ball from her jacket pocket. No larger than an average caterpillar egg, it was still proving an almost undefeatable challenge for Prince Isaac. "Take it."

Isaac eyed the malevolent gray ball a moment before reaching for it. It was just small enough and just soft enough that if he pushed hard enough against Rosie's palm, he was able to work the ball past his stiff, curled fingers and into his own palm. As always, what followed was seven consecutive minutes of excruciating concentration.

Squeeze the ball. Roll the ball. Drop the ball. Rosie issued each command in a dry, matter-of-fact tone of voice, rotating through them at intervals and watching Isaac's face closely as it changed shade by shade from faded tan to a sort of dark pale without him voicing a single complaint. He was a stubborn one, that was for sure.

"Enough." Rosie allowed him to pry the ball free with his left hand, glad he was willing to do it himself. It hurt her just to watch some of her patients. Taking the ball from him, she dropped it in her pocket. "Well done."

"Just in time." Isaac managed a semi-convincing smile in an attempt to cover his weariness. "Sir Stuart has arrived to collect me."

"Not so fast." Rosie nodded at the glass of doctor's water. "Drink that first. Then you can go."

Isaac glared at her. "I will not drink that…foul potion," he informed her coldly. They had the same argument, more or less, after every session.

"You will," she shot back at him. "You will if you have to stay here all day!" Finding that Isaac continued staring at her obstinately, she closed his file with a thump. "Very well. I will tell Sir Stuart that he is not needed and…"

"Wait." Isaac held up his right hand in protest, wincing a little with the gesture. Why could he feel sore muscles in his arm when he could not actually move his fingers? "Alright." Remembering in time to take up the glass with his left hand, he held it up as if toasting her. "Anything to set a good example for the others."

Rosie did her best not to smirk as Isaac drained the glass in a single gulp. Nor did she allow herself to look impressed when he kept a straight face. That would ruin their game.

"If that is all, then?" Isaac handed her the empty glass. He already felt a little better, though he would never have admitted it.

"Just about." She raised both eyebrows for emphasis as she reminded him, "Do your sun basking today."

Sir Stuart walked over to them, arriving in time to hear Rosie's admonition. While he knew full well why Isaac was resisting the treatment, he had not yet found a solution. Winter would soon be here, too, its chill temperatures and shortened daylight hours further hampering the sun basking treatments. He shrank back a bit when Rosie looked over at him.

"I will hold you responsible if he does not bask today."

"Yes, ma'am," Stuart answered at once. It was the first and only response that occurred to him. His own mother was a doctor, too, so his training on the subject had begun very early. Besides, sun basking would do his best friend, Isaac, a world of good. If only there was a way to do it without exposing the ugly scars that covered Isaac's torso, the scars that made even Stuart flinch. They were not the neatly sewn, or at least moderately gruesome, type of scars that Wranglers so often boasted of and showed off with pride. Despite the surgeon's best efforts, and he had been summoned almost immediately through fairy dust to the scene of the battle, the wounds had been too severe to heal smoothly. Potions and salves alike had failed to reduce the color of the scars, or even to ease the taut skin around them.

Abruptly, Stuart realized that Isaac was glaring at both himself and Rosie.

"By your leave," Stuart held out his hand to Rosie, who automatically reached for it, "fair lady." Brushing a courtier's kiss across the back of Rosie's ever-so-slightly wrinkled hand, Stuart turned to Isaac. "I suppose you know how much we have to do today?" Without waiting for a response, Stuart moved into position behind the chair. Releasing the hand brake, he continued, "And yet here you still sit, whiling away your time with a lovely lady."

Isaac rolled his eyes as soon as he was sure Rosie could not see what he was doing. Stuart might think he could cajole him into sun basking, but he could just think again. There was no way Isaac was going to embarrass himself like that. Belatedly, Isaac returned Bert's wave as Stuart wheeled him out of the room.

Stuart, on the other hand, was not so sure. In fact, he had that very moment had a brilliant idea. It would take a little doing…a far cry from impossible, though.

Isaac waffled between indignant and curious as Stuart stopped the chair, excused himself, and went to talk to one of the city guards. The half-smile Stuart was wearing when he returned did nothing to relieve Isaac's mind on the subject of the conversation, which he had a sneaking suspicion had been himself. Whatever it was, the guard hurried away like it was important. All the way back to his quarters, Isaac was ready to object at the first sign of a detour, but there was none. He might have given up and asked once they were in private, but he did not have to.

"Here we are," Stuart announced, bringing the chair to a halt just inside Isaac's rooms. The floor-to-ceiling windows, which had been heavily draped for the last few months by Isaac's order, were now thrown wide open by Noland, Isaac's valet. Sunlight was streaming in and bathing the room in the fresh, golden light of morning. "For the next few hours the palace guards will enforce a no-fly zone in this area, giving us peace and quiet to sun bask in."

Isaac swallowed hard. Only a handful of fairies besides the senior medical staff had seen the extent of his scars. Stuart and Noland were two of them. Maybe—just maybe—this was possible. He could already feel his spirits lifting.

"Us?" Isaac inquired as casually as he could manage around the lump in his throat.

"Us," Stuart confirmed.

"Impossible." Isaac announced suddenly. Eyeing the ointments and bandages Noland had neatly set out in preparation for protecting his scars from the sun's caress, Isaac let the silence stretch out as long as he dared. "Life is neither peaceful, nor quiet with you around, Stuart."

It took a moment for Stuart to fully digest the joke, such as it was. Then he and Noland burst into laughter, with Isaac joining them a heartbeat later. Oh, it felt good to laugh. Stuart had shared many experiences with Isaac, everything from the bone-weariness of Wrangler apprenticeship to the glory of triumphant returns. Isaac could hide very little from Stuart, including a bitterness that was not unusual during the adaptation period. Like the uncommon friend that he was, Stuart was determined to remain at Isaac's side, to fight the darkness as resolutely as he fought the animals and insects that endangered fairy lives.

Chapter 2

Refreshed after the sun basking and a quick, cool wash to get the ointments off his chest and legs, Isaac was almost jovial as Noland wheeled him to his mother, the queen's, quarters for lunch.

"Flowers." Isaac snapped his fingers, then sighed. "I should have thought to bring some flowers."

Noland cocked an eyebrow that he knew Isaac could not see before suggesting smoothly, "I could have the gardener add some to the luncheon trays."

"Hmm," Isaac mused aloud and tapped his chin lightly. When his sensitive fingertips encountered scar tissue on his face, his mood faltered. "Yes, I…" He dropped his hand to his lap. "Just be sure that they are fresh-cut." The frown he was trying gallantly to suppress abruptly surfaced when he saw that the doors to his mother's quarters were closed. "How odd," he muttered under his breath. As a rule, the Wood Fairy Royal Family was openly available to their subjects. Unless, of course, they were engaged in private business.

Noland brought the chair to a halt in front of the closed doors and knocked to announce their arrival.

~ 17 ~

Isaac's gloomy thoughts were no match for the curiousity that the ensuing commotion that the knock incurred. Both of his dark brown eyebrows went up when he realized that he could hear three distinct female voices. He recognized his mother's and his sister's voices, but the third voice…? Perhaps if he was not having to sift through the additional noises of shuffling papers and rustling material, he might be able to identify it. All he could be sure of at that moment was that it was pitched a little lower than the other two voices. A warm, pleasant voice.

Noland, equally taken aback at the odd occurrence, nearly jumped when the doors were thrown open. He was silently grateful that they opened inward instead of outward.

"Ah, Isaac." Princess Gallica, Isaac's younger sister, motioned for Noland to step aside. "Late, as usual." Moving swiftly around the chair, she grasped the handles and forced it forward into the room. "Close the doors, will you, Noland?"

Completely thrown off balance by his sister's odd behavior, Isaac opened his mouth to protest. And promptly shut it when he spied his mother on the far right side of the room—with a stranger. The two of them were pretending to examine the portrait of his maternal grandparents that hung on the wall before them.

His mother was of average height and a slender, lithe build, a rare beauty in a tribe of rough-and-ready fairies.

Isaac naturally assumed that the woman beside her was the owner of the unidentified voice he had heard moments before. But what an odd woman. Her hair was bound up in a cloth, entirely hidden from view, a style completely at odds with the current court fashion for ladies to wear their hair loose, down to their shoulders or even waists. She was nearly a third of a twig taller than his mother and—strangest of all—the hand that she raised to touch the painting's frame was white as milk, as if it had never seen the sun.

"Isaac," Queen Fiona looked over at last, relieved to see the doors firmly closed again. Leaving her guest still examining the painting, she flew over to kiss her son lightly on his forehead. "Mmm," she smiled. "You smell of the sun."

Isaac flicked a glance at the stranger, willing his mother to drop the subject of sun basking, and smiled back.

"Excellent." Fiona beamed at him and deftly changed the subject. "A letter arrived today from Prince Cambrian that I think you will find very interesting."

"Arrived today?" Isaac did not bother to hide his surprise. "It must be urgent for him to risk sending a windship out this late in the season." Prince Cambrian was a Sky Fairy and lived in the mountains to the west. Perhaps the letter carried some explanation for winter's delay. Perhaps—his gaze strayed again to the mysterious woman—it had something to do with her.

"It came by special courier," Gallica volunteered from where she had seated herself beside him on the couch.

Hearing a note of strain in her voice, Isaac cocked his head at her.

"Yes," Fiona interjected calmly. "By the Lady Cassidy Clark, of the Water Fairy Tribe." Her voice rose slightly on the last few words.

Isaac froze in place, the shock of his mother's announcement seeming to stop even his heart's beat for a moment. Fairydom was home to four tribes: the Sky Fairy Tribe; the Plant Fairy Tribe; the Silver Fairy Tribe; and the Wood Fairy Tribe. The fact that there was a fifth tribe was a king's secret, passed only from father to his heir when said heir came of age. The secrecy was of vital necessity, stipulated to in a treaty signed hundreds of thousands of years ago when they severed diplomatic ties and completely withdrew from the rest of Fairydom because the other tribes were engaged in terrible wars. Hearing his mother speak of them, in the presence of his sister and some unknown guest, was almost enough to make Isaac question his sanity.

"Please." Three pairs of brown eyes turned towards the stranger when she spoke; she reciprocated by turning to face them. Intelligent, hazel-green eyes shone from her milk-white face as she continued, "Call me Doctor Cassidy."

Isaac stared without realizing it. *Doctor* Cassidy had a lovely oval face, brilliantly pink eyebrows, and a firm set to her mouth that indicated she was accustomed to responsibility. The slender fingers of her hands rested lightly on her folded arms, her shoulders relaxed as though she was completely at ease even under these unusual circumstances.

"Welcome." Isaac, having completely forgotten himself, tried to rise. Because his legs failed to respond, he put his hands on the arms of his chair and lifted himself into a standing position. His right hand protested a little, but he ignored it.

Somehow Cassidy realized what was happening before anyone else in the room. Her wings, slightly stunted from generations of life in the relatively cramped undersea cities of her tribe, spread to their fullest and managed to lift her across the room to his side. Reaching Isaac just as he was transferring his weight to his legs, she slipped under his near arm and did her best to support him. Her sudden proximity seemed to snap him out of his daze.

Isaac flushed an unbecoming shade of red and clung to his guest in a completely undignified fashion. What else could he do? If he tried to drop himself back into his wheelchair, he would dump her on the floor beside him; or worse, she would get caught between him and the chair and be injured.

"Steady," Cassidy murmured. "It is fine, just fine." She tried to smile up at him and found that her face was only a few fingers' width from his. "Together, yes? Easy now." Her experience in the hospital allowed her to continue as though completely unaffected by the stimuli that assailed her senses.

Fiona and Gallica held their collective breath while Doctor Cassidy assisted Isaac back into the safety of a seated position.

"Good." Cassidy smiled at Isaac, privately relieved to have a little distance between them. "You are as strong as your mother said."

Isaac, sensing that Cassidy was offering him an excuse for nearly catapulting himself onto the floor, decided wearily not to be disagreeable about it. She was the one who rescued him, after all.

"Doctor Cassidy," Fiona spoke to fill the silence, "has come to share her tribe's medicine with us."

A slight frown creased Cassidy's smooth features. "Yes," she agreed, then clarified, "and also to investigate a concern."

A knock at the door sent Fiona and Cassidy scurrying back to the painting, while Gallica moved to answer the door.

"Thank you." Gallica waved the butler away and brought their lunch in herself, setting it on the low table that sat in front of a comfortable plush couch. "All clear," she called to her mother, having closed the door behind her with her foot.

"Oh, thank goodness." Queen Fiona was not accustomed to hiding things from her subjects, especially things of such grave importance.

Isaac sat where he was, silently sorting through half a dozen questions until he decided which of them was the most important.

"Will Father be joining us?" he nodded at the lunch tray as if checking to make sure there was enough food for them all was the only reason he was asking.

"I have already spoken with King Walter," Cassidy answered for the others. Her family held a position of great importance within the Water Fairy Tribe, not quite royalty, but as close as the culture of her tribe came to it. She instinctively discerned the question Isaac had not asked.

"I see." Isaac's eyebrows drew together as he considered his next question carefully. He did not understand how it was that his father had chosen to have his mother be the one to introduce him to their important guest. And *after* she had been introduced to his sister? What exactly could Doctor Cassidy be investigating? Whatever it was, it was important enough for her to leave her tribe, travel this late in the season, and risk discovery nearly every moment. Not to mention the fact that she would simply have to winter with them.

"You have many questions," Cassidy observed shrewdly. "If you will permit me, I will be happy to answer them."

"Gallica." Fiona nodded at the lunch tray. "This may take a while and I for one am famished." Together, she and Gallica took the lunch tray over to Fiona's desk, where they could finish preparing it without interrupting the others.

Cassidy fluttered over to join Isaac, settling herself on the couch beside his chair in very nearly the same spot his sister had just vacated.

"Thank you." Isaac looked her in the eyes and held her gaze a moment longer than was necessary. He was thanking her for more than her willingness to answer his questions and he wanted her to know it. After all, this was hardly the time to give in to the supreme embarrassment he felt over forgetting he was crippled; he would save that for later.

"Of course." Cassidy smiled back.

"Perhaps you would be willing to," Isaac shrugged slightly, "well, to start at the beginning. Why is your tribe reaching out after so long?"

Cassidy, accustomed as she was to hours either alone in her laboratory or in her own surgery, thought nothing of chewing lightly on her lower lip while she debated the answer to that question for the thousandth time. Even with her excellent command of the language common to the four tribes who lived above the sea's surface, she had not decided what the simplest explanation was.

"I am here," she began slowly, "not at the request of my tribe, but of my cousin, Kuntza Botere. You will not have heard of him, for his mission was guarded most carefully by the Sky Fairy Tribe."

Isaac's intestines twisted themselves into a hatchet knot as the worst-case interpretation of her statement leapt forcibly to mind. The treaty with the Water Fairy Tribe, simply put, insured that they would be allowed to slip from the memories of the surface tribes' general populations. No contact, and *especially*, no interference from outsiders—that was the price the Water Fairies had exacted from them, under threat of certain death from polluted waters, dried up streams, etc., should they dare transgress.

"He is with the Sky Fairy Tribe?" Isaac maintained a neutral tone, reminding himself that Cassidy had already met with his father. And his mother.

"He was," Cassidy confirmed. Her keen eyes automatically took note of the changes in his body: the tension in his shoulders; the abrupt jump in his heart rate, as seen in his jugular vein; even the way he forced himself to lean against the high back of his wheelchair. "Because winter will soon arrive, he returned to our capitol city, Cachora, bringing witnesses to testify against the pirates."

Isaac blinked. *Pirates?* What did pirates have to do with the Water Fairy Tribe?

Cassidy chose her next words carefully. "Many months ago, pirates stumbled across some of my tribesfairies. Since that time, the pirates have been trying to convince us to join with them in fighting their oppressors." She held up both of her hands, palms forward in a gesture of peace, when it looked like Isaac might explode all over the room. "Kuntza has found their claims to be false." When she thought Isaac had regained sufficient control, she continued, "He was also told of many brave fairies who fought against the pirates and were injured." She looked down modestly, then back up at Isaac, completely unaware of the havoc her looking up at him through her lashes wreaked on him. "I have come to help as a doctor, a surgeon. But, additionally, to see and to hear. After I return home in the spring, I too will testify." She deliberately made no mention of the contents of her testimony. Good scientist that she was, she fully intended to keep an open mind.

Isaac's intestines slowly began to unclench, but the knot remained. It had reworked itself especially for Cassidy when she smiled up at him. Water Fairies lived in cities under the sea and, if he had been asked, he would have readily supposed that they smelled like brine. That their eyes would match the sea's murky depths and be wholly unappealing. That they would be…nothing like Cassidy.

"Well." Fiona approached, a plate of sandwiches in each hand. Since the plates were destined for the low couch table anyway, she set them there as she ventured, "I hope that everything is all straightened out?"

Cassidy declined to reply, looking at Isaac instead. Only he could answer that at this point.

"I have the answers I need for now," Isaac nodded. Even in his somewhat-dazed condition, he felt a faint relief when he saw that he would not have to wrestle left-handed with spoonsful of liquid in front of their guest. Sandwiches were much more cooperative in his experience.

Gallica promptly appeared at her mother's elbow and handed Isaac a tray with four empty glasses on it. Her other hand held a pitcher of freshly squeezed juice, which she promptly began pouring into said glasses.

Cassidy noted that Isaac did not even bother to voice a protest at his sister's treating him like a serving table. The relaxed manners of the Wood Fairy Tribe were going to take some getting used to. On the other hand, she felt a slight flutter when she saw how easily Isaac handled the heavy tray; professional interest, of course.

"Mother." Isaac offered the tray to his mother, nearly taking off Gallica's nose as she bent to set the half-full pitcher on the table.

Fiona shook her head in mock horror at her children's antics, secretly glad that Isaac was feeling up to it.

"Doctor," Isaac moved the tray away from Gallica before she could snag a glass. "And you." He feigned a glare at Gallica, smoothly depositing the tray in her hands and snatching up a glass without spilling a drop from either his drink or hers.

"You must not mind them." Fiona smiled at Cassidy, delighted at Isaac's display of hand-eye coordination. If only the Chief Nurse, Rosie had seen it! They compared notes routinely on the subject of Isaac's recuperation, so Fiona knew all too well how much trouble Isaac was having with his dexterity. "They are a full hundred years apart in age and I am not always sure which of them is the younger."

Cassidy accepted the sandwich Fiona offered her with a smile, then let it rest on a napkin on her knee until they had all been served. It was a simple case of propriety for her.

Noticing her reticence, Isaac held off also. Besides, there was one more question he wanted to ask.

"Doctor." Isaac let the word hang in the air a moment. "What kind of medicine will you be sharing with us?"

"My specialty is reconstructive surgery," Cassidy answered.

"Oh, Isaac," Fiona admonished her son. "Let her eat."

"Wings, delicate neural reconstructions," Cassidy continued, not having really heard Fiona' protest.

Isaac's meat sandwich dribbled through the fingers of his suddenly clenched fist, pieces of it bouncing off his knee to land on the table and floor.

"Did you say wings?" he asked hoarsely.

Cassidy, her sandwich halfway to her mouth, stopped what she was doing and looked him straight in the eyes.

"Yes. Wings." She nodded at his wheelchair. "Spines, as well." She exuded quiet authority as she advised him, "I will need to examine you before I am certain that I can help."

Isaac nodded numbly. *Wings. Spines, as well.* It was too much to process.

"I am sure that can be arranged." Fiona finally managed to squeeze a few words past the lump in her throat. The implications of what Cassidy was offering were enormous. And not just for Isaac. Fiona shook herself free of speculation. "After you have rested, of course."

Cassidy, humbled by the way they were all looking at her, returned her sandwich to the tray. All trace of her appetite had vanished, anyway.

"It is most important that I have the proper space to work," Cassidy explained, focusing on Fiona to keep from having to watch Gallica help Isaac clean up his sandwich. If she had ever doubted how much what she could offer would mean to him, she was now absolutely certain. "You have medical rooms, of course."

"Of course," Fiona agreed. "However," she shook her head as Cassidy eagerly began to rise from the couch, "the halls will be filled with guests and staff right now. And the hospital with patients. We could not keep your identity a secret very long if we allow you to be seen."

Disappointed, Cassidy sank back onto the couch. Her logical nature told her that the queen was quite correct. She could hardly endanger her tribe's privacy just to please the brown-eyed man beside her. Even if his eyes did remind her of dark, liquid chocolate just before it was poured into its mold. Distressed at the turn her thoughts had taken, she gave herself a firm mental shake.

"If you will tell me what you need," Isaac's deep voice filled the silence, "I can talk to our doctors for you, try to find the best option."

"Do you have so many medical rooms?" Cassidy asked, surprised enough to turn towards him. From what little she had seen since her arrival early that morning, she would have thought that most of the Wood Fairy kingdom was given over to athletic pursuits.

"I am afraid we do." Isaac, still caught somewhere between the shock of her announcement and the lurch he felt each time he looked into her dazzling hazel eyes, spoke as quietly and gently as if he was trying to calm a spooked dragonfly. "Wrangling is very dangerous work—most of the injured are brought here for their recovery and therapy."

Seeing that Gallica was about to join the conversation, Fiona caught her eye and warned her off with a barely perceptible shake of her head. Despite their best efforts, both at preparing Wranglers for the possibility of paralysis and at preventing it, the adaptation period was always challenging. Like so many before him, Isaac had gone from witty and charming to withdrawn and irritable. A harmless winter's flirtation could be very good for Isaac's self-confidence.

"And are there so many injured?" Cassidy probed, her brow furrowing at the thought.

Isaac raked one hand through his hair, this being the subject of many sleepless nights for him from long before the time that he joined the ranks of the *so many*.

"Too many," he acknowledged tersely.

"I see." Cassidy cocked her head to one side. She waved her fingers, breaking whatever spell they had been under. "But you must not trouble yourself about me. I must speak with your doctors anyway. We can discuss accommodations as well as medical records."

"Of course." Isaac was about to congratulate himself on hiding the strange pang of disappointment that he felt at Cassidy's dismissal of his offer, when he caught his mother and sister exchanging knowing glances.

Chapter 3

Later that evening, Isaac waited impatiently in Rosie's outer office. Ordinarily he would have been glad of a delay, especially since it was his turn to review his progress with her, such as it was. But, because he knew that his mother, sister, and Cassidy were planning to arrive shortly after he did, he watched the water clock anxiously as the water dropped from the main container into the lower dish, splashing through the seconds since his arrival.

Sir Stuart's duties requiring his presence elsewhere, the task of driving Isaac had fallen to his valet, Noland, who was so affected by his prince's anxiety that he, too, jumped a little when the door to Rosie's inner office finally clicked open.

"Yes, Rosie." Patricia, Rosie's second-in-command and a perpetually solemn-faced woman, paused in the doorway, arms full of files. "Right away, ma'am." Stopping just long enough to stack the files on her desk, Pat scurried off into the maze of tunnels that led to the various hospital rooms.

Isaac held up a hand to Noland when his valet reached down to release the chair's brake.

"Rosie?" Isaac called out. Something was

wrong, very wrong. Unless his ears were playing tricks on him, Rosie was sniffling.

"Just a moment, Your Highness."

Isaac lowered his hand and looked over at Noland. It was worse than Isaac had thought.

Rosie appeared in the doorway, her arms piled just as high with files as Pat's had been. A faint redness about her eyes and a damp drop-spot on her blouse was the only visible evidence of her distress.

"My apologies, Your Highness." Rosie fluttered across the room to Pat's desk. "I hope you have not been waiting long."

Isaac's faint wave sent Noland fading out of the room as if he had never been there. When Rosie began sorting through the files—to avoid looking at him?—Isaac half-smiled. As a rule, nurses and doctors did not treat the Wood Fairy Royal Family with much deference. They were usually too busy bandaging a scrape or scolding them for…well, for being typical Wood Fairies. Even Isaac's father was semi-regularly in need of medical assistance. What a role reversal this was! He had better handle it tactfully, too, if he wanted Rosie to be open-minded about letting Cassidy, a stranger, into her domain.

"Rosie." Isaac modulated his tone somewhere between a wheedle and a command. Coaxing. Yes, that would do for a start. "Rosie, look at me." It was a moment before she obeyed, but he did not mind. Her vanity aside, and he thought she looked fine, there was the cause of her tears to be considered. "If those files can wait a moment," he nestled his injured right hand in the palm of his left, "I should like to know why you have been crying."

Rosie blinked once, looked away, then began blinking rapidly.

"Oh, Rosie." Distressed, Isaac silently cursed his wheelchair and his dependence on it. "Have a heart," he pleaded. "I cannot even offer you a handkerchief from over here."

Rosie looked at him, surprised. She had never been fooled by his readiness to participate in the standard therapies. After centuries of nursing, she could sense when a patient had made up their mind that they were never going to walk again, despite any and all evidence to the contrary. Not that there had been much positive physical evidence in Isaac's case. Hearing him bring up his condition of his own accord was a good sign as far as his adaptation progress was concerned.

Producing her handkerchief from her pocket, she dabbed at her eyes, trying to smile for Isaac's sake. "I tell them and I tell them not to overdo it." She shrugged and stuffed the damp handkerchief back in her pocket. "Daily we warn them that they can reinjure themselves if they are not careful." Her false calm evaporated in a burst of anger. "That boy from the Songaa troop, the Wrangler with the traumatic shoulder injury? He was feeling so good this morning that he talked his apprentice into a few more minutes and a few more and…" She took a deep, shuddering breath. "It was shortly after you left. He not only undid all of his progress towards healing, he tore another, supporting muscle."

Isaac sat there, unhappily admitting to himself that there was nothing he could say to make her feel less responsible. They remained in silence for several seconds, the water clock splashing them off with monotonous precision.

"Is the apprentice alright?" he asked eventually, head cocked to one side, not quite looking at her as he spoke.

Rosie half-laughed in response. The other, still-angry, half of her slammed her fist down on the desk.

"I removed him from the rotation."

Isaac flinched. Any apprentice who did not complete his yearly volunteer hours could be held back from progressing to the next level come spring.

"For a week." Rosie shook her head. "Maybe I am an old fool, but I am convinced he truly believed he was doing the right thing by my patient."

"Which makes him a young fool," Isaac

offered gently. "I am glad you are giving him another chance."

"But if anything like that ever happens again and he is involved…" Rosie glared meaningfully at Isaac.

"I would hope so!" Isaac responded earnestly. On the one hand, he was impressed with Rosie's ability to think beyond the event itself; on the other hand, he knew that the apprentice would have plenty of time to think about what they had done wrong while polishing boots, sharpening swords, etc., instead of volunteering for the next week.

Rosie surprised them both by laughing. "Well, now that that is over with," she shuffled the stack of files she had finished sorting, "I suppose we should get down to business."

"Yes," Isaac glanced through the open outer door at the tunnels, remembering how well voices carried. "In your private office, perhaps?"

Rosie's eyebrows went up. Rather than asking questions, however, she fluttered over and released his chair brake. Like all nurses, she was required to be able to maneuver all of the wheelchair models currently available. Like any sane nurse, she was grateful that Prince Isaac had chosen a lightweight metal model, with a tight turning radius, modified only slightly to include a high, cushioned chair back for him to lean against. Parking it easily in her office, she put on the brake out of habit, and closed the door out of instinct. Patient progress reviews were confidential, of course, but Isaac's tone of voice just now made her think they were not merely going to discuss his therapy results. With that in mind, she parked herself in her own chair, across the desk from him.

"I need to officially inform you that Prince Cambrian has sent a surgeon to spend the winter with us. He is quite confident that she can help me."   Isaac's mother had finally produced Cambrian's letter of introduction for Cassidy and to say that Cambrian's expectations were high was to understate the matter.

Rosie frowned, the matter from earlier slipping to the back of her mind while she focused on this new development.

"Your Highness," she slipped into a formal address without meaning to, "I hope she can. However…" She looked down at her hands, clasped in front of her on the desk. Strong hands, a little weathered from centuries of being scrubbed clean.   "Doctor Rutherford, who operated on you initially, is the finest surgeon in all of the Deep Woods. That is why he was here." The fact that he had accepted a position elsewhere, one that some considered a step down, shortly after the pirate offensive was something she rightly attributed to the wear and tear on a fairy's heartstrings. They could only be stretched so tight before they snapped, and as their finest surgeon, he had spent hours amounting to days applying himself to reconstructing shattered windfairies when their fighting fleet limped home.

"Despite his skill, there is little to no chance that I will ever walk again," Isaac summed the situation up for her. He met her gaze steadily when she finally looked up at him. "I have believed that from the first time my head cleared after the battle." He had vague memories of being attacked from three sides while onboard the *Zelkova*, by one pirate on the right, one loose cannon from behind, and by half a mast that fell on him from above. He even thought he remembered when Princess—now Queen—Rebecca used wild fairy dust to wish up Rutherford for him.

"I am sorry." Rosie almost choked on the words. She hated admitting defeat, even when it was not her fault. Perhaps her heartstrings were stretched tight, too.

"Rosie." Isaac waited for her to look up at him. "This surgeon, Doctor Cassidy Clark. She is young and full of hope. She says she knows of medicine we have only dreamed of." Despite his best efforts at remaining reasonably skeptical, Isaac found himself growing more attached by the minute to the idea of walking and flying again. "She has asked to see my charts, my medical records. I know she wants to talk to you about finding somewhere to work, also."

"Fine." Rosie shrugged noncommittally, this morning's accident having left her more weary than cynical. "Have her come by my office."

"I…" He looked over his shoulder as the door clicked open. He nodded at Noland, who opened the door the rest of the way for the Queen and the others. Once they were inside, Noland promptly shut the door, posting himself outside to guard against intrusion.

Rosie half-bowed to the queen from her desk, nodded at the princess, and turned curious eyes on the hooded stranger. Rosie assumed the stranger was the new surgeon, but when the hood was finally thrown back, Rosie's mouth fell open.

Hundreds of loosely-formed pink ringlets framed Cassidy's face, bouncing slightly as if enjoying their freedom from both the cloth wrap from earlier and the hood just now. Intelligent hazel eyes met Rosie's evenly, then lowered slightly in respect.

"Nurse Rosie," Cassidy acknowledged her peer.

Rosie came halfway out of her chair to bow, then sank limply back into it. She had treated patients from every tribe, including a few that were of mixed heritage, but never had she seen such brilliant pink plumage.

Cassidy's paler pink wings twitched slightly, the only indication of her amusement at the shock her presence was creating.

"I am told you assisted the surgeon who operated on Prince Isaac aboard the *Zelkova*," Cassidy gently nudged Rosie back into the conversation.

"Yes." Rosie nodded once, then again. "Yes, I did."

"Excellent." Cassidy beamed quite without realizing it. "I will need your help in reviewing Prince Isaac's file, if you would be so kind." Scientist and doctor though she was, Cassidy was also something of a student of fairy nature. A little humility went a long way, as she had discovered early on in her career.

"I," Rosie swallowed, still distracted by the color and almost hypnotic motion of Cassidy's hair, "would be honored."

"The doctor will need access to rooms large enough for herself and her two assistants," Queen Fiona interjected, pleased with the sincerity she discerned in Cassidy's behavior. "They will need complete privacy, and will eat and sleep there."

Rosie felt her eyebrows starting to rise again and sternly held them down, so much so that she inadvertently frowned.

"We wish in no way to interfere with the efficiency of your facility," Cassidy assured her, troubled by the frown. Perhaps the royal family was incorrect as to the size and number of available rooms?

Rosie managed a smile at that. "I would never have believed otherwise," she returned graciously. "And I think I know just the place."

"I knew you would," Queen Fiona smiled at her dear friend. "Please see to it that the doctor and her associates receive all of the help you can give." Motioning to Gallica, Fiona led the way out of the room, Noland shutting the door behind them. As interested as both Fiona and Gallica were, they had agreed between them that they could serve their guest, and their tribe, best by behaving as if nothing out of the ordinary was taking place. Hiding a Water Fairy all winter, when every single Wood Fairy in the area would be taking refuge in Weetu, was going to be quite a feat.

"If you will follow me?" Rosie invited. She took a moment to get Isaac's complete file from her cabinet, which allowed Cassidy to reposition her hood.

As they left the office, Noland slipped back into position behind Isaac's wheelchair.

While following Rosie, Cassidy marveled at the use of bioluminescent mushrooms—what they called 'cold fire'—to light the tunnels and rooms. It would take her a while to get used to the green light, but it was really quite clever. Weetu came as something of a relief to her. In his letter, her cousin Kuntza had described the Sky Fairy cities as 'clinging to the mountainside by sheer willpower' and being 'alarmingly open.' Both Cassidy and Kuntza were accustomed to the cozier, volcanic-glass domed cities of their own tribe, and while she would certainly miss the colorful display of the sea creatures, at least it was unlikely that she would accidentally look out a window and see the land stretching out before her. She felt queasy just thinking about it.

Isaac, meanwhile, was trying not to think about Cassidy's hair. He might have scoffed at himself for being so distracted by naturally curly hair if it had not been so very pink. Still, he reasoned with himself, that was no reason to assume it would feel any differently from any other woman's hair. When he caught himself thinking about touching her hair, he scowled. She was a doctor, well, a surgeon. She wanted to cut him open and rearrange things so that he could walk again, possibly even fly again. That was better than fine with him, but it surely meant that she was off limits. No teasing—and especially, no hair-touching.

Cassidy and Rosie, oblivious to Isaac's quandary, flew lightly along, discussing

Cassidy's needs as far as rooms, equipment, and so forth.

"Ah, here we are." Rosie, comfortable with Cassidy now as a medical professional, stopped in front of the door to a large room. "We can have a door installed this evening, to insure the privacy of yourself and your associates."

Cassidy entered the room just behind Rosie and looked around. She vaguely heard Rosie mention something about providing proper sleeping accommodations—the mattresses were apparently old and lumpy, as the room had been out of use for some time—but was absolutely captivated by the abundance of wood. It was all about her. Wooden walls, a wooden ceiling, even wooden tables and chairs. She reached out and stroked the top of the wooden desk near her. It was very different from her fishbone desks at home. And the wooden filing cabinets seemed drab compared to the vibrant pinks and oranges of the coral furnishings in her laboratory.

"And a thorough dusting." Rosie added that to her mental list, her cheeks pinking slightly with embarrassment when she saw the trail Cassidy's fingers left on the desktop. "These rooms are well away from the beaten path, and have fallen into some slight disrepair," she began to apologize, but Cassidy just smiled.

"Dust," Cassidy held up the fingers she had run over the desktop. "Is that what this is?"

Rosie found that she simply had no response to that.

"Yes." Isaac smoothly answered when he saw that Rosie had been rendered speechless. "Over time the wood, the paper, and pretty much everything in here, breaks down and turns into dust. The air can carry it from one place to another, but eventually it lands somewhere and builds up if it is not removed routinely."

"I see." Cassidy felt her wings twitching and focused on stilling them. "Please do not concern yourself with removing this dust," she turned to Rosie. "My nurses and I will remove it ourselves. It will be good," she clasped her hands in front of her, oblivious to the fact that she had just smeared dust on the front of her travelling cloak, "to begin working."

"I…yes." Rosie was still not quite up to formulating a response.

"Is that Isaac's file?" Cassidy nodded at what Rosie was holding.

"Yes." Rosie held it out to her.

"Excellent." Cassidy accepted it with a smile. "If you will have the door installed and my nurses brought to me, please?"

"Wait!" Isaac spoke quickly when he saw that Cassidy was about to remove her cloak, hood and all. "Noland, go get two master craftsfairies and a door. I want it up before suppertime."

Startled by both his words to her and his tone with Noland, Cassidy stared at Isaac in bewilderment.

"It might be best," Isaac turned back to Cassidy, "if you waited in one of the inner rooms until the door is in place."

"Oh!" Cassidy could not believe how quickly she had forgotten the need for secrecy. She was just so accustomed to travelling freely throughout her home region…

"It is most unlikely that anyone will venture into this part of the maze," Isaac spoke soothingly. "Nevertheless, I will feel better once you are all safely installed here. Door and all." He flashed a winning smile at Cassidy and felt the tight skin around his scars stretching uncomfortably.

Cassidy watched in confusion as Isaac's smile vanished. It had seemed so sincere…

"Rosie, I hate to trouble you." Isaac shrugged slightly, trying to keep all traces of the embarrassment he felt well-hidden as he asked for her help.

"Rosie has a dozen things to do," Cassidy objected, setting his file down on the desk. "Please allow me to drive you." She was acutely aware of the way Isaac's left hand gripped the arm of his chair to the point of being white-knuckled.

"You are very kind," he agreed, his voice

sounding hoarse even to his own ears. As she released the brake, he reminded himself again that she was just another medical professional. She was going to put him on a table and…and a whiff of her perfume sent shivers down his line of thought, tangling it right up. He might as well face it. He dearly hated having beautiful women drive his wheelchair.

Chapter 4

Cassidy and her two nurses, exhausted from the work of sweeping, dusting, and effectively scrubbing down the entire area they had been given, lingered over their suppers. The rags and things used to clean the rooms had already been whisked away when their supper arrived. Cassidy took a sip of her beverage, a delightfully rich, tangy liquid provided with their evening meal, and wondered if Rosie brought their supper herself to protect their secret or because she was the type to be involved in every detail. Probably both.

"I ache all over," announced Daphne in the language of their tribe, Margua. "From my hallux to my scalp." Rolling a small hunk of bread between her fingers, mashing it into a smaller hunk, she remembered aloud, "I thought that we would never finish cleaning the surgery." She threw a mock scowl at the room to her left, the largest of their five rooms. The room where they presently sat would become the recovery room in time.

Cassidy laughed, unsurprised. Daphne was a brilliant scientist, a better than average nurse, and just a little spoiled by the fellows back home. Personally, Cassidy was glad for the work. It took her mind off certain things, off a certain…prince.

"It was a good thing that we started with the bedrooms," Cassidy observed. Rosie had wisely arranged to have the old, unusable mattresses removed while Cassidy worked with her nurses in a different room, away from prying eyes. That was also when the packing crates they were presently using for furniture had been delivered. "Or they would not have been ready when the new mattresses arrived." Warned by Rosie when it was time, they had moved into the furthest room, the surgery, and worked their way out from there.

"How are you, Agnes?" Cassidy looked over at where her dear friend and confidant sat in the room's one good chair on the far side of the small desk.

Agnes, having already finished supper, took a sip of her nightly hot tonic, a medicinal blend discreetly prescribed by Cassidy to ease the effects of time, such as arthritis of the hands and other maladies common to women after spending eight or nine thousand years in near perpetual motion.

"If we had not done it ourselves," Agnes thought aloud, "I would have been anxious about it having been done properly."

Cassidy hid her smile behind her napkin, dabbing lightly at the corners of her mouth. "I am certain that if Rosie had anything to do with cleaning these rooms," she observed dryly, "the floors would have been clean enough to perform surgery on."

"Hmmm," was Agnes's only reply.

"Please tell me we do not have to unpack tonight," pleaded Daphne after waiting a polite moment. Professionally, she was sorry that they had not been able to bring all of their equipment and instruments. Personally, she was already dreading the process of sorting through packing paper and finding enough places to put everything they had brought.

"Would you rather have to get up and do it in the morning?" Cassidy laughed.

"Morning." Daphne frowned wistfully. "How will we know it is morning from inside this cave?" Like the others, she was glad for the enclosed space of their rooms, but already she missed seeing the lightning eels darting across the sea floor, and watching the seahorses cavorting and nibbling plankton.

"Well, after we wake up because we have slept long enough," Agnes nodded at the water clock that sat on the long dresser on the far side of the room, "we can always check that to make sure."

Cassidy nearly choked on her drink. Agnes had a very dry wit, which still occasionally took Cassidy by surprise, even after all of their time together. She looked up gratefully when someone knocked on the outer door. Instead of supplying just one door, for the entrance to the main tunnel system, they had been offered five doors, four of which they accepted: one for the main entrance; one between the antechamber and the recovery room; and one for each of the bedrooms, which branched off of the recovery room.

"I will get it," Cassidy volunteered, knowing that she spoke the surface language better than either of her companions. Rising, she fluttered into the antechamber, closing the door to the recovery room behind her. "Who is it?" she called in the surface tongue.

"Rosie," came the answer.

Cassidy opened the door and stood back to let her in. The door opened inward, so Cassidy was able to stay behind it and out of sight of anyone who might be passing by.

"I came for the dishes," Rosie said once the door was securely shut.

"Now really," Cassidy smiled at her. "You must not wait on us like this."

Rosie, having mostly recovered from her shock at learning that not one but *three* Water Fairies were going to winter in the depths of the medical maze, managed to smile back.

"It may well be unavoidable." Rosie shook her head. "The fewer of us who know that the

Water Fairy Tribe exists, the better." After disappearing briefly, Isaac had returned long enough to explain in terse but definite language the exact terms of their treaty with the Water Fairy Tribe.

Cassidy nodded slowly. She could hardly disagree, even though she knew her family had been subtly nudging the other tribal leaders towards rejoining the rest of Fairydom for over a century now.

"Nevertheless, if you are spending all of your time in the maze, others will notice. That would hardly serve our purposes," Cassidy pointed out reasonably. "Is there no other trustworthy fairy who could perform such simple things for us?"

Rosie frowned thoughtfully. "My own assistant, Pat, would be the ideal choice, but I need her elsewhere. She is almost as involved in the day-to-day operations of our facility as I am." After a little more thought, Rosie's frown eased slightly. Of all her nursing staff, there was no one that seemed quite suited to the task of keeping a secret this large while performing tasks so small. "I suppose we could ask Sir Stuart."

Cassidy hesitated, not sure she liked the idea. Glancing at the closed door that led to the recovery room, she asked quietly, "Is he young? Handsome?"

  While Rosie's eyebrows twitched violently, she managed to prevent them from actually rising.

  "Yes, I am afraid so."

  "Oh, I am not asking for myself," Cassidy explained. "One of my companions is young and pretty." Unable to interpret the twist in Rosie's lips in response to her words, Cassidy continued, "She has not yet allowed it to interfere with her work."

  "Still, it could be quite risky," Rosie finished for her. Rosie had trained far too many new nurses, male and female, to be ignorant of just how big a problem a small distraction could become for someone in their profession. Still, she found it quite amusing to realize that Cassidy was apparently oblivious to her own feminine charms. "Let me discuss it with Prince Isaac. I am sure he will know what we should do."

  "Prince Isaac?" Cassidy was puzzled.

  "Why, yes. Sir Stuart was Prince Isaac's comrade at arms, and is still his best friend." Rosie went on to add, "In fact, the more that I think of it, the better I think it would be in the long run. Prince Isaac will need a friend while he recovers."

  "Yes, that is quite true," Cassidy agreed. "Very well. If Prince Isaac will vouch for Sir Stuart, I will accept that."

"Excellent," Rosie smiled. She was about to ask after the dishes when her gaze fell on Prince Isaac's file, still resting on the now-clean desk. "May I ask…" She began, then faltered.

Cassidy, following her gaze, guessed what it was that she wanted to ask.

"I will examine his file in the morning," she promised Rosie. "And hopefully, I will examine him in the afternoon."

"Can you really help him walk again?" Rosie asked a little breathlessly.

"It is possible. I will know more after I have studied his injuries." Cassidy would have liked to give Rosie a definite answer, but she knew better. Even with the advances she and other Water Fairy scientists had made recently, there were still limitations.

"Can you tell me something of how it would be done? The procedure?"

Cassidy took Rosie by the hand and led her towards the recovery room. "I will do my best." Opening the door with her free hand, a little clumsily because she was not yet accustomed to the knobs the Wood Fairies used instead of sliding doors, she preceded Rosie into the room.

"Rosie, allow me to introduce my two assistants—Agnes," she nodded to the woman on her right. "And Daphne." She nodded to her left.

"How do you do?" Rosie asked politely.

Agnes, assessing Rosie's clean but worn white coat, squared shoulders and tired eyes, instantly liked what she saw.

"We are quite well," Agnes answered a bit haltingly, having switched to the surface tongue for Rosie's sake. "Thank you."

"My pleasure." Rosie, likewise recognizing in Agnes's steady gaze and firm chin the kind but uncompromising qualities of an excellent nurse, was truly pleased. Curiousity compelled Rosie to look next at Daphne. Honesty demanded that she agree with Cassidy's assessment—Daphne was both young and pretty, the type to turn a man's head without much, if any, effort. Still, Cassidy had brought her along on this vital and risky mission. That was enough to make Rosie offer a smile and nod.

"Yes. Thank you," Daphne responded, uncomfortable in her first brush with needing to speak the surface language. She knew Cassidy spoke it fluently, and that one of the reasons Cassidy had chosen her over the other nurses was the slightly exaggerated impression Daphne had given of her command of the language. Now that she was here, Daphne felt distinctly insecure on the subject. Her only comfort, in fact, was that Cassidy's grandma, Damaris, had approved her competency on the subject.

"Agnes," Cassidy gestured towards the crate they were using as a table, "I am afraid that we need to unpack Bobby."

Extremely curious as to who—or what—this 'Bobby' was, Rosie waited impatiently for the minute or so it took for them to clear the top of the crate, produce the prybar that had been left, and remove the lid.

"Rosie," Cassidy set aside the packing material and lifted out a skeleton, "meet Bobby. He is made almost entirely from fish bone and is a precisely accurate recreation of an average adult male." Seeing that Daphne had set up the stand, Cassidy hung Bobby on it by the cords about his shoulders. "Here," she turned Bobby so that his 'back' was to them, "we see silken threads that represent the spinal column."

Rosie, who had graduated at the top of her class, regarded the artificial spinal column with considerable awe.

"Can you show me approximately where Prince Isaac's injuries occurred?" Cassidy asked Rosie.

Rosie looked at Bobby carefully. "The worst injury to his back is about here," she indicated the lumbar or lower portion of the spine.

"Yes, as I thought. He still has command of his upper limbs." Cassidy paused. "Though I noticed his right hand is not fully functioning?"

Rosie shook her head in agreement. "His sword hand."

"I do not understand," Cassidy prompted when Rosie lapsed into silence.

"I am not sure I can explain," Rosie answered reluctantly. "Or that I should."

"Please, Rosie." Cassidy looked her in the eyes. "I must know all that I can."

"We are not even sure," Rosie began to protest, then shrugged slightly. "You are right, of course." Shoving her own, fully functioning hands into the deep, square pockets of her coat, Rosie gave in. "It is not uncommon for a Wrangler or a windfairy to physically exhibit injuries of the mind. In Prince Isaac's case, being so badly injured during the pirate offensive, it is our belief that he feels he failed in his assignment to lead the Wood Fairy Fleet into battle."

Cassidy listened in growing dismay. She was here as much to learn the truth of the pirates as to heal Prince Isaac. How could she have overlooked the possibility that the two would be interconnected?

"So it is his sword hand that does not function," Cassidy slowly interpreted, "because the battle was lost."

"Oh no." Rosie shook her head vehemently. "We won the battle. The pirates were routed and sent scurrying back to their nests like the rats that they are." Her tone while she spoke of the pirates was pure venom, a startling change from the warm, friendly one she had been using. "But because Prince Isaac was prevented from doing more than participate in a brief skirmish, we think his mind is not allowing him to use his sword hand."

Cassidy mentally filed this new idea for review at another time.

"Who led the Wood Fairy Fleet," she nearly tripped over the alliteration, "after Prince Isaac was injured?"

"Sir Stuart."

"*The* Sir Stuart?" Cassidy clarified, appalled at the idea of having another violent man anywhere near her delicate instruments. "The one you were speaking of earlier?"

"The very same," Rosie agreed. "He is a hero of that battle, decorated by King Walter himself."

Cassidy turned away to hide her distaste at the thought of celebrating aggressive, if necessary—and she was as yet unconvinced of that—behavior. It was clearly a matter of pride for Rosie, and Cassidy had no wish to offend her. Their customs on the subject were obviously completely different.

"I see." Settling Bobby back on the display stand, Cassidy considered carefully. "If the damage is not too bad, I may be able to administer a decoction that will revitalize the cord and allow it to heal more or less on its own. It would take most of the winter." Folding her arms across her chest, she added, "Most patients respond very well to the decoction, with eighty-nine percent of them healing completely. Of those who do not, nearly nine percent are still able to walk short distances, take care of their basic practical necessities, and so on."

"What of the remaining two percent?" Rosie asked bravely. She wanted to be ready when it came time to help explain this to Isaac and the royal family.

Cassidy deliberated carefully before replying. "In the event that their spines do not respond to the decoction, there is one other, rather remote possibility. An experimental procedure that we have only just begun to use." From the corner of her eye, she saw Agnes frowning slightly. "Time is a critical factor in whether or not this procedure will work. In this case," she shook her head, "too much time may already have passed."

Rosie was noticeably paler than she had been upon entering the room. "Please tell me about the procedure." Seeing Cassidy's reluctance, she hastily defended her question with, "When you are ready to present this to King Walter and Queen Fiona, I must know as much as possible so that I can help to make sure they understand."

Cassidy agreed. Rosie would be a very useful advocate, able to explain the complicated procedure in terms of Wood Fairy medicine, at least as much as that was possible. After she understood it herself, that was. Cassidy nodded at Daphne, who retrieved a small, bright red packing crate.

Gingerly applying the prybar, Daphne delicately removed the lid. Nestled within layer upon layer of the best packing materials, lay a rectangular case, no longer than Daphne's arm from wrist to elbow. This was the other reason Daphne had been chosen for this trip. Her last fifty years of apprenticeship were spent studying under the first surgeon to successfully use this procedure.

"Open it," Cassidy instructed Daphne. "This is a very dangerous operation," she told Rosie while Daphne produced the tiny key that she wore on a chain about her neck. "It has only been performed a handful of times. And one of those times, the patient died."

Daphne opened the case to reveal strands of gold so thin and fine that they resembled nothing so much as the minute, silken threads that made up Bobby's spinal cord. After allowing Rosie a good, long look, she shut the case and locked it again. Returning it to the inside of the packing crate, she set it back on the counter where she found it.

"In some cases," Cassidy told Rosie, "when the spinal cord is badly damaged, surgically inserting a number of those gold wires can, along with the decoction, allow the spinal cord to overcome the damage, and eventually, the wires would be removed. With time and intensive physical therapy, some patients have successfully learned to walk again."

Rosie was silent for several seconds, her gaze locked on the small, red packing crate.

"I must ask you not to discuss this with anyone," Cassidy stipulated. "Especially not Prince Isaac."

"No." Rosie cleared her throat and tried again. "No, I understand." *And yet...* "I am just sorry his hopes are so high."

Cassidy patted Rosie's arm lightly. "The fact that he has the use of his arms is a very good sign."

"He also has some control of his legs," Rosie all but blurted out.

"Oh? Wonderful!" Cassidy smiled. "How much?"

Rosie did not respond immediately. "While seated, he can raise and lower his feet."

The information was somewhere in Isaac's file, Cassidy was sure, and yet something drove her to probe Rosie's statement further.

"How far can he raise and lower them?" Cassidy's heart sank deeper into the pit of her stomach the longer it took Rosie to reply

"Nearly a finger's width."

"I see." Cassidy kept smiling and strictly avoided asking whether *a finger's width* meant the distance from one side of a fingernail to the other or the height of an average finger from the pad to the top of the fingernail. It was not that she did not care. It was simply that, either way, the answer did not bode well for the young prince. Besides, Cassidy would have to run her own tests before she could make an informed decision regarding the suitability of either procedure for Prince Isaac's condition. "Well, we both have a lot to think about."

Agnes, correctly assuming that Rosie had returned to collect the dinner dishes, and that the interview had run its course, made a point of allowing a metal fork to slip through her fingers and onto the metal serving cart. The water clock had not stopped splashing off the seconds, and there were still a lot of more important things to do than speculate before they would finally be able to retire for the night.

"For-give, please," Agnes shrugged with her hands.

"No harm done," Rosie answered a little too brightly. "Those are designed to survive being dropped by apprentices." Her smile froze a little when she registered that she had said *survive*. "It is late. I better get this back to the kitchen and let you get some rest." Her eyes strayed again to the red crate.

"Before you go," Cassidy remembered something abruptly, a matter of some sensitivity. "We would like to," she held out her hands hopefully, "wash up before retiring."

Rosie waited for her to continue, then looked at the others. Rosie herself had shown them how to work the sinks, so she was briefly puzzled. Daphne averted her eyes, but Agnes watched her expectantly. A thought came to Rosie's mind. While giving them the short tour earlier, had she neglected to go over the finer points of their indoor plumbing?

"Of course." This was not the first time Rosie had to explain such matters, for more than one of the apprentices, and even a few of her junior nurses, came from outlying communities where 'indoors' was where one went during the winter and the plumbing was antiquated at best. "If you will follow me?"

Chapter 5

On the far edge of Weetu, Isaac was nursing a glass of nectar while he watched the sun fade beneath the horizon through the window of his room. Even the sweet tang of the imported kiwi concoction could not quite hide the bitter taste of the medicinal potion Noland had stirred into it to help him sleep. Isaac did have to admit that the potion was working. He recognized the symptoms by now; his eyelids growing heavy, his attention wandering where it would. He hated the dulling effect it had on his senses. What kind of a Wrangler did not sleep with senses on the alert? Only the promise of a night without dreams prompted him to accept it once or twice a week.

Abruptly, Isaac gulped down the rest of his drink. He did not trust himself to keep the secret of the Water Fairies while half-asleep, especially not from his old friend.

Noland's eyes were wide with surprise as he accepted the empty glass from his master. It usually required several not-so-subtle hints from himself, coupled with well-aimed jibes from Sir Stuart, to get Isaac through an entire glass of this stuff. Noland routinely tasted it after stirring it, just a drop or two off the edge of the stirring spoon, and so knew just how terrible it tasted in every nectar he had tried.

Stuart, too, was startled. He had grown to enjoy spending the evenings in Isaac's company. Many of Isaac's responsibilities fell to Stuart after Isaac's injury, with the King's blessing, and Stuart usually managed to work a report of the day in between sitting down and when it was time to leave. He greatly valued Isaac's guidance, but also felt that it gave Isaac something besides his recovery to focus on.

"Well." Stuart looked at his half-full glass sorrowfully. The potion would knock Isaac flat on his back in just a few minutes once it was fully consumed. Possibly sooner given that Isaac had most of it in a single swallow.

"Forget it," Isaac told Stuart when he saw that Stuart was about to set his glass down. "Kiwi is your favorite. No need for you to leave just because I have to retire." He grinned a little. "Stay, please. I will feel very badly if you do not."

Stuart settled back into the chair he had been subconsciously preparing to absent. "I should hate to have that on my conscience," he grinned back.

"Good." Isaac began unbuttoning his jacket. "Alright, Noland, I am ready."

Noland moved the wheelchair closer to Isaac's bed, where a pair of clean pajamas was waiting patiently. Between the two of them, Noland managed to get Isaac out of his dress clothes and into the pajamas. Isaac was basically asleep before Noland finished buttoning his sleep shirt.

"Here." Stuart knelt on the bed behind Isaac, slipping his arms around his friend's torso. Gripping the front of Isaac's back brace through the thin sleep shirt, he nodded at Noland, who was ready with Isaac's legs. Months of practice enabled them to smoothly reposition Isaac so that his head was on his pillow. Stuart even helped to pull the blankets up from the foot of the bed to Isaac's chin. It was a simple service, but something Isaac, who could not sit up on his own, would not have been able to do for himself even if he had been awake.

"How is he doing?" Stuart asked Noland. Of everyone in court, they spent the most time with Isaac. If his moods took a turn for the worse, they quickly conspired to return him to the privacy of his own chambers. Once they had even turned away Queen Fiona, though neither of them was quite sure whether it was for her sake or Isaac's. The dark wood of the walls of the bedroom bore a few new scars where Isaac had thrown things a time or two.

"Better," Noland nodded, transferring Isaac's dress clothes to the laundry chute. "He had a curious meeting with the queen for lunch, but afterwards he was in high spirits."

"Curious how?" Stuart asked, intrigued.

"I was not permitted to join them," Noland shrugged. That in itself was odd. "I also got the impression that someone else did." Producing a small, soft brush from the drawer Isaac had given him to store cleaning things, Noland turned careful attention to brushing off the arm cushions on Isaac's wheelchair. There were crumbs on the seat, too, making Noland frown when he noticed them. "When the butler brought the tray, there were four cups."

Stuart flew over to his glass and passed it just under his nose, eyes half-closing in delight.

"It could have been the king," he suggested before taking another sip.

"The king was in conference elsewhere at the time," Noland pointed out. "It must have been important, too; he called the full Council." Satisfied that he had gotten all of the bread crumbs, he put the brush away. Taking up a small container of axle grease, he began daubing it meticulously on the wheel shaft. Too much and it would slop everywhere when he tried to drive the chair. Too little and friction built up, causing unnecessary wear and tear on the components. "I also heard from one of the hostlers that a small party arrived at daybreak this morning."

Stuart looked around at that, his drink forgotten. "Arrived? You mean someone chanced travelling this late in the season?" That was unbelievable. "Was that the same hostler who reported a sharp drop in temperature on our shores?"

"Yes, I believe so." Noland replied. "The temperature drops every winter," he shrugged. "The party is what I find most curious. No one has seen them since they presented the king's secretary with a letter bearing Prince Cambrian's royal seal."

Stuart tried to connect the dots, but none of them seemed to have anything to do with each other. Why would the Sky Fairies be sending a party out this late? Winter always started in the Sky Fairy mountains, then blew its way around Fairydom until spring. As for the members of this party, Stuart had personally seen the Sky Fairy Ambassador at supper, and there had been no new faces at his table. Nor had the ambassador seemed the least bit distracted, joining a few of the others at the evening's entertainment and remaining the entire time. Stuart was not in the habit of spying on the tribal ambassadors, but he had been there as well, at the insistence of Lady Lorna, the guest he was assigned to escort that evening. Another of Isaac's tasks that had fallen to him, yet it was hardly his favorite. Lady Lorna was as physically attractive as she was cold and calculating. Truth be told, he intended to ask Isaac for advice in handling her for the next few days until his assignment rotated.

"I suppose that would explain why Isaac was so quick to finish his potion," Stuart mused aloud.

"That could be." Noland, having buffed up a spot or two on the toes of Isaac's boots that must have brushed against something during the course of the day, put them away. "The potion does seem to rob him of his hold on his tongue."

Stuart winced, thinking back to the first month of trying to get Isaac to take the stuff. Isaac's anger had flowed unchecked with only half a glass of the stuff in him. Anger at himself for being 'so stupid' as to get injured, anger at the doctors who could not cure him, anger…at his situation.

Stuart had seen this kind of reaction before, knew that it was perfectly normal despite the fact that their culture taught that injury was almost inevitable. Why, even as children they knew the stories of how their teachers had come to leave the Wrangler Corp. An unfailing respect for them was drilled into every child, be they prince or blacksmith's apprentice. It might have seemed rather glamorous except that they spent their days in direct contact with ex-Wranglers and saw for themselves what the various injuries prevented them from doing. Whatever their culture taught, it was a cold, hard fact that these fairies were no longer Wranglers. Many of them could no longer walk or fly; some few could not even feed themselves. In short, no one was eager to be injured.

Tossing off the rest of his drink almost without tasting it, Stuart set his glass down. "He did alright at therapy today. Jared had to calm him down at the leg machine, but that is normal."

"Do you think he will ever walk again?" Noland asked. He had wondered about it many times, without daring to bring it up.

"I suppose he could." Stuart ran his fingers through his wavy brown hair. "The doctor is not very hopeful, though."

While the setting sun was nearly gone, there was enough light from the cold fire for Stuart to easily see the bare spots on Isaac's wall. Two circles and one large rectangle, darker than the rest of the wall, marred the area around the one remaining picture. Isaac had insisted, almost violently, that the other paintings, which depicted him engaging in various athletic pursuits, be removed. The round picture that had survived his demands was a portrait of the royal family a few hundred years ago. Gallica was still a gangly youth at the time the painting was done, and Isaac not far ahead of her. *Gallica.* It was too late to expect the king to tolerate what could be seen as prying questions. Stuart's favorite tomboy, on the other hand, would probably be much more accommodating.

"Carry on." Stuart left abruptly.

Noland looked down from where he was preparing to pull the nightshade over the prince's bed. The sun set every evening, but the mushroom's cold fire burned on and he was not about to let it disturb Isaac's slumber.

"Carry on?" he asked the empty room. Sighing, he shook his head and tugged the coarse, black cloth into place, stretching it between the ceiling and Isaac's bed like a canopy, then snapping the restrainers with exaggerated force. "What did he think I was going to do?" Noland was a fourth generation valet to the Royal Wood Fairy family and very proud of it.

Stuart, oblivious to the feathers he had ruffled, flew silently through the tunnels towards Gallica's rooms. Gallica always joined her mother and brother for lunch. To the best of his knowledge, today had been no different. In that respect at least. He was cutting through the empty amphitheater when he heard a familiar laugh, arresting him in place.

"Do you always offer auditions mid-season?"

Gallica's voice drifted out from somewhere towards the front of the room to Stuart's waiting ears. The stage lights having been removed after the performance, he had some difficulty in locating her at first. When he saw who she was with, he bristled angrily.

"Hello!" Stuart sent his voice ahead of him, but not by much. Landing on the stage with an unnecessary thump, he faced the princess and the head of the acting troupe, Phil Girard. Phil was probably as tall as Gallica, if he kept his shoulders back, and seemed to be having some trouble with his collar. Judging by the way Phil was tugging at his collar, it was either done much too tightly or Phil was decidedly nervous. "I believe the Princess asked you a question."

Gallica tried to laugh it off. "Nonsense, I was just…making conversation."

"Alright, I will play." Stuart fixed her with a hard stare, then turned genial eyes towards Phil. Nothing like confusing one's enemy to make them easy prey. "Do you often give auditions mid-season?" That was something of an exaggeration, since their engagement was for the entire winter, but Stuart did not really care.

Phil opened his mouth, but nothing came out. "Sometimes," he finally managed.

"Of course you do." Stuart's mouth kept smiling, but the humor did not reach his eyes.

"After all, your lead might come down sick. Unexpectedly."

"Lena?" Phil spluttered. "Oh, no, Lena never gets sick."

"Lucky for you." Stuart waited for Phil's nod before continuing. "Well, then, I suppose you had some smaller part in mind for the princess." Belatedly, he realized he was ruining his chances of getting any information out of Gallica. She could not have been more furious with him if he had told her mother about the time he caught her posing as a dragonfly jockey at an edge city.

"Right." Phil figuratively grabbed the straw Stuart had offered. "Just a, well, a line." Catching site of the princess' eyes, he stuttered, "Or…or two. Yeah, two lines. Plenty for a beginner!"

"Really Phil," Stuart allowed his smile to come down a few notches and injected false admiration into his tone. "You are much too kind, offering *two* lines to a rank amateur." Tugging thoughtfully at his ear, he made a decision. It was going to cost him. Plenty. Not that it would be a total loss… "I wonder if you knew that Lady Lorna had some acting experience?"

Phil, understandably wary of Stuart after being caught alone with the young princess, managed a noncommittal, "Oh?"

"Why yes. She was telling me about it at dinner this evening. In fact," Stuart faked a frown, "given the proper, mmm, persuasion, she might be convinced to be available as a stand-in for a few of your cast. Just in case someone, not Lena, of course, were to become ill."

"Say, that is a good idea." Phil knew Lady Lorna, mostly by reputation, but certainly enough to be sure she did not have a young, strong protector lurking in the shadows. "I should ask her about that."

"Now." Stuart's smile vanished like a magician's assistant. "Ask her now."

"Y…yes…" Phil was back to stuttering. "I was just leaving." He disappeared in a rather spectacular fashion himself, fleeing via the stage exit.

Gallica was about to let Stuart have it when he turned to face her.

"How dare you think what you are thinking?" she flared, distressed to find that she was suddenly more hurt than angry. After all, Stuart had known her all of her life.

Stuart considered the question while he flew the short distance between them.

"I apologize." Seeing that his humble tone had further taken her off guard, he offered her his arm. "Seeing you with," he glanced in the direction of Phil's hasty retreat, "him, I guess I overreacted. Forgive me?"

Gallica struggled to recapture some of her anger, but it was gone.

"Why should I?" At least she could act angry. They were on stage, after all.

Stuart stared down at her, noticing for the first time that her hair was down. For the most part, the Gallica he knew decried fashion in favor of wearing her hair up and out of the way.

"For old times' sake?" he suggested hopefully, finding himself unable to bear the thought of her being truly angry with him. As she had not yet taken his arm, he gently reached for her hand. Instead of resting it on top of his arm, a more formal position, he tenderly tucked it in the crook of his elbow. "And because I am willing to admit now that you could take Phil Girard any time you wanted to."

Gallica laughed, caught herself, then laughed again. It was true that Phil, whose broad shoulders were beginning to fail at hiding his increasing girth, would not have stood a chance against her in a straight-up fight. Her Wrangler training saw to that.

"Oh, you," she reached up with her free hand to squeeze his forearm. "Are you ever going to realize that I am all grown up?"

Stuart had to look away at that point or risk putting her statement to test. Her lips were just a little too near, the dim lighting just a little too romantic for even his iron restraint.

"I give you my word," he lifted off carefully, making sure that she came with him. "I am completely convinced."

Something about the timbre of his voice set Gallica's heart to doing all sorts of gymnastics. She resorted to humor in self-defense.

"Sure," she agreed, bumping him with her near wing. "Until the next time you think I need rescuing."

Stuart laughed with her a little, knowing that it went far deeper than that. Unless he was seriously mistaken, the little girl he had helped with her math homework; the tomboy he had taught to ride; even the semi-serious youth he oversaw during weapons training, had complete possession of his heart. It was a sneak attack, that was what. He had never even seen it coming, just trusted her implicitly with piece after piece of his heart until there was nothing left that he could call his own.

"Gallica." He cleared his throat when he heard his own tone. "Gallica," he tried again, "please try to understand. Weetu is full of good, honest men who would be thrilled to have your attention. Does it really surprise you that I object to you spending time with someone like Phil Girard?"

Gallica blushed a little. "It surprises me that you think I had any romantic interest in him."

Stuart turned to face her and immediately

wished he had not. Once again she was too close for comfort. "Then what…?" He stopped himself just in time. "I have no real right to ask that."

"Are you sure?" Gallica asked, tilting her head back to look up at him. "Best friends can usually ask awkward questions."

Best friends. Stuart smiled and resumed his course for the royal quarter. He was a realist. Friends who were 'all grown up' did not fall in love with old playmates.

"Alright. Tell me."

Gallica leaned a little closer. "The Chief Steward reported seeing three separate members of his troupe in the south corridors." She was disappointed when he did not respond. "The *south* corridors," she repeated. "Where the treas…" Her words trailed off with a gasp when Stuart abruptly stopped and took her by the shoulders.

"I know what is in those corridors," he reminded her in a low tone, his eyes boring into hers. The tribe's second treasure room was discreetly tucked in behind a false wall, a fact most fairies had hopefully forgotten. "In fact, I am sworn to protect it."

"I know." Gallica decided this was her chance. "So let me help you."

"How?" Stuart's recently discovered feelings made his tone harsher than he would have liked.

"You tell me." Gallica shook free of his grasp and came to her full height to glare haughtily at him. "I had a plan until you ruined it back there."

"And I will ruin any other plans, do you hear me?" Judging from her wide-eyed expression, Gallica had heard him only too well. "You are not to make another move until you hear from me. Clear?"

Torn by conflicting emotions, Gallica settled for a frosty, "Clear." Head high, she whisked herself off to her rooms.

Left to stare after her, Stuart tore at his collar. *What just happened?*

Chapter 6

The next day dawned cold. So bitterly cold that a layer of ice had formed overnight around several of the smaller portholes—including the handful of portholes that the kitchen staff had left open for fresh air. They were immediately reported to the Chief Steward, who immediately relayed it to Prince Isaac via Sir Stuart.

"What are we to do?" moaned the Head Cook. "All of the breakfast food is frozen solid!"

"Might do the court good to miss a meal for a change," Isaac muttered, not quite to himself. "For now, the more important thing is to check the bark ring apartments. Here, you." He pointed directly at one of the butlers. "Get this ice melted and seal that porthole for winter."

"Winter?" The bewildered butler took a second look at Isaac's scowling face and decided it would be simpler—and wiser—to just obey. "Look alive," the butler barked at the staff. "Fetch wood for a fire. You lads," he caught two of the more experienced fellows by the arms, "double-check the chimney, make sure it is not blocked."

Satisfied, Isaac motioned for Stuart to drive him out of the kitchen. Isaac's sharp ears caught the order for the breakfast food to be brought over by the fire, and he chuckled a little. That butler was apparently just as smart as he looked. Starting a fire was a necessary step to defrosting the porthole and the water pipes, but could also be used to thaw the breakfast foods. In effect, they would be sorting out two problems with one solution.

"Put out an alert," Isaac ordered Stuart. "That ice means winter has hit—with a vengeance. I want every last bark ring apartment emptied out; it is far too dangerous to leave anyone there. Even check…no, *especially* check the apartments that were supposed to have been transferred to an inner ring already." Isaac grimaced. "Lord Dean was particularly resistant to the idea of leaving his 'spacious apartment' for the 'cramped' inner quarters."

"I thought he always wintered at his private estate," Stuart remarked in surprise.

"Not this season," Isaac muttered. "Be sure to tell the medical staff to stand by for any cases of hypothermia."

Stuart looked at Tom, his eldest apprentice. Tom nodded that he had heard and vanished down a side tunnel.

"Where are we going now?" Stuart asked.

"To report to my father."

Accordingly, Stuart drove a silent Isaac to the king's offices.

"Prince Isaac." The Captain of the Guard who was guarding the king's office saluted. "His Majesty, King Walter, instructed me to admit you as soon as you arrived." He frowned apologetically at Stuart, who was still in position behind Isaac's chair. "Just the prince, Sir Stuart."

Baffled, Stuart moved out of the way so that the guard could take over driving. Hearing the doors click closed behind the guard was enough to make Stuart wince slightly. He was accustomed to being taken into both the prince's and the king's confidence. It was absolutely no consolation to him when the guard reappeared and resumed his post moments later.

"Sir?"

Stuart looked back at the guard, his mind already half-occupied with thoughts of joining the search of the bark ring apartments. The other half of his mind was still thoroughly involved in trying to figure out how to get back in Gallica's good graces.

"His Majesty would like you to wait."

Accordingly, Stuart did just that. The large water clock in one corner kept him company, providing the only noise in the room besides the regular breathing of its occupants. Unlike most of the water clocks in Weetu, this one was designed as much for entertainment as for function. Tiny wheels and paddles were meticulously positioned between the upper container, where the drops originated, and the lower container, or receptacle, which eventually caught the falling drops. On one side of the clock was a small bell, which attached to the wheels and paddles via a lightweight cord. The water drops, falling at a constant rate, eventually spun the wheels and paddles to the point that the attached cord built up sufficient tension to ring the bell. That happened once every hour.

The bell rang once while Stuart waited, and was approximately halfway towards another ring when the heavy doors clicked open. The guard leaned close to hear what someone inside said, then made eye contact with Stuart and motioned for him to enter the office.

From the far side of his desk, King Walter watched as Stuart entered the office and stood at attention. Glancing at either side of his desk, Walter pondered briefly which situation to address first.

"You wanted to see me, Sire?" Stuart silently considered the facts. Prince Isaac, Princess Gallica, Nurse Rosie, the king, and himself were the only ones present. That probably meant they all knew something that he did not.

"I did," Walter acknowledged. "I have something of a very confidential nature to discuss with you." Stuart's greeting helped Walter decide. He was more than fond of Stuart, he trusted him. Everyone else in the room knew the full details of the arrival of the Water Fairy Doctor and her nurses; what Gallica had brought to him, on the other hand, was not common knowledge.

"Of course, Sire."

"Stuart." Walter leaned forward a little. "Relax. If I did not trust you, you would not be here."

Stuart complied with a half-smile. "Thank you, sir." He had tried many times to come to terms with his close ties to the royal family, something he had never anticipated when he joined the Wrangler's, and yet he still found himself tongue-tied and awkward around the king and queen.

"Rosie has just been telling me that our medical staff has done all that they can for Isaac. The injury to his spine is simply too severe, well beyond our current level of medicinal understanding. It is her considered opinion that, without additional treatment, Isaac will never walk again." Walter watched with grim appreciation as Stuart's face drained of color until it was almost as white under his tan as the dress shirt he was wearing. Truth be told, when Walter got the news, he felt exactly like someone had hit him in the stomach with a sledgehammer.

"Sorry to hear that, sir." Stuart's voice was a whisper. He would not have spoken at all except that the pursuant silence seemed to indicate it was expected of him.

"As am I." Walter now leaned back in his chair, gripping its arms so that his hands would be hidden from view under his desk. "I suppose you are aware that we had some new arrivals last night."

"I am, sir." Stuart, thrown off by the change of subject, answered at once. "It was quite dangerous for them to travel so close to the onset of winter."

"Exactly what have you heard about them?"

Stuart took a moment to gather his thoughts. "I heard that three fairies, hooded and cloaked to the point that observers were not sure if they were male or female, arrived just after the doors opened yesterday morning."

"Is that all?" Walter's tone had a slight edge that belied his casual posture.

"No, sir. I have also heard that they presented a letter bearing Prince Cambrian's official seal and were brought immediately to see you. After that, they seem to have disappeared, but," Stuart hesitated. "I believe one of them joined Queen Fiona, Princess Gallica, and Prince Isaac for lunch yesterday."

Walter searched Stuart's face, but if Stuart was curious, he was not giving himself away.

That meeting with his wife was supposed to have been completely unobserved.

"Is *that* all?" Prince Isaac asked, resting his chin on his good left fist. He half-expected Stuart to tell them that he knew the two nurses spent lunch in his mother's private dressing room, or that they were currently sequestered in the medical maze. Stuart had a positive talent for keeping his eyes and ears open.

"It is."

"Alright. What we are about to tell you is not to be spoken of with anyone besides those present and the queen. In fact, if you can avoid speaking of it at all outside of this room," King Walter's glance took them all in, "that would be for the best."

"Understood." Stuart automatically snapped back to attention.

"Stuart." This time it was Isaac who spoke. "Sit down, will you please?" He cleared his throat when he heard how irritated he sounded. Soon enough, he promised himself, he would able to stand at attention again.

Sheepishly, Stuart took the chair Isaac pointed at.

"Now, we know something of great importance has recently occurred in the Sky Fairy Kingdom," Isaac began, "but we know almost nothing about it. While the three fairies that arrived yesterday did bring a letter from

Prince Cambrian, it was intended merely to introduce them as scientists and surgeons from another tribe. To express Cambrian's confidence in them."

Stuart noticed that Princess Gallica was holding her breath. What was going on?

"They are Water Fairies." Isaac looked over at Gallica and flashed her a grin. "You can breathe now. The secret is out." Resuming eye contact with Stuart, Isaac sobered slightly. "They say they can help me walk again. Even," he shrugged slightly, "even reconstruct my wings."

That did it. Stuart's mouth dropped open slightly and stayed there. He was no medical expert, but fairy wings were deceptively powerful when fully functional and exceptionally fragile when injured, almost impossible to repair. They bore some resemblance to butterfly wings in that a healthy set of fairy wings consisted of a larger top pair and a smaller lower pair, yet were in the shape of bird's wings. Stuart's own wings, currently gathered and tucked under his jacket like a bird's so that he could sit comfortably, were twitching with excitement despite his best efforts to control them.

"How?"

Nurse Rosie, responding to looks from King Walter and Isaac, answered.

"I discussed the process of spinal repair with their surgeon, Doctor Cassidy, last night. They have procedures and medicines that I have never heard of, or even considered. The best hope is that they will be able to insert a decoction that will enable his spine to repair itself." Since she had already explained all of this to the king and queen that morning, she omitted the second, more dangerous option.

"And my wings?" Isaac asked anxiously. With his wings and spine restored, he could resume active duty in the Wranglers. He and several thousands of other, similarly injured, Wood Fairies. The implications were staggering.

"I have not as yet asked about that," Rosie shook her head. She intended to, naturally, but had been so overcome by Cassidy's words last night that asking about another, no doubt equally astonishing, procedure had completely slipped her mind.

"Your Majesty." Stuart wished he was standing. "How can I help?" It was the only thing that made sense. Even knowing nothing about a tribe of Water Fairies—a very strange circumstance in and of itself—Stuart was absolutely certain that he would not have been apprised of the situation without a very good, very specific reason.

Walter smiled at him. "There is actually

something we need you to do. It might seem beneath your office, Sir Stuart."

"I would muck out the entire stable if it meant Prince Isaac could resume his duties."

Isaac burst out laughing, spoiling the moment.

"Sorry, Stuart," he apologized, still chuckling a little. "I did not realize my duties were so overwhelming."

Stuart grinned back, relieved to have the joke explained to him. He made a mental note to get Isaac back later.

"I think we all know your intentions," King Walter reassured Stuart once his own smile was under control.

"Thank you, Sire."

"What we need you to do is this: whatever the doctor and her associates need, you will provide. You will take them their meals and return their dishes to the kitchen. Paper, ink, towels, laundry service…anything, for the duration of their stay." King Walter was again watching Stuart closely. Mucking out the stables was not a pleasant job, but it was at least something Stuart could do openly. Being apparently 'reduced' to performing odd jobs about Weetu, without the option of explaining himself, might be more than a Wrangler could take.

In point of fact, Stuart was at that moment

wrestling with his pride. As an apprentice, he had been at the beck and call of both the senior apprentices and the active Wranglers. While this assignment might not seem so very different from that, he regarded that period of his training with acute loathing. It had been such a relief to move past it, to promise himself he would never again… At some point, his loyalty got the upper hand. Loyalty to his friend, to his tribe, to his king.

"You can count on me, Sire."

"Good." Walter leaned forward again. "Rosie, Sir Stuart will join you in your office within the next half hour. At that time, you will introduce him to our guests and make sure he understands all aspects of his task. In the meanwhile," he refrained from looking at his unusually silent daughter, "if you would take Isaac to his morning therapy, please?" He nodded briefly at his son before they left.

When the door was closed behind Rosie and Isaac, Walter stood and walked over to Gallica. He had a feeling she had not told him the full story of last night, but could not figure out what she was withholding. She had been perfectly relaxed while she told him about the suspicious behavior of the performing troupe members; likewise while she listened to Rosie and Isaac. It was only when Stuart entered the room that she retreated into silence.

"I understand that you had a little trouble with Phil Girard last night," King Walter finally said to Stuart.

"Is that what he told you, Sire?" Stuart asked carefully. That seemed highly unlikely, but Stuart needed a moment to think about how to answer. Gallica looked at him for the first time since he entered the room, and quickly dropped her eyes.

"No." King Walter shook his head, confused by the obvious tension his question had caused between them. "Gallica did. I believe it had something to do with concerns about the safety of the tribe's second treasury?"

"Oh." Stuart was almost disappointed. If Gallica had told her father the whole story, Stuart might have thought she was, however unwittingly, interested in him. "Yes, she told me just last night that three different troupers have been found suspiciously near the south corridors."

"And you approached Girard to ask him about it."

Stuart frowned. "No, sir." In all honesty, he had not.

"Well, then, what did happen?" Unless Walter was mistaken, Gallica was borderline squirming now.

"I engaged Girard in conversation about the health of his cast."

"The health of his cast?" Walter repeated blankly. "Why?"

"I was trying to keep him off balance." That at least was true. "I also suggested that if he needed a substitute performer, he might try Lady Lorna."

Walter's lips twitched. Lady Lorna had spent last winter at Weetu as well, much to Isaac's chagrin. It looked to him as if Stuart was trying to get her taken off the roster of unattached guests who were routinely escorted by members of the royal household. It would probably work, too; the woman had a streak of vanity as wide as the woodgrain of a hedge tree.

"I see."

Stuart hoped not.

"And the wandering troupers. What have you done about them?"

Stuart blinked. He no doubt should have done *something*. Except that he had been wholly distracted at the time. And he had no wish to explain to the king by whom he had been distracted.

"As yet, nothing. An increase in guards near the south corridors would only confirm any ideas they might have regarding the location of the tribal treasury. As would asking questions about it, or doing anything to make them think we care overly much about whether or not they visit the south corridors."

"They should already know better than to trespass in the south corridors," Gallica interrupted. "Only guests of the royal court have any business in that area."

"Her Highness is right, of course," Stuart agreed, stifling his annoyance with her for blasting a hole in his logic. Everyone who came to work at Weetu was advised of that fact, though exceptions could be made upon request. "I will ask the Chief Steward to review court etiquette with them again. And while it is true that adding guards would draw even more attention to the area, I could always assign different guards. I can think of a few I would trust to watch, listen, and report."

King Walter considered the idea and them at the same time. Gallica and Stuart had been friends since he could remember, with the usual number of tiffs and squabbles. Today, however, their behavior towards each other rivaled the chill outside. He assumed it would blow over, like always, but decide to prod the matter along. Wintertime spats had a way of getting out of hand as tempers got shorter.

"Proceed with your plan," he agreed. "Tell the steward as much or as little as you think wise." An idea struck him as Stuart rose to leave. "And as for that other matter, I have decided that I want you to share it with Princess Gallica." He held up a hand when they both attempted to protest. "After additional thought, I realized it is more than one fairy could handle without the change from ordinary being noted. This way, you two can spell each other, rotating so that you can each appear around Weetu as you ordinarily would through the course of the day." Feeling that he had explained enough, and certainly more than he needed to, he nodded dismissively to Stuart. "Be a good girl, now, Gallica, and run along. I have a busy day ahead of me."

Gallica literally bit her tongue to keep from reminding her father that she had been flying for the last century.

"Thank you, sir!" Stuart hastily saluted and ushered Gallica out before she erupted.

That suited King Walter just fine. In fact, he was smiling as he began reviewing one of the stacks of papers on his desk. The second reason he had assigned them to work together was to force them to work out whatever was bothering them. Rather clever, he thought.

Chapter 7

"Let go of me," Gallica hissed as soon as they were out of earshot.

"With pleasure." Stuart instinctively slipped into the role of command for his own protection, emotional and physical. Gallica had a superb right hook. "Now, you listen to me," he ordered when he saw that she was still simmering. "We have a job to do, right? Well, we are going to do that job and do it correctly. Just like always." He allowed his voice to soften a little at the end, hoping he had reached beyond her anger to her good sense by then. In his experience, Gallica was one of the more level-headed women in Weetu. Of course, that had been before she began insisting she was old enough for romance. "You can be mad at me later, alright?"

"Alright." Gallica twisted her hands together, distressed at her behavior of late. What had gotten into her? "Stuart? Do you," she paused to reconsider asking him if she was going crazy. She was still mad at him, after all. She would figure out why later. "I suppose we should do what Dad suggested. Take turns, I mean."

"I think we should," Stuart nodded. "Will you take them breakfast?" he asked. A wry smile tugged at the corners of his mouth. "That is, if there is any available? Breakfast got frozen solid last night when the kitchen staff left some portholes open."

"Oh, no!" Gallica immediately extrapolated on the statement. "Not all of the bark ring apartments have been emptied!"

"They better be empty by now," Stuart retorted, scowling. "Isaac ordered that before we went to report to your father."

"That is a relief." Gallica tried to remember hearing Isaac mentioning that, but to no avail. Wrapping her arms about her waist, she half-turned away from Stuart. If she were honest, what really distressed her was that there was some unidentified emotion driving her erratic behavior. How could she solve what she did not understand?

"Your Highness?" Stuart waited a beat, then tried, "Gallica?" The expression on her face when she turned to look at him told him that she was not really seeing him. She looked almost frightened. "Gallica." He took her gently by the shoulders. She was perfectly safe in Weetu. "Do you know where the surgeons are?"

"I…" She leaned towards him, almost as if about to rest her head against his shoulder. "Yes."

"Good." He choked back the word 'girl.' "If you will take them their breakfast, so that I can follow-up on the ice?"

"Course." Gallica straightened. "Of course I will."

"I think I will start by checking in on the kitchen," Stuart half-offered, wanting to stay with her as long as he could. He felt intense relief when she smiled and nodded. Slipping one arm between her upper and lower wingsets so that she would still be able to fly comfortably, he led off.

"They must be starving by now," Gallica remarked as they wove through the tunnels leading to the kitchen. "Say, I wonder what they like to eat?"

Stuart shrugged. "I have absolutely no idea. But it is a great question." He smiled down at her instead of reminding her that he had only just found out the—what was it? Oh yes.—the Water Fairy Tribe even existed. "We want them to be as comfortable and happy here as possible."

Gallica smiled back. In the past, her world had always landed on its feet when Stuart was around. Last night had been one of a very few times where he had added to her troubles. At the moment, though, it felt as if last night never even happened.

"Well, get another bucket!" snapped a harried cook as they entered the kitchen.

Stuart frowned, taking in the situation at a

glance. The skirts of both the cook and the lass who was running to obey her were sopping wet halfway up to the knee. Everyone not involved in the mad dash to prepare some sort of breakfast was on the business end of a mop or a bucket, but puddles and small streams of ice water were still forming with exasperating irregularity. Despite the blazing fires, more than one of the staff was shivering.

The ice was obviously thicker than they had originally believed. Instead of melting and running down the outside of the tree so that they could fasten the portholes and put up winter seals, the melted ice was flooding the kitchen.

Stuart caught one of the younger lads by the arm as he dashed past. "Go find a page. Go find a dozen if you have to," Relieving him of his full bucket, Stuart added, "Have them round up a dozen Wranglers and their firesticks." A pebble thrower might be more effective, but he hoped they could avoid discharging a weapon in the kitchen. The cooks would never forgive him, not even if he helped clean up the residue gunpowder on his hands and knees. Realizing he was still holding the lad by the arm, Stuart released him. "Hurry."

In turn, Gallica tried to take the bucket from Stuart, but he refused.

"Anyone of us can carry a bucket, but only you can take care of the other matter," he reminded her.

Gallica could not argue with that, so she took a mental step back and assessed the kitchen from another angle. Half of the kitchen staff was battling the flood while the other half was trying, unsuccessfully, to carve a meal out of the semi-frozen foods. She could hardly serve what did not yet exist.

"Here," Gallica leapt forward to rescue a slender scullery maid who was trying to carry a pot that was almost as large as she was.

"Thankee." The lass—Dottie to her friends—blew out her breath towards her bangs, which flipped up, then landed back in her eyes. "I never done this before," she explained. "Figured I could carry it."

"You can," Gallica grinned bravely as she helped the maid lug the heavy pot of oatmeal towards the fire. "With a little help." Together they managed to lift the pot onto one of the massive iron pot hooks and swing it into the heat. "Need anything else?"

"Not till she finishes cookin'," grinned Dottie. She took up a long handled ladle and began stirring the oatmeal.

Gallica promptly found someone else to help. Always at her best in an emergency, she exuded a cheerfulness that began to turn the tide of despair amongst the staff. Popping through the kitchen, she completed odd jobs for anyone who needed a hand. When things began settling down, she found something a little more challenging.

"I can do this," she told a sous chef who was making croissants at a blinding speed. "What should you be doing?" Shooing him off to assist one of the Chief Cooks with the bacon, Gallica washed her hands and donned an apron. Her dress was a simple brown barkcloth, and she might have begun shivering if she had not found work to do, but she still did not want it covered with flour.

She was halfway through filling the pan when the Wranglers arrived. The mops and buckets were laid aside so there would be enough room for the Wranglers to do their jobs, and Gallica yielded the dough to the regular staff. Looking for something else to do, she placed an abandoned mop so that it would divert a steady stream of ice water from its course through the middle of the kitchen floor.

Stuart, constantly aware of what Gallica was doing, traded the mop he had been using for a firestick. A minimum of ten twigs long, firesticks were hollow iron tubes that they ran various combustible cores through. The core could either be made to extend from the far end of the firestick or, which would be more useful in this case, could contain the burning core and be used to melt through the ice.

Stuart and the others flew forward to inspect the problem. The three iced windows were each large enough for two fairies to pass through shoulder to shoulder, and without stooping. It was a practical necessity for bringing supplies in. As for the ice, it took very little prodding to conclude that it was still quite solid.

A burly Wrangler whistled softly. "Firesticks may not be enough," he warned. "Especially not in an enclosed area like this."

"We only have to melt out enough ice to close and seal the portholes," Stuart reminded him. The kitchen was the only place in Weetu's bark ring that remained active during the winter, but even the cook fires could not be expected to keep it warm enough unless they got those windows closed and sealed.

"Without flooding the city, you mean." Another Wrangler chuckled and shrugged off his cloak. "After you."

"Not without these," Gallica muttered, popping up beside Stuart with a pair of protective goggles that she had commandeered from one of the equipment-carrying apprentices. Without even giving him a chance to protest, she slipped them over his head and settled them in place. "Too tight?" she asked.

Stuart shook his head. "They seem alright. Thanks." Spying the breakfast cart that was waiting for her, he smiled. "Good luck."

"Thought that was my line." Squeezing his upper arm lightly, Gallica fluttered to one side so that they could get the firesticks safely past her.

Stuart promptly flew over to the cook fire and inserted the far end of his firestick. He waited until it was red hot, then pushed the core—a combination of powdered magnesium and wood dust, pressed together—out far enough for it to catch fire. Beside him, the other Wrangler was doing the same.

"Ain't you gonna stay and watch?" asked Dottie as Gallica started off with the cart.

"I want to," Gallica admitted, recognizing the lass she had helped earlier, "but I am already late."

Stuart, absorbed in his task, did not even see her leave. Naturally the magnesium in the core began spitting and sparking as soon as it touched the ice water, but even that was not enough to keep the iron firestick head hot. By alternating the firesticks as the iron cooled, they began making some headway in clearing the upper rim of the center window. Seeing that his technique was working, the other Wranglers split into teams and tackled the two side windows.

Coughing in the smoke, Stuart stepped away from his window to let another take his place.

"You!" Stuart pointed at a chef. "Tell the pump room we need circulation in here."

"Take this." Stuart's partner passed his firestick off to one of the waiting apprentices. "You keep on with the edges," he told Stuart. "I will try to shave these rough spots down enough to get a proper seal."

Stuart nodded. "Good idea."

Working with his hand axe, his partner began scraping at the lumps and bumps on the far side of the window, giving Stuart plenty of elbow room to continue working on the right hand side of the sill. When they were both too cold to continue, they traded places with the two waiting Wranglers. It was dangerously cold and they were relatively dry. Stuart was glad to note that the wetter kitchen staff members had been sent off to change clothes and warm up.

"About time," Stuart remarked when the circulation fan finally began sucking out the smoke the firesticks were producing.

"And maybe about time we tried the window," his partner suggested.

"Wait." Stuart held up his hand. "If we try to close it before the ice water has finished running off, and it will not close all the way, it will probably freeze in place."

"Whereupon we would no longer be able to get in there and remove more ice," the other Wrangler conceded the point.

"Let it drain a minute. Then we will try."

Hearing that, the Wranglers working on the center window with them both began carefully checking the rims for ice water that had refrozen. After they gave the thumbs up, Stuart called for an apprentice to hold their firesticks.

"Keep them hot," he ordered, halting the lad as he moved towards the sand bucket.

"One on top, one on the bottom of each side?" suggested a Wrangler.

"Exactly what I had in mind," Stuart agreed. Once all four of them were in position, Stuart counted it off. "One. Two. Three. Heave!" Steadily, they began to push. Stuart wished for earplugs when the recently-frozen hinges shrieked in displeasure at how they were being treated.

"Hurray!" A handful of the remaining kitchen staff began to cheer when they saw the latch snap smartly into place.

Stuart chuckled and gasped for breath at the same time. "Better get the seals in place."

Three craftsfairies appeared beside them, seals behind them on carts. First they snugged the wooden cover in front of the window, loosely screwing it down. Moving in careful unison, they then attached a boxy glass cover over that for added insulation.

"Window number two?" Stuart smiled as another cheer rippled through the kitchen. Using the cuff of his ruined dress shirt, Stuart mopped some sweat off his face and removed the goggles.

"Latched and sealed." Stuart's partner swiped at his own forehead, smearing firestick ashes across it. Frowning at Stuart, he asked, "Am I as dirty as you are?"

"Naturally." Stuart grinned. Firesticks always managed to spit on the fellow wielding them, especially when a magnesium core was exposed to water; the ten twig distance only guaranteed safety from the dangerous heat, not the mess.

"Well, I hope you wash up before you keep any appointments!" He ribbed Stuart.

"Appointments?" Stuart looked over at the kitchen clock, then down at his suit and groaned. "As a matter of fact," he handed over the firesticks he had been holding. "I am late for one right now!" Without further explanation, he began making his way towards the tunnel that wound closest to his quarters.

"Oh, go right ahead," he called after Stuart. "No worries. We can finish this up!"

Stuart waved at him but did not bother to look back.

The other Wranglers grinned a little, buried the heads of their firesticks in the bucket of sand they brought for just that purpose, and joined the kitchen staff's bucket line.

"Another day," one of them sighed, "another adventure."   He stuffed his and Stuart's firesticks in the bucket as well. "The exciting life of a Wrangler." Rolling up his sleeves, he went to join the bucket line as well. There was no room, so he tapped a scullery maid on the shoulder. "My turn."

Stuart, confident that the emergency in the kitchen was in capable hands, raced towards his room, where he tossed his soiled jacket and shirt into the laundry chute. Turning on the water in his sink, he quickly washed his arms to his elbows and scrubbed his face before toweling himself dry. The hangers that fell to the floor when he reached into his closet for a fresh shirt and jacket he left to be picked up later. After a moment's hesitation, he even swapped out his britches so they would match the jacket a little better.

When Isaac looked up from where he was waiting in the pump room, a funny expression crossed his face.

"Thanks for keeping me company, Bert," Isaac grinned at the windfairy he'd been talking with. "Let me know how that meeting goes and if there is anything I can do to help out."

"Thank you," Bert caught himself, "Isaac. I will!" He had dabbled in playwriting before he decided to join the Royal Wood Fairy Fleet, and last night's theatrical performance had piqued his interest in it once again. Winter was the perfect time to try a new play from an untested playwright. By mid-winter, the audience would be so desperate for distractions from their forced confinement that they would sit through nearly anything. Even some of his adventures, he hoped!

"I was starting to worry," Isaac stated mildly when they were clear of the room.

"The kitchen was worse than we first thought." Stuart likewise maintained a casual attitude. "We had to use firesticks." By now everyone would know that winter had snuck up on them, but they did not need to know how bad it almost was.

Isaac grimaced. "That explains the urgent call for the kitchen fans." He had ample experience with firesticks and knew just how unpleasant using them in an enclosed area could get.

"It turned the trick, though," Stuart was happy to report. "That and the idea of shaving the center ice down."

Isaac decided that explained the half a dozen or so tiny cuts he had noticed on Stuart's knuckles. Ice was one of their crueler weather-based enemies: if it did not freeze one to death, it could crush them, cut them, etc.

"We better go see if Rosie has something for your hands," Isaac suggested.

Stuart was about to laugh off the idea of seeing a doctor for such a small matter when Isaac winked at him.

"Oh. Yes, just to be on the safe side," Stuart agreed hastily. "We are practically there already." Just a few turns and they would in fact be at Rosie's. Where she was, however, was another matter.

Isaac's stomach rumbled just as they were cornering to enter Rosie's office.

"I guess you missed breakfast, too," Stuart grinned.

"Just like training camp," Isaac grinned back, reflecting on their time together as Wrangler apprentices. Noting that they had the corridor to themselves, he signaled with his left hand for Stuart to keep going.

"Being a Wrangler," Stuart squared his shoulders and lowered his voice in imitation of one of their former instructors, "means being the best. Especially when the conditions are the worst." Following another of Isaac's hand signals, he turned left.

"We cannot, therefore," Isaac took over the narrative, "risk sending you into active duty without fully acquainting you with the dangers. Hunger. Thirst. Fatigue." His stomach rumbled again and they both laughed. They were still in the well-traveled part of the maze, so they were acting natural.

"I thought I was going to starve to death every time they asked us to complete the obstacle course before breakfast," Stuart laughed at the memory. A growing boy at the time, mealtime had naturally been his favorite times of the day.

"And I almost died of fright that first night they woke us up after an hour of sleep," Isaac snorted. "Remember that?"

"When the dummy chipmunk 'attacked' our camp?" Stuart shuddered. "Fright was the only real danger and we still lost part of the class to other professions afterwards." Apprentice Wranglers were sworn to secrecy about the training program, whether they finished it or not, because the trials were so important in determining who had the right combination of mental and physical toughness to become Wranglers.

Isaac nodded. "Seemed like a rotten trick at the time."

"And after," Stuart snorted. "Right up until we needed to be able to roll out of our blankets and come up fighting." Stuart glanced down at his left thigh, home of a twig-long scar from the morning that the spider they were hunting found them first. They had been lucky; no one died that morning.

"Right," Isaac agreed. He had come out of the experience physically unscathed, partly because Stuart was there when he needed him, a burning twig from the campfire in one hand, lance in the other. He felt certain that neither of them would ever forget seeing the wildly dancing torchlight reflected in each of the spider's ten eyes.

Chapter 8

Gallica, who had been sitting politely wondering why she neglected to bring a breakfast for herself to consume while the Water Fairies were eating, clenched her stomach muscles to suppress yet another growl. She was embarrassed enough by bringing their breakfast so late; having her stomach betray her own hunger would only compound it.

At least they were kind enough not to show it if they were upset. Of course she had explained about what happened. And they seemed to be making a special effort to speak her language instead of theirs, though the younger nurse—Daphne—was really struggling in that area.

"You say this bread is made with acorn flour?" Agnes asked, holding up the half a roll she had just buttered. Just as she expected, the young princess stared at the roll a mite too long.

"That is correct," Gallica smiled. "What sort of flour do you use?"

"Jackfruit flour," Cassidy replied. Too late she realized that she was not authorized to be fully transparent. Her tribe might still, on the whole, wish to remain apart. Revealing the existence of the tiny island farms the Water

Fairy Tribe maintained would be a serious violation of that wish.

"Jackfruit," Gallica repeated. "I am not familiar with that." She was puzzled when the others exchanged glances. She even thought she saw Cassidy shake her head ever so slightly.

"It does not grow in the woods," Agnes finally responded.

"Oh." Gallica's curiosity was about to get the better of respecting their reticence when someone knocked on the outer door. "I will get it," she rose.

"Wait." Cassidy looked up sharply. "How will it look to have the princess hiding with a breakfast cart in this…this medical maze?"

"Better than it would look to have a Water Fairy answer it," Gallica answered without thinking. "Forgive me," she reddened. "I just meant that I am expecting my brother and his comrade at arms. Possibly with Rosie. But I will be sure of who it is before I open the door."

Leaving it at that, she flew into the other room, closing the door to the inner room behind her. Approaching the outer door, she rapped her knuckles against it in a predetermined rhythm. Predetermined over a century ago, but she felt reasonably certain that if she could remember the 'secret' knock of her youth, either Stuart or Isaac would as well. Sure enough, the answering knocks came seconds later.

"About time you got here," Gallica laughed when she opened the door to admit them. "I am famished," she lowered her voice.

"Join the club," Isaac winked at her, pleased with his wittiness at tying the secret knock back into the conversation.

"Well, I had to do something to be sure it was you," Gallica explained, her voice still low. "They were worried it might be some random fairy out hunting for gossip or whatever." She waved one hand dismissively.

"Hmm," Isaac frowned. "They have an entire tribe to protect, Gallica. I can understand their wariness. I know you can, too," he held up his hand to forestall her from apologizing or getting mad, whichever came first. He was too hungry to try to figure her out right then. "We should probably keep using that knock. That way, if the right knock is not given from outside, the door stays locked and no one was ever here." It was a simple plan, not terribly brilliant or anything. Effective, though. "And speaking of famished, we all are."

Gallica's eyes widened and she looked over at Stuart, who tilted his head dismissively to one side.

"Are they still working on the windows?"

"No, that has been taken care of," Stuart assured her. "By now I imagine they have even got the ice water mopped up and are getting back to their regular routine."

"Then why did you come hungry?" Gallica looked accusingly at Isaac.

"My fault," Isaac acknowledged sheepishly. His own hunger had been unimportant, but he should have thought of Stuart's comfort. "We came directly here from my therapy."

"I wonder if you are hungry enough to rescue us from all of this food?" Cassidy, recognizing Isaac's voice, had opened the door between the two rooms. She paused briefly when she saw the stranger, then forced herself to relax. By his very association with the prince and princess, the second man was probably Sir Stuart. She had been expecting something quite different, though she was not sure what. A brace of swords on his back and daggers all around his belt, perhaps? Gathering her scattered thoughts, Cassidy proceeded, "I am afraid we are not accustomed to eating a heavy breakfast. If you would care to join us?"

"You are too kind," Isaac hesitated. But when Stuart cast a sidelong look at him, he nodded. "If you are certain you have extra, we would be most happy to join you."

"Please." Cassidy stepped back from the door to allow them entrance. Agnes and Daphne were busily arranging the remaining food on the serving trays so that their guests would have clean things to eat from.

"Finally," Isaac grinned as he saw the serving fork they had set for him, "a fork the size of my appetite." The leftovers were not really enough to satisfy any of them, especially split three ways, but the snack would at least stop the embarrassing rumbles for now.

Gallica waited uncertainly, feeling more than a little foolish after trying so hard to hide her hunger for so long, until Stuart drew back a chair for her. The faintly stubborn look in his eyes told her that he was not going to eat unless she did.

"Thank you."

Stuart carefully slid her chair in for her, then glanced around the room for another place to sit.

"May I?" he asked, pointing to an empty packing crate. "I can hardly sit while you ladies stand," he added when Cassidy seemed to be about to indicate one of the remaining chairs.

"Of course." Cassidy watched with some interest as Stuart retrieved the packing crate and seated himself. She had hardly expected such gallantry from a warrior.

"My apologies," Isaac spoke up when they were all seated. "I neglected to introduce my friend and companion, Sir Stuart of Ouray."

Cassidy waved aside Stuart's attempt to rise, marveling at how similar the etiquette of their tribes was after so many generations apart.

"And I am Doctor Cassidy Clark." Gesturing at her nurses in turn, she introduced them. "This is Nurse Agnes and Nurse Daphne."

"My pleasure." Stuart managed a seated bow of sorts.

"*Our* pleasure," Isaac corrected, bowing as well. "Nurse Agnes. Nurse Daphne."

"We are so grateful that you have come," Gallica offered.

"Indeed we are," Stuart agreed.

Gallica stiffened slightly when she saw that he was smiling mostly at Nurse Daphne. Like the others, Daphne's hair was pinned up in a business-like fashion. Unlike the others, it was a very dark pink, almost red. A cute nose sat atop full lips, and those lips seemed to be smiling back at Stuart.

Cassidy noted the silent exchange as well and sighed inwardly.

"Will you have time this morning for an examination?" she asked Prince Isaac abruptly.

"I certainly will," Isaac answered, delighted that they were finally getting around to him. He could not have stood waiting much longer.

"Should we wait for Rosie?" Stuart asked and took another bite of roll. The bacon was cold, but that did not keep him from eating his share.

"Yes." Cassidy nodded. "I have been studying your file," she looked at Isaac, "and I have some questions that I need her to answer." It was amazing to her how quickly they had finished eating what looked like so much food to her and her nurses.

"I will fetch her," Gallica offered, setting her utensils down. She needed the space.

"And I will take these things back to the kitchen," Stuart volunteered, rising with her. The glare Gallica gave him was only a split-second long, but devastating. They had arranged a truce, he thought, after meeting with the king.

Isaac and the others made short work of gathering the breakfast dishes, so that Stuart was only a few steps behind Gallica in the tunnel.

"Gallica." When she refused to stop, Stuart left the cart and caught her by the arm.

"What do you think you are doing?" she flared at him.

Deep down, Stuart knew he was out of line stopping her that way. He was about to let her go when she decided to add something.

"You forget your place, Sir Stuart."

"My *place*?" he repeated, incredulous. Conflicting emotions tore through him until he released her arm. Slipping one arm about her waist, he pulled her close. It was wholly unpremeditated. The results were beyond his wildest expectations. Ice water and magnesium, that was what they were: her cold, callous remark and his newly-discovered, highly volatile feelings towards her. Sparks could not help but fly when they came in contact with each other.

Tenderly, he cradled her head against his chest while he tried to pull himself together. He was breathing like he had just completed a distance flight trial.

"Stuart?" She could not have been more surprised by his actions—and her reactions—if he had suddenly grown another head. All she was sure of at the moment was that she needed some space. No matter how badly she wanted to stay where she was.

"Shhh," he murmured, smoothing her hair. Thank goodness she had been wearing it down. He might have gotten all sorts of pins stuck in his hands otherwise.

"Stuart," she repeated, pushing against his chest with her hands. "Let me go."

He drew back enough to look her in the eyes. "Why?" She blushed adorably and he proceeded to scatter kisses around her face.

"Stuart," she protested, "stop."

Sighing, he obeyed. "Are you sure?" he teased. He had never been in love before. Oh, there were a few romantic encounters in his past, harmless flirtations—certainly nothing he was ashamed of. Right now, he simply wanted to hold her as long as he could.

"Yes." Her eyes closed when he rested his forehead against hers. "I am mad at you, you know." She felt his answering chuckle rumble through his chest. "I…I mean it."

"Alright." Carefully he stepped back, allowing his hands to fall to his sides. "With the princess' permission, I would like to talk to her after supper?"

Her slowly fading blush came back in full force. "I think you had better ask my father first." Gallica's hands flew to cover her mouth, both out of shock at what she had said and because his gaze had dropped to her hands. Abruptly she lifted off and flew away.

Stuart stared after her for a moment, wondering if she had meant to say what she did. According to Wood Fairy custom, asking a woman's father for permission to court her was the final step before proposing. Judging by the way she kissed him back, Gallica's feelings for him went a lot deeper than friendship. Truth be told, he was not sure which of them had been more surprised to find that out! Whether she meant it or not, he decided it was a good idea. Then he could proceed to woo her with a clear conscience. A most delicate task, fully converting years of friendship into the love of a lifetime…and a most enjoyable one.

Returning to the cart, he whisked it off to the kitchen, where he spotted the Chief Steward.

"Sir Stuart," the steward greeted him without ceasing to review the suggested menu for the rest of the week.

"Steward," Stuart smiled back. "Do you have a moment?"

The steward lowered the menu at once. Sir Stuart, as a knight of the realm and hero of the court, was a well-respected Wrangler in a society where nearly everyone wanted to be a Wrangler when they grew up.

"Of course."

Stuart allowed his smile to dim slightly as he made a show of looking about to see if he could be overheard.

"It has come to my attention," he began, "that certain troupers have been found wandering the corridors on the south of Weetu."

"Yes, a grave trespass." The steward shook his head. He kept his surprise at Sir Stuart's interest to himself. "I instructed them personally regarding the restricted areas."

"I assumed so." Stuart's smile was back in full force. "That is why I came to you first. I thought that if you could find the time to speak to them, just once more, it would solve the whole difficulty. No doubt they simply got turned around." Unfortunately, all troupers had been tarred with the same brush as those who left their performances carrying someone else's valuables, and Stuart wanted to be sure the steward knew there were no accusations being made.

"I interviewed this troupe myself, Sir Stuart," the steward stated the obvious, since part of his duties included arranging diversions for the winter season. "I can assure you it is a simple misunderstanding."

"Excellent." Stuart was still smiling. "I knew I was right to come to you." Taking a peek at the menu, he made a show of delight. "Orange custard tonight? My favorite. But I have taken up enough of your time. Carry on." Spinning on his heel, Stuart checked the kitchen clock as he headed towards the tunnels. It would probably be some time before Isaac needed him again. Maybe even long enough for him to beg an audience with the king.

Stuart's whereabouts was the furthest thing from Isaac's mind just then. With Rosie's help, he had removed his jacket and shirt and been made semi-comfortable face down on an examination table. Any concern he might have had over revealing his scarred torso and back to Cassidy evaporated when she began checking them against the report from his most recent surgeries. If they did not bother her, why should they bother him?

While he lay there, he could hear everything Rosie and Cassidy were saying, but could not understand much of it. The first aid classes required by the Wranglers were extensive, but not fancy. They called an arm an arm and a leg a leg. It did make a kind of sense to him that they would use more specific terms for what went on under the skin on a complicated thing like a spine…he just wished he could follow them better. Was what they were saying good or bad?

"Regardless of whether or not we ultimately decide to implant the strands," Cassidy was referring to the gold strands Isaac knew nothing about, "injecting the decoction will stimulate healing."

"And when would you know if surgery was indicated?" Rosie asked.

"If there is no marked improvement after the first week of injections, I would consider surgery."

"Would you know more if you were able to inspect his spine for yourself?"

"Absolutely. But I cannot recommend exploratory surgery at this time. The incisions would be only partially healed if and when I did the implant."

"Is that your experience?" Rosie asked, surprised.

"No, not mine personally," Cassidy clarified. "It is the reported result of earlier attempts at the implantation." Tapping Isaac's file she continued, "Based on the accounts of his initial and subsequent operations, I believe that he has a good chance of regaining seventy-five percent of his mobility from the decoction alone."

"Not good enough." Isaac spoke up. Turning his head on the pillow so he could look at them, he urged, "Rosie is right about the exploratory surgery. You need to know for yourself. I do, too."

Rosie looked curiously at Cassidy. "Does your tribe have potions or any form of medicine that helps wounds heal faster?"

"Yes, we have several salves and potions that aid in healing. Why do you ask?"

"What you said about the incisions from the exploratory surgery taking so long to heal." Rosie shrugged slightly. "The cuts would not be deep. I could prescribe medicines that would help them to heal within a couple of days."

Cassidy glanced at Agnes, not sure if she believed Rosie's assertion. How could this tribe, which clearly had no concept of lightning beyond something that came and went in storms, have medicine superior to anything she had ever heard of?

"I would like to see that," Cassidy hedged at last.

"Then allow me to assist in the initial surgery. That way, you can explain to me what you see, and I can explain it to the king and queen."

Cassidy frowned slightly. If she understood Rosie correctly, the nurse had already 'explained' the options of decoction or implantation to the king, without Cassidy being present. There was a very real risk involved in the implantation, and Cassidy was more than a little concerned that vital details were going overlooked. It was a worst case scenario, but she had to consider it.

"Very well. I will allow you to assist me if you will promise to bring the king and queen to me so that I may report my findings to them directly. I have no doubt that your help will be needed in explaining the finer points, but I must insist on this."

"I cannot speak for the king and queen," Rosie began.

"I can," Isaac interrupted. "They will come. I give you my word."

Cassidy nodded. "Then let us begin the surgery."

Isaac grinned suddenly. "I like the way you think, Doctor, but I have a few things I need to do before we do that."

Cassidy, her stomach fluttering in response to his grin, did not trust her voice and simply raised her eyebrows questioningly.

"Sir Stuart has already taken over most of my court duties, it is true," Isaac explained. "But it would still cause a commotion if I just disappear for a couple of days. Especially now that winter has struck. There is no chance that I could have been called away on assignment or sent somewhere by my parents."

"Very well." Cassidy frowned thoughtfully. "We shall begin the decoction treatment instead," she decided. Together, she and Rosie helped him sit up. "Agnes, prepare an injection of the decoction."

"May I watch?" Rosie asked, intensely curious.

Cassidy nodded first, then Agnes did. Agnes led Rosie into the surgery, where such things were stored because the room was large enough.

Isaac was acutely aware of his shirtless state as he leaned on Cassidy's arm for support. "Can you pass me my shirt?" he asked hopefully. The examination was clearly over.

"It will only get in the way of the injection." Cassidy turned to look at him and found herself quite literally eye to eye with him. "Daphne?"

"She is in the other room somewhere," Isaac said. The fact that they were alone should have made him more uncomfortable, but he found himself thoroughly distracted by her eyes. He had never seen anything like them. "How many colors do you have in your eyes?" he asked.

"My eyes?" Cassidy could barely breathe, despite her best efforts at forcing herself to think of him as just another patient. It should have been easy.

"Mhmm." Isaac stared at first one, then the other. "They are so beautiful. And your hair…" He was reaching to touch it when he heard Rosie's voice.

"You actually insert that needle under his skin?"

Cassidy managed to smile when she saw Isaac's attention abruptly redirected towards Agnes. Just in time, too. She took a deep, steadying breath, and passed Isaac's support off to Rosie.

"Here is the topical anesthetic, Doctor." Agnes held out a vial of greenish blue salve.

"Thank you." Cassidy took a short swab from the tray beside the examination table and transferred some of the salve onto it. "This may tickle," she warned as she moved behind Isaac to smear the salve on his back. "Syringe." She and Agnes traded items.

"Would you mind talking me through this, Doctor?" Isaac hated to admit that he was nervous, but that needle put him in mind of some of his mother's letter openers.

"Of course." Cassidy finished checking the

syringe for bubbles. "The decoction is here, in the glass barrel." Knowing he could not turn towards her, she held it out so that he could see. "The barrel is connected to the hollow needle, which will allow me to inject the decoction under your skin, near your spine." *Inside* his spinal column, actually, but she saw no need to mention that right then. Cassidy had been watching the water clock while she spoke and now she began inserting the needle gently into his back, relying on her memory of his medical records and using the scars from his surgery as a map to determine the correct location for the injection. The needle was treated with an even more powerful variation of the topical anesthetic, so as she slowly slid it further in, it numbed the area around it, reducing the pain of the experience significantly. "How do you feel?"

"Fine for now," Isaac tried to laugh. "Ask me again when you are ready to put that needle in me."

Cassidy shot Agnes a knowing look and they both smiled slightly at Rosie. The decoction was nearly half-injected already.

"Why, it is in you now," Cassidy said, playing for time. The decoction was very thick and had to be injected slowly.

"What?" Isaac's tone accurately reflected his shock. "I was expecting it to hurt!"

"It usually does," Cassidy acknowledged. The decoction injected, she withdrew the needle, leaving a small, red hole in Isaac's back. "Agnes?"

While Agnes put a bandage on the hole to keep it from getting compromised while it healed, Cassidy unscrewed the needle from the barrel and set the syringe in the sink to be washed and re-sterilized.

"Because the spine is such a sensitive area," Cassidy wiped her fingers on a clean hand towel, "it is necessary to numb you before inserting the decoction."

"Are there other uses for that," the word 'syringe' escaped Rosie, who nodded at the sink instead, "thing?"

"Quite a few," Cassidy nodded.

"I would love to stay and discuss this," Isaac interrupted before what he expected to be a long conversation could begin. "But I do have arrangements to make?"

Chapter 9

"I see." King Walter drummed the fingers of one hand on his desk thoughtfully. While he found the news disturbing, he was half-expecting it after Gallica's warning. "Did they see you?"

"No, sir." Chief O'Reilly, of Weetu Security, shook his head. "I knew they were turned back a few nights ago, so I just kept quiet and followed them."

"How close did they get?"

"Within a few turns of it." O'Reilly shrugged. "Maybe I accidentally gave myself away. Maybe they were looking for something else..."

"But they were looking for something? Not lost, not wandering?" Walter stressed the question because it was so important.

"No, sir." O'Reilly shook his head again. "At first, when I was following the trouper, he was real interested in specific objects along the way. The painting of your great-grandfather. The sword and shield mounted at the cross tunnels. Various other relics," he waved his hand expansively.

"Then he did know exactly where he was going." King Walter sighed. This was the kind of headache he did not need. The tribe's reserve treasure had been concealed safely since…well, so long that, as far as King Walter was concerned, it was just another pile of octagonal bits of marked metal and so-called precious rocks.

"Afraid so." O'Reilly scratched his chin. "What puzzles me is why." He shrugged in response to King Walter's upraised eyebrow. "Winter just hit, sir. A few days back, it might have made sense for them to be poking around, looking for an easy score. Could be they planned to steal something and get away while the weather was good. But now?" He shrugged again. "Nobody can leave Weetu until the spring thaw."

Wonderful, King Walter thought. *A mystery that is also a puzzle.*

"I suppose they could plan to hide it until then?" he suggested hopefully.

"Might be." O'Reilly did not sound convinced. "Could'nae say that is how I would handle it. Too much time for something to go wrong."

King Walter nodded, conceding the point. Then someone knocked on his office door.

"Come!"

A guard appeared, saluted, and waited for permission to speak.

"What is it?" King Walter felt that he would welcome a diversion.

"Sire, Sir Stuart would like to see you."

"Stuart?" Walter frowned. "Send him in." When O'Reilly started to rise, Walter waved him back to his chair. "This will only take a moment."

Stuart entered with a bow and a glance at the chair before King Walter's desk. There were two chairs, but only one was turned so that its back was to the door. If memory served, that was a favorite tactic of…

"Sorry to interrupt, Your Majesty. Hello, O'Reilly."

O'Reilly flashed a grin of appreciation at the king, impressed at the lad's deduction.

"Come in, Stuart." Walter leaned back in his chair, faintly amused at how easily Stuart had determined who his guest was.

"Thank you, Sire." Stuart stayed where he was. "I was hoping to speak with you privately. Mayhap I could return later today?"

Concerned now, Walter straightened again. This was just not his day.

"Stay, lad, stay." O'Reilly levered himself off the chair and slid it back into place, square with the desk, so precisely that the chair legs fit into their original indentations in the carpet. "I will continue looking into this matter, Sire, and report back when I know more."

Walter grinned at his old friend from Wrangler days, not minding the presumption of dismissal in the least.

"Very well." Walter's grin dimmed a little when O'Reilly's back was turned and he was limping out of the room. O'Reilly's wings got clipped during a routine animal wrangling, then his leg was severely wrenched by a rogue frog. His knee never healed properly.

Realizing that Stuart was still waiting by the door, Walter shook himself free of the past and waved him over.

"Sit down, Stuart. Twice in one day, eh? Just how bad is the situation in the kitchen?"

"That has been handled, Sire." Forgetting the telltale scrapes on his knuckles, which he had also forgotten to have treated, he folded his hands around his knee. "We had to use firesticks and shave down the centers, but the windows are latched and sealed for the winter."

"Well done." Walter waited. "What brings you here, then?"

Stuart took a deep breath. "I am here to present myself for your approval, Sire, as a fit suitor for Princess Gallica's hand."

Walter almost asked him to repeat himself. The Wood Fairy Royal Family had a long and proud tradition of openness with their subjects. Also, he knew he would be pleased to have a Wrangler like Stuart for a son-by-law. But...Walter knew Gallica considered Stuart a trusted friend and that friends occasionally had spats.   However, unless Stuart told him something that made him think Gallica regarded him as more than a friend, he would not be able approve the courtship.

"Tell me, Stuart. Why was she so angry with you this morning?" Walter waited semi-patiently for the answer.

"Because of…something I said to her last night."

"What did you say?"

Stuart hesitated, torn between protecting Gallica and being honest with her father.

"She told me she wanted to help find out what the troupers were doing near the south corridors."

Walter scowled slightly. Gallica could be headstrong, true enough.

"But what did *you* say?"

"I…informed her that I would ruin any plans she had for doing that."

Walter looked down at his desk to hide a smile. No wonder Gallica had been ready to spit nails when she came to see him that morning!

"Stuart, I realize you have known Gallica for a good many years. You two are very good friends. But what you have just told me makes me think that you see Gallica as someone to protect. As a little sister?"

"No, Sire, there is more, much more to how

I see her."

Walter stared at Stuart, startled that the lad had interrupted him. Thinking back to his own interview for Fiona's hand, he tried to remember how it felt to be on the other side of the desk.

"You are in love with her?"

"I am," Stuart declared himself stoutly and without reservation.

"Why?"

It was Stuart's turn to be startled. He had a hunch that the king was looking for more of an answer than, 'Because!' In fact, he would be pretty disappointed in himself if that was all the better he could do. Rising, he stuffed his hands in his pockets.

"Your Majesty. Princess Gallica is as sweet as she is fiery. As kind as she is stubborn. And as much as I loved the tomboy that she was, I love the woman she has become even more. I find her very attractive."

Walter was not expecting that. He was impressed again by the way Stuart looked him straight in the eyes, not dodging the issue at hand.

"What if she thinks of you as an older brother?" Walter was nearly blinded by the answering light in Stuart's face.

"I am confident that she has feelings beyond that for me, Sire."

Walter was beginning to believe that, too.

"I cannot answer you now, Stuart. Come back tomorrow morning, and I will answer you then." As he expected, Stuart's face fell slightly.

"Thank you, Sire." Bowing, Stuart let himself out of the office.

"You heard?" Walter turned towards the door that adjoined his inner den, the place where he retired whenever possible to share a meal with his wife. Stuart had obviously been too distracted to hear Fiona gently open the door a crack.

Fiona opened the door the rest of the way and stepped through. "I certainly did." Coming over to her husband, she kissed him lightly on the forehead. "What do you suppose brought that on?"

Walter shook his head. "How should I know? I have only attended every birthday party either of them ever had. Watched them crawl and toddle, and sprout like weeds in the spring. How was I supposed to know they were old enough to fall in love?"

Fiona bit her lip and kept her motherly observations to herself. If Walter had not seen the signs Gallica was exhibiting, it was understandable. In fact, it rather reminded her of her own father, who had married at five hundred years old and thought she was too young at two hundred and seventy. Smoothing his hair, she leaned against his shoulder.

"Do you want me to talk to her?"

Walter sighed. "Yes. And no." He captured the strong, brown hand that was so gently ruffling his hair and turned to face her. "What kind of a father would I be if I let someone else, even you, do my job for me?"

Fiona kissed his forehead again. "A busy one." Since she was already so close, she leaned in to kiss his lips.

"Where did the time go?" Walter asked, easing her onto his lap. Her head resting safely against his shoulder, he lifted her right hand so that he could see the wedding ring he had placed there. "Feels like I just put that on you yesterday."

Fiona captured his hand in turn and wrapped his arm about her waist. "You did." She was so close to him that she could hear his heart, beating in his chest.

Walter chuckled and gave her a gentle squeeze. "Alright, now. Any advice on how I should approach Gallica?"

"Love is complicated," Fiona mused aloud. "It involves all of our emotions, the bad as well as the good."

"She certainly has been emotional lately," Walter recalled belatedly.

"Mmm," Fiona murmured noncommittally. "Are you really worried that she would reject him? Or that she will accept him?"

Walter pressed his cheek to her hair. "Yes."

They remained like that, just holding onto one another, until the sound of the foyer clock ringing the hour reached them.

"I have to go." Fiona made no move to rise. The chair's arm was digging into her leg, but she hated to end their rare moment.

"And I should be halfway through these reports on my desk." Walter's tone betrayed his lack of enthusiasm for the idea. If anything, he pulled her closer.

Sighing, Fiona straightened away from him. Rising, she went to the mirror to smooth her hair.

"Shall I send her to you?"

"Not right now, thank you, Darling. If I finish these reports before supper, I will find her myself."

"Alright." Fiona blew him a kiss and disappeared, shutting the door behind her.

Gallica, meanwhile, was 'lost' in the medical maze. It was partly by design and partly because she had not been paying attention to where she went after she told Rosie that she was needed. Walking usually soothed her, but today it was just no good. Stuart's kiss turned her inside out and she was still trying to figure out if she liked the way she now saw herself.

"At least I know why he was so mad last night," she muttered as she turned another corner. The cold fire was barely glowing here, and she made a mental note to have their resident Plant Fairy pay the area a visit. The mushrooms probably just needed to be watered.

"Whoa!" She stopped abruptly, startled to find that she had reached what appeared to be a dead end. "Huh." Looking around, she confirmed that there were no branch tunnels leading off from the chamber she was in. "Weird." She trailed her hand along the wall. "Feels solid." It had always been her belief that Weetu's tunnels were never-ending. They might turn, they might branch off, and several led to bark ring and exits, but this was the first time she had ever encountered a true dead end.

When a cool breeze fanned her cheek, she squinted up into the darkness. A faint motion, almost more of a sense of motion, in the same direction that the breeze was coming from prompted her to remark, "Well, at least the ventilation system reaches this far." Shrugging off the peculiarity of it all, she moved to brush her hand off on her slacks—but her hand was clean. "No dust?" That was just bizarre. Whatever the chamber had been initially used for, and it was too dim to see more than vague shapes of what might be shelves along the walls, it had to have been empty for centuries.

Probably ever since the Great Sap Flood, when a particularly wet spring resulted in sap breaching several chambers despite the coat of sealer that went on every wall, ceiling, and floor in Weetu.

Gallica suddenly chuckled. "Here I have been so preoccupied with Stuart that I walked halfway 'round the city trying to clear my head, and all it took to joggle me loose is an old, empty room!" Subconsciously, she took note of the room's designation as she retraced her steps. There might be some record of it in the old blueprints of Weetu. Might even prove interesting.

Her stomach began gurgling about the same time that she reached corridors she recognized. Ordinarily she would have joined her mother and brother for lunch, but after the events of the morning, she simply did not feel up to it. Her assignment to help take care of their guests was the perfect excuse, so she made a beeline for the kitchens.

"Look out," warned a scullery maid, both hands fully occupied with a heavy tray of dishes.

Gallica, startled out of her thoughts, leapt aside just in time to prevent a messy collision.

"Your Highness," one of the senior butlers, pale at the scene he had just witnessed, appeared at Gallica's elbow. "Please forgive the commotion."

"Of course," Gallica agreed amiably. The smoke had cleared and the floor was dry. She really should have known that things in the kitchen would be functioning at peak efficiency already.

"How may we assist you?"

"I need luncheon cart for three, um, four." This time she remembered to add herself. Any leftovers could easily be served to the menagerie or even the farm animals.

"One moment." The butler excused himself and flew off to begin preparing things.

"Hi."

Gallica looked towards the sound of the voice, momentarily surprised to find that it came from the scullery maid.

"Sorry I snapped at ya just now. It ain't that I ain't grateful for yer help this morning."

Gallica smiled and flew over to where Dottie was now scraping off the stack of dishes.

"Forget it," Gallica advised, rolling up her sleeves. "How about letting me help you again?"

"I dunno." Dottie cast a look about the kitchen. "That butler looked awful mad at me fer snapping at ya."

"Let me worry about him, alright?" Gallica found a long-handled serving spoon and started to scrape a plate.

"Ain't that something?"

"What?" Gallica asked.

"A princess knowin' how to do dishes, what else?"

Gallica chuckled. "Every Wrangler knows how to do dishes. It is part of our training."

"Yeah, I know." Dottie ducked her head and reached for another dish. It was several seconds before she spoke again. "I wanted ta be a Wrangler when I was a kid." She watched a half-eaten roll and lunch meat sandwich fall into the bucket at her feet. "Tried it fer a while, too."

Gallica debated whether or not to ask what happened, but Dottie decided for her.

"Found out it was too hard fer me. It was all too much. Too cold, too hungry, too tired." Dottie scraped off another plate. "Course, others washed out with me."

Gallica nodded, vividly remembering how her own class size shrank from over two hundred apprentices to less than fifty before they were sworn and assumed the rank of Wrangler.

"How come you reckon I failed?"

Gallica was taken completely by surprise. "Who said you failed?"

"I did."

"Oh." Gallica stacked a scraped plate in the sink beside her. "I can only tell you what I believe to be true." Seeing that the cart was nearly ready, she rinsed and dried her hands. "You did not fail as a Wrangler. You are succeeding as a maid."

"Some success." Dottie shook a glop of oatmeal off the long-handled spoon she was using.

"Listen," Gallica put her hand on the younger woman's arm. "We all had dreams when we were kids. Suppose I wanted to join a troupe, as a singer or something. If I could not control a single note but I could cook meals that made them sing my praises, would I be a failure or not?"

Dottie shrugged. "Who sings to scullery maids?"

"You just keep doing your best," Gallica admonished. "Consider this your apprenticeship for assignment in the linens, or maybe even a chef."

Dottie, whose hands had never stopped working, smiled a little at that.

"Apprenticeship, huh?" She looked around the big kitchen as if she was seeing it for the first time. "Yeah. Maybe I could."

"I know you can." Gallica gave the girl's arm a friendly squeeze before flying over to take charge of the cart. "Magnificent," she beamed at the anxiously waiting butler. And it was. Fresh churned butter, thick slices of acorn bread, and a pot of lightly spiced stew. "If you will just cover it for me, I will get out from underfoot."

She laughed while the butler protested that she was always welcome in the kitchen and took herself off to the medical maze. More than one of the patients and nurses sniffed hopefully as she approached, but she steeled herself against them. She even took a different route this time, in case someone decided to follow the tantalizing trail of odors she knew she was leaving behind her.

When she was sure she was alone, she rapped out the 'secret' knock on her side of the door.

"Your Highness." Cassidy stepped back to allow her in. "Oh, you must not trouble yourself with us."

"It is no trouble," Gallica insisted, wheeling the cart into the so-called recovery room. "Is my brother still here?" She suddenly hoped not. There was not enough food for five, even with the way the others picked at their food.

"No, he left at least half an hour ago," Cassidy answered.

Gallica lifted the cover from the cart to reveal the waiting deliciousness. "I brought enough for myself this time, if I may join you?"

"But of course." Cassidy smiled. She had been contemplating the other half of her mission, wondering how she was going to research conditions above the surface while sequestered in a five-room space. Now she realized that she had some of the best contacts in the tribe. The Wood Fairy Royal Family, Sir Stuart, and Rosie. Surely she could piece together what they told her and arrive at the truth of the cruel accusations.

Chapter 10

The pump rooms were regular beehives of gossip and speculation by the next morning. Most of the stories agreed that the rumors began with the butler who served the king's table the night before. Naturally, there was conversation during the meal, and while butlers were usually the souls of discretion, this conversation had shattered the poor fellow's silence.

"My apprentice told me they have found something to help Prince Isaac walk again, but it is so expensive it would bankrupt the tribe!" One Wrangler insisted to another as they did their therapy.

"Your apprentice is wrong," scoffed the other Wrangler. "I have it on very good authority that he is already walking. And if it works out alright for him, it will be freely distributed."

"You are both wrong," laughed one of the nurses, who had come to make sure they were working as well as talking. While she checked the tension on their pedals she explained, "This has been in development for quite a while." She felt that was a reasonable assumption, since she knew hundreds of experiments along that line had been funded by the royal family. "But there is no such thing as an instant remedy for paralysis. Even if it proves effective for Prince Isaac, he will have a lot of work to do." Again she spoke with authority, having spent some of her apprenticeship working under a doctor investigating just such a cure. It was the dream of every Wood Fairy physician to come up with a cure for the spinal paralysis that so many suffered.

"Good morning!" Isaac sent the cheery salutation before him into the pump room. Then he did his best to look taken aback when almost every fairy in there began pelting him with questions.

"Prince Isaac, is it true?"

"When do the rest of us get it?"

"Why are you still in your chair?"

That last question hung in the air as the others faded.

Isaac drummed the fingers of his left hand on the arm of his chair and chewed on his lip. He had spent most of the night working out how much he should say, so this was only partly an act.

"From your questions," he began after a glance over his shoulder at Noland, "I take it you have all heard something about a new procedure." He paused just long enough for them to chorus that they had. "And as usual, no two of you have heard the same thing." He grinned, which encouraged them to chuckle sheepishly. "This is as good a time as any, I guess, but keep in mind that I am no physician. I cannot explain exactly how it works or why." Taking a deep breath, he gave it his best shot. "There is, in truth, a new procedure that has great potential to help overcome paralysis of the spine." He held up his hand to forestall the comments and questions that erupted from the group. "There is also a very real danger." Cassidy had gone over the implantation process with him after his decoction injection that morning.

"I have already begun treatments, but," Isaac raised his voice when another round of murmurs began, "it will be weeks if not months before we know anything for sure." He had also discussed wing reconstruction with Cassidy that morning and agreed with her that she would know more after she had explored the damage to his spine. The same muscles that powered his wings could wrench his healing spine, but she was cautiously optimistic. Apparently repairing his wings would take time, too.

"And if it works?" The question came from a nurse.

"Rosie is already checking medical reports to determine who else this procedure might help." Isaac could barely keep the grin from splitting his face at that announcement. He broached the subject with Cassidy earlier that morning, and she said she would need some supplies, but that she would be happy to treat as many as she was able.

"Well then." The nurse tapped her pencil on her clipboard, settling things down a bit. "Back to work everyone." She smiled at the happy chatter that filled the room. Not everyone would benefit from this new development, but everyone was happy for those who might.

"Jared," Isaac smiled at the apprentice. "How are you today?" Isaac was more than satisfied with how things were going. Now that the 'secret' of the procedure was out, he could finish his therapy session and go back to Cassidy for the delicate, exploratory operation. Between Stuart and the Chief Steward, most of his duties would be covered, with his mother and Gallica filling in on the rest.

"Happier'n a bear in a berry bush!" Jared removed Isaac's footrest and began setting up the straps. "That new percedure is going to change a lot of lives!"

Isaac had to settle for a smile and nod or risk laughing aloud at Jared's mispronunciation of 'procedure.'

"Right, then." Jared reset the marker and reached for the station's sandglass. "Ready…go!"

Isaac forced himself to move slowly and steadily. His excitement made that almost as difficult as his anger had. Dozens of occupations could be filled by fairies with spinal paralysis. As prince, Isaac was already part clerk and part historian, for example. When he became king, his duties would shift even further into desk work. At least after this procedure it would be by choice. His own choice, not an accident. This thought carried him through the entire therapy session.

"Alright, now." Jared handed him the glass of doctor's water. "You guzzle that down while we wait for Sir Stuart."

"Sir Stuart is otherwise occupied this morning," Isaac responded. Apparently it was Stuart's turn to eat breakfast with their guests this morning. Taking a deep breath, he poured the medicated water down his throat. It tasted as terrible, as always. "Noland will come for me soon."

"Noland is here," Jared announced, using his pencil to point towards the doorway.

"Excellent." Isaac relaxed into his chair. "This procedure will keep me from coming to therapy for a few days, Jared. Nothing to worry about, alright?"

"Sure thing!" Jared was still grinning as he watched Noland wheel Isaac away. It looked to him like the talk about how long it would take for Prince Isaac to get back on his feet was exaggerated, so folks would be surprised at how fast it happened. Yup. Sure enough did.

Noland, meanwhile, was more than a little curious about his master's plans for the next few days. He was hurt. Had he not served Isaac faithfully for the last hundred years? More than that, had he not gone above and beyond his duties as valet to protect Prince Isaac these past few months? Of course he had. Sir Stuart knew everything Noland had done, too. So why was he, Noland, being cut out of their important plans?

"Noland, is that Stuart over there?" Isaac pointed to where he thought he had glimpsed his friend.

"I believe it is, sir," Noland answered stiffly.

Isaac frowned. "Very strange. He is supposed to be…" He stopped there.

"He appears to have been going towards the King's Offices," Noland offered. "Shall we follow him?"

"No, Noland, never mind." Isaac waved the suggestion away. "Just take me to Rosie's office, please." Stuart was obviously about something important. Isaac just hoped Stuart had remembered to order enough breakfast for him, too!

Stuart, oblivious to most everyone around him, was indeed hurrying to the King's Offices.

A page had hunted Stuart down in the kitchens to tell him that he was to report there as soon as he could.

"Sir Stuart, reporting at the king's command," he informed the guards, whom he had startled with his rapid approach.

Rigidly adhering to protocol despite his obvious impatience, one of the guards knocked and asked permission for Stuart to enter. The longer he had to wait, the more anxious Stuart became. This summons could be in reference to any of a hundred things going on in Weetu, including the troupers' peculiar behavior. Or, it might be about the thing closest to his heart. He had not seen Gallica since their encounter in the tunnels yesterday, so had no idea what, if anything, her father asked her.

"You may enter," the guard finally intoned.

Stuart smoothed his hair once and obediently flitted through the open door.

"Stuart." King Walter tapped ink back into the well from the end of his quill pen. "Have a seat, if you would. I will be with you in a moment."

"Thank you, Sire." Stuart selected a chair and seated himself. His present state of heightened anxiety was not all that different from peak hunting mode. His senses were on high alert, enabling him to smell the faint scent of the soap King Walter washed his hands with recently, probably after breakfast. He could even see dust that he cared absolutely nothing about on one of the carvings that adorned the king's desk. Worst of all, the sound of quill scratching on paper was driving him quite mad.

"I spoke to Gallica after supper yesterday." King Walter examined the letter he was writing and signed it. Drying the quill end off on a bit of scrap cloth, he set them both aside.

"Oh?" Stuart could think of nothing else to say.

Since the letter had all winter to dry before King Walter could send it to King Wilson of the Plant Fairies, he leaned back in his chair and ignored it. He had only pulled out the letter to King Wilson so he would have something to do with his hands while he made Stuart wait. The blasted thing was just one more formality in his life, anyway.

Steepling his fingers, Walter watched Stuart watch him for a moment. Up until now, Walter's morning had been more or less wasted, his mind wandering back to his daughter's situation as if there were no petitions to read or decrees to sign.

"I did not question her directly, you understand." Walter seriously doubted Stuart, or any other childless man, *could* understand, but he said it anyway. "I wanted to test her feelings for you." As Walter remembered it,

Fiona's father had made him wait for what felt like forever before giving his answer.

"Thank you, Sire." Stuart sat up a little straighter.

That was not the answer Walter expected. It surprised him so much, in fact, that he dropped all pretenses.

"You have our consent to court her." Walter watched in amazement as the imperturbable Sir Stuart now leapt to his feet, took two quick flying laps around the room, and reseated himself. When it became evident that Stuart was simply going to sit there, beaming, Walter swallowed the lump in his throat. Gallica was a lucky woman.

"My wife and I agree that she has feelings for you, as well."

"Thank you, Sire." They were the same words he had spoken before, but Stuart's tone had softened from formal to personal. He had always honored and respected his king; it was easy with a man like King Walter. Now he looked forward to the day that he could call him 'Father.'

"Thank you, son."

They stared at each other for several seconds, each more or less lost in his own thoughts.

"By your leave," Stuart stood and bowed from the waist. "I have some arrangements to make for this evening."

Walter suppressed his curiousity and waved him off. "Yes, go along now. Shoo. I have most of a morning's work to catch up on."

Stuart, suddenly grasping how difficult it must have been for the king, Gallica's father, to give him permission to court her, barely made it outside before clearing his throat so he could swallow. Eyeing the clock, he came to the conclusion that he had just enough time to get things started before he needed to report to the surgery with lunch. First thing first, of course.

Isaac, having finally reached the surgery with Rosie's help, was dismayed to learn that he was to have no breakfast.

"Not even a piece of toast?" he half-complained, half-wheedled.

"Sorry." Agnes was adamant. The amount of food left on the breakfast cart would have appalled her if Princess Gallica had not taken the time yesterday to explain how leftovers in Weetu were used to feed the farm animals. "You have to have an empty stomach during surgery for your own safety."

Cassidy chuckled to Rosie from where they were sitting at Cassidy's desk, taking a final look at the old surgery reports.

"Has he always liked food this much?" Cassidy asked.

"He used to." Rosie smiled fondly at her prince. "Thought he lost a little weight after the pirate offensive and was scarcely eating enough to keep a caterpillar alive for a while."

"Tell me about the pirate offensive," Cassidy encouraged. "I have heard it mentioned before."

Rosie sighed and rubbed cold fingers against tired eyes. "Are you warm enough down here?" she asked, tugging her jacket a little closer about her torso.

"Yes, quite." Cassidy smiled politely. "We are accustomed to laboratory temperatures, which can be quite chilly under the proper circumstances."

Rosie smiled back, amused at the idea and comprehending it at the same time. Not all medicines could be produced at the same temperatures or in the same conditions. Cassidy must have spent an awful lot of time working on medicines, Rosie decided.

"The pirate offensive." Rosie sighed again. "The four surface tribes joined forces against the pirates, the first combined fleet since I can remember. And we still lost so much. Nearly half of our fleet was shot to splinters on the edges of the Mists. When Queen Rebecca and King Hugh of the Silver Fairy Tribe finally subdued the Mists with the wild fairy dust, we stood a fighting chance…there was just very little left to fight with."

Cassidy reached out to touch Rosie's hand

sympathetically.

"By the time the pirates were routed, over eight thousand of the bravest fairies we had were already dead. Fleets were reduced to minimal strength, and many of the windships that made it home were sailing on the hope and grit of their crews."

"Did the pirates attack?" Cassidy kept her tone sympathetic, not sure how Rosie would take the question.

"They were going to attack the Sky Fairies." Rosie scowled, the first time she had done so in Cassidy's presence. "When Silver Fairies realized that, they called the rest of the tribes together to decide what to do. Even working together to lay a trap for the pirates, we still almost lost everything."

"You have records of this?" Cassidy could barely contain her excitement. The records might be biased, it was true. Nevertheless, obtaining a copy to take back with her would be ideal.

"Yes, of course," Rosie nodded. "Royal Historians from all four tribes were present during the battle. Records were exchanged and histories updated before the leaves began to turn." Noticing the confused look on Cassidy's face, Rosie laughed softly. "Forgive me. I fear I have said something you do not understand."

"Yes." Cassidy nodded. "Do you use turning leaves to measure time?" She was familiar with the water clocks her hosts provided, but this bit about leaves made no sense at all to her.

"Oh, yes, I see." Rosie smiled. "I was not speaking of an actual rotation of leaves." She moved her index finger in a circle to emphasize her point. "Every year in the autumn, the green leaves of the sugar maple trees change color from green to different shades of yellow, orange, and red. When they do that, we say 'the leaves have turned.'"

"They really change color?" Cassidy was impressed. Color was what she missed the most about her home. "I wish I could have seen that."

"It is lovely," Rosie smiled. "The air begins to change, too, from heavy, humid warmth of summer to the crisp, cool air of autumn."

"The air in the forest is usually fairly cool all year long," Isaac interjected, having caught himself staring at the slow smile forming on Cassidy's lips. The faraway look in her eyes seemed to call to him, too. "But in the meadows and near the sea, the heat and humidity can weigh on you like a tangible burden you must bear."

"I had no idea," Cassidy responded honestly. "Conditions in our regions are all very much alike. The volcanic areas are a little warmer than the others, I suppose."

"*Volcanic* areas?" Rosie shivered. "I could not abide to live near a volcano!"

"No?" It was Cassidy's turn to laugh. "I grew up near a volcanic trench, watching the orange magma cool and surrender to the sea's touch." Her eyes met Isaac's and she suddenly could not swallow. The fire in his eyes reminded her very strongly of the volcano she was just speaking of. Did that make her the sea?

"Everything is ready, Doctor," Daphne announced from the doorway to the surgery.

"Excellent." Cassidy broke eye contact with Isaac to look down at the reports she had spread across her desk. "Shall we?" She smiled at Rosie and faked a look at Isaac. Rising, she led the way into the other room.

A sink full of hot water waited for her, so she rolled up her sleeves, buttoning them in place above her elbows. While she lathered her hands and arms, Agnes and Rosie helped Isaac out of his jacket and shirt. He was already on the table by the time Daphne had tied Cassidy's surgical gown. Once Daphne was scrubbed, Cassidy helped her into her gown.

Agnes used that time to explain the sedation mask to Isaac and Rosie.

"Do you remember the salve we used before we injected the decoction?" Agnes asked. After they nodded, she pointed at the inside of mask. "This is lined with a very similar substance." Holding the mask up near her face, being careful not to breathe on it, she showed him how it would fit in place. "After I put this over your nose and mouth, I will spray a little warm water on it, which will allow the sedative to reach you. In just a few breaths, it will put you to sleep and Doctor Cassidy will be able to operate without causing you any pain."

"A few minutes? And he will be safely out for the entire surgery?" Rosie was astonished. The traditional potions used by the surface tribes could require close to an hour to take full effect. Some did work more rapidly, but those were only meant to aid in sleeping and would never stand up to the rigors of surgery.

Cassidy gave the cold fire a short, doubtful look; it was more plentiful in this room than the others, thus forming part of her decision to make this the operating room or surgery. However, now that she was preparing to use it, she could not help but compare it to the much brighter beams of the lightning bulbs used by her tribe.

By then, Agnes had settled Isaac comfortably on his stomach, damp sedation mask in place. At her nod, Cassidy began.

"Scalpel." Cassidy held out her hand to Daphne for the instrument. Her precise cut opened his skin just above his spine. "Retractors."

Chapter 11

When Isaac stirred later that evening, Cassidy looked up from where she sat. The copy of the history that Rosie had readily provided to her was surprisingly interesting reading. She checked the clock, marked her place, and put the history down so she could check on him.

"Hi." Isaac blinked groggily at the shape beside him, hoping he was not talking to an armoire or some other piece of furniture. Still, this being only his second visit to the recovery room as a patient, he supposed he might be excused for such a mistake.

"Hello." Cassidy took his wrist between her thumb and two fingers. His pulse was rapid, but strong. "Try to relax." She patted him lightly on the shoulder. "The surgery went very well."

"Tell me about it, Cass."

She blinked and hesitated, not sure at first that he was actually speaking to her. Telling herself that he was still coming out from under sedation, she opted against protesting the terrible nickname.

"You fell asleep, just like you were supposed to." She gently lifted the covers back into place. "Your spine was right where it should have been." From the table near his bed, she retrieved a mug of water with a straw and offered it to him. "I found a few bone slivers embedded in your spinal cord. Another sip?" she coaxed when he seemed about to wave the mug away. "Good," she patted his shoulder with one hand while she replaced the mug with her other hand. "It will help clear your system."

"You found bone slivers?" Isaac's head was clearing already.

"Yes, a few. They were interfering with your spinal cord, preventing it from healing properly." She checked the clock again, wanting to keep him awake and talking as long as she could. "I was able to see them because of a special magnifying glass I sometimes wear during surgery."

"Like a spyglass?" Isaac was familiar with those, having used them often during active Wrangler duty.

"More like a jeweler's glass, I would imagine." Without stopping to think, she reached out to smooth his hair from his forehead. "You really should turn your head," she advised hastily, as if that could somehow disguise their mutual response to her action.

"Why is that?" Isaac asked, taking her hand in his since she had not pulled it completely back, but allowed it to rest on the bed near him.

"Your neck…it will stiffen up if you stay that way much longer."

"Might be worth it." Forgetting his resolve not to get involved with her, Isaac lightly kissed the back of her hand.

"Now really." Cassidy withdrew her hand from his and moved so that she was on the other side of the bed. Deciding that the surgery was a safe topic, she resumed her simple account of it. "With the bone slivers removed, and continued injections of the decoction, I am confident that your spine will heal quite nicely."

Isaac gave in and turned his head so that he could see her. He had to use his arms to raise himself a little to do it, and was glad for her strong arm under his chest to help support him during the process. Her cuff caught for a moment on the buttons of his shirt, but she freed it easily enough.

"That sedation mask is very effective," he observed after he was resettled.

"Does that mean you do not want supper?" Agnes asked cheerfully from the doorway.

"Supper?" Isaac perked up visibly at the suggestion. "Bring it in, bring it right over here." He pointed at the table beside his bed.

"Easy now," Cassidy warned when he tried to rise. "We will help you sit up in the morning, alright?"

"But what about supper?" His tone was

nothing short of pleading.

"Agnes will feed you." Cassidy produced a pillow and together they got it positioned under his chest. She flattered herself that she hid her breathlessness until she was back over by the counter where she had left the history.

"You go onto bed now," Agnes instructed Cassidy from where she was arranging the supper tray on the table beside Isaac. "I will wake Daphne if I get tired."

"Thank you." Cassidy smiled brightly at her. "Goodnight."

"Sweet dreams."

Isaac's deep voice resonated in Cassidy's ears as she, still smiling, turned to leave. According to the water clock beside her bed, it was hours before she actually managed to fall asleep, though—and that was after she gave up trying to read. The clatter of dishes in the recovery woke her entirely too soon.

"Sorry," Gallica's voice whispered. "I hope I did not wake her."

"It would hardly be the first time she did not get enough sleep," Agnes' voice stated practically, making Cassidy smile.

Breakfast was served by the time Cassidy completed a short toilette and changed into fresh clothes for the day.

"Oh!" Gallica started guiltily when she saw Cassidy come out of her bedroom. "I woke you."

"No apologies, Gallica," Isaac chuckled from where he leaned against the wall by his bed, supported by various cushions. He had already choked down one of Rosie's pain-relieving potions, so his pain level was better than tolerable. "They woke me at least twice last night to ask if I was sleeping alright."

Daphne laughed at his teasing, making such a merry noise that Gallica and Cassidy had to join in.

"Here," Gallica was still grinning as she brought a tray over to Isaac's table. Tucking an oversized napkin in the neck of his shirt she explained, "In case I spill."

Isaac might have felt ridiculous, being fed breakfast by his little sister, a ready-made audience looking on…except that Cassidy and her nurses were busy eating and talking amongst themselves. His stress level fell considerably when he realized that they were helping Daphne practice the surface tongue.

"Ready?"

Gallica's body language told him all he needed to know. Her eyes were a little wider than normal; her shoulders were a touch too tense for anybody who could juggle knives as easily as she did. She was obviously genuinely afraid of spilling his eggs or drink on him.

"Thanks, sis." Isaac's smile was as warm and genuine as his feelings for Gallica at that moment. He did not feel up to fighting his less-than adept left hand for breakfast that morning.

Gallica smiled bravely and offered him a forkful of eggs.

Cassidy watched surreptitiously, telling herself that it was in case Gallica got in some difficulty. She thought it quite impressive how quickly the brother and sister established a rhythm, so that the fork never caught him with his mouth closed, the drink always connected with his lips before Gallica began tilting it, and so on.

"They seem very different from the advena at home," Agnes observed quietly.

Cassidy stiffened reprovingly. The *advena* Agnes was referring to were surface fairies—mostly survivors of windship crashes—and their descendants being held by the Water Fairy Tribe to protect the secret of its existence. Cassidy somehow doubted that Prince Isaac and Princess Gallica would be happy to learn about them. It was, in fact, a practice that her own family had been working to discourage for the last few centuries. It helped that more and more of the Water Fairies coming of age were expressing an interest in visiting the surface, but they were still a long way from a resolution.

Agnes, sensing Cassidy's discomfort, ate the rest of her breakfast in relative silence. As the oldest Water Fairy present, she felt that she should have known better than to bring up something they could not explain.

"I guess that does it," Gallica announced as soon as Isaac used the napkin to wipe his lips with a flourish.

"Give the cook my compliments," Isaac said. "And tell Stuart my nurse is prettier than his." He watched in astonishment as Gallica nearly dropped the tray she had just picked up from his table. "That was a joke." He protested her obvious distress at his words without really understanding it. Surely she did not care who Stuart was seeing, if anybody? He only meant to compliment his sister.

"I know." Gallica felt her smile start to wobble and turned quickly to leave. She was still too confused about what was happening with Stuart to be able to formulate a coherent response. "If I see him, I will, um…"

"Thank you so much for bringing us these lovely meals," Cassidy smoothly inserted. Rising from the table, she helped load the last few things on the serving cart, still talking so that Isaac could not. "I realize you cannot tell your cook how much we enjoy these new dishes, but they really are quite nourishing and appetizing."

Daphne and Agnes covered their retreat by converging on Isaac with medicinal intent, allowing them to escape without further embarrassment.

Gallica paused at the door to the tunnel and smiled shyly at Cassidy. "Thanks."

"As one woman to another," Cassidy patted her arm lightly, "you are quite welcome."

Gallica blushed and smiled at the same time.

"Here." Cassidy moved so that she would be hidden behind the opened door and let Gallica out with the cart. Motivated by very definite medicinal intent, she then returned to the recovery room, shutting both doors behind her.

Gallica was still scolding herself for overreacting to Isaac's comment when she sensed someone watching her. Looking swiftly behind her, she saw no one. Looking ahead of her, she found Stuart, leaning against the wall of the tunnel, arms folded across his chest.

"Morning, Beautiful." Stuart was more than pleased with the effect of his compliment on her. Flying over to her, he kissed first one, then her other delightfully pink cheek.

"Stuart, I…" Unsure of what to say, Gallica hid her face against his shoulder, her hands cupped against his chest. Her uncertainty faded like mist before the sun as his arms settled about her, warming her.

"I did what you told me," Stuart murmured into her hair. He was disappointed to find that she was wearing it up that morning.

"Hmm?" Gallica shifted so that her cheek was resting against his shoulder. That made it easier to look up at him.

Stuart smiled down at her, aware that she had no ulterior motive in mind. With a different woman, he might have thought she was trying to tease him into kiss her. To help her understand the difficult spot she was putting him in, having to resist the temptation she inadvertently presented, he began lightly kissing her face.

"I spoke to your father."

"Mmm?" Gallica did not fully register his remark until after a few more kisses. Her eyes opened wide. "You did what?"

Stuart allowed her to pull away from him, but not quite release her.

"Gallica." He waited for her to look him in the eyes. "I told him I loved you."

"Why?" That declaration rattled her more than she could even comprehend at that moment.

"Because I do." Stuart eased her back into his embrace, coming halfway himself rather than demanding she be the only one to yield. "He gave me permission to court you."

Gallica was feeling dizzy, so she quite naturally rested her head against his chest. Her feelings—since she had been old enough to have any—for Stuart had always run deeper than mere friendship, though she did her best to hide them for fear he would laugh at his young chum. When had his feelings changed? Had she done something to change them? She tried to think back over the last few days, wondering what she could possibly have done…and wishing she had done it sooner!

"Gallica." Stuart slipped a finger under her chin, gently forcing her to look at him. "I want your permission, as well."

Her response was to slip her arms around his neck and kiss him. He kissed her back, leaving her completely breathless. With her nestled in his arms, his hand on her hair, he felt whole. It was more than the triumph of completing his Wrangler training and being sworn. It was more than the feeling of belonging when he sat at the king's table with Isaac. And it was infinitely more than the friendship he had built with Gallica over the centuries. This changed everything for him.

The sound of someone coughing made Stuart look up.

"Good morning, Your Majesty," he greeted the queen quietly.

"Mother." Gallica drew away from him and flew to her mother's welcoming arms.

"I see you wasted no time, Sir Stuart." Fiona smiled affectionately at him. As embraces went, the one she had just stumbled on was probably the sweetest she had ever seen. Stuart was indeed Gallica's first love, something Fiona had quietly suspected for a long time.

"Thank you, ma'am." Seeing the approval in her eyes made Stuart feel ten twigs tall.

"And now." Fiona held Gallica away from her for a moment, inspecting her closely. As expected, she found eyes full of stars. "If you will pardon us, Sir Stuart, I require my daughter's assistance this morning." Her original intent had been to check on her son's recovery, but since she was confident of his caretakers, she felt not the slightest twinge of conscience at her change of mind.

"Yes, ma'am." Stuart did not hesitate to agree, but he had eyes for Gallica alone.

"Thank you for taking the cart back to the kitchen." Fiona assumed his acquiescence on the subject and swept Gallica away for a breath of fresh air. First loves were heady enough without an overabundance of seclusion.

Stuart, finding himself alone with a cart full of dirty dishes, dutifully returned it to the kitchen as the queen had bidden him.

"Please have a lunch cart for five ready at noon," he instructed the butler who took the cart from him. Rather than sticking around to watch the butler and other kitchen staff engage in speculation, he took himself off to play a hunch. The indoor airball courts were open now, a little earlier than usual, in an effort to help Weetu's populace adjust to the fact that they were officially cut off from their outdoor excursions until spring. That meant just about everyone would be at the morning's games, a series of one-on-one challenges against the Wranglers posted there for the winter. By the time Stuart arrived, the competition was in full swing. It should have been the perfect opportunity for him to slip in relatively unnoticed.

"Sir Stuart!" From the eight corners, where the spectators watched safely from behind protective netting, came a spontaneous cheer for him.

Disappointed at being made so conspicuous, Stuart waved at them as if he had just come to watch the game. In an attempt to blend back in, he quickly joined the group of Wranglers on the sidelines.

"Stuart!" A broad-shouldered Wrangler thumped him on the back. "Thought you might be too tangled up in red ribbon to come compete." He roared at his own joke about the supposedly endless paperwork a Wrangler of Stuart's rank had to complete.

Stuart protested as much as he dared, but in the end he had to give in. He was a Wrangler; he was posted at Weetu for the winter; and *of course* he thought the Wrangler reputation was worth defending. The matter settled, he abandoned all hopes of eavesdropping on Lady Lorna and Phil. As expected, they were together among the spectators.

"That feller over yonder has beaten all but one of us so far," a nearby Wrangler growled.

"Does he have a name?" Stuart asked curiously.

"Answers to Dizzy," grunted another of the Wranglers.

"Is that it?" Dizzy chose that moment to hurl a verbal challenge from the far side of the court. "Have you clodhoppers given up?"

Stuart's eyes narrowed. "Give me a hand here," he ordered the nearest Wrangler. Seating himself, Stuart swiftly removed his jacket and rolled up his sleeves.

"I do not like the way he is looking at you," the Wrangler muttered as he helped Stuart exchange dress boots for the more pliable sports slippers with their padded soles.

"Oh?" Stuart glanced at his opponent, a wiry young man with pine-green hair.

"He looks like lunch just wandered in."

Stuart laughed aloud at that. He and Isaac had been teammates on the local championship airball team. One-on-one was a little different, naturally, but then that was all that he and Isaac had been able to find time for over the last few decades.

"That makes things more interesting."

Slapping a few of his friends lightly on their shoulders, Stuart turned and ducked under the protective netting that kept spectators from getting an airball in the mouth.

An official rose to hover mid-court, airball in hand. The fist-sized ball was made entirely of rubber. It could be kicked, head-butted, punched, bumped, thrown, or bounced through any one of the six goals that adorned the ceiling, walls, and floor of the court. This being an indoor game of one-on-one, the first to reach a total of fifteen goals would be proclaimed winner.

"Take your places," the official called.

Stuart and Dizzy faced off on the court floor. They both tensed when the official held the ball out, away from his body; slowly it tipped, allowing the ball to fall. Dizzy shot off the floor the millisecond the ball was no longer touching the official's hand.

Stuart waited a discrete moment longer to see if he could anticipate Dizzy's play. A faint sideways motion of Dizzy's body suggested that he planned to turn completely around for a reverse shot at the goal on the far wall. Surging up and forward, Stuart was in position to block Dizzy's shot with a sidekick that sent the airball hurtling towards a different wall goal.

"Point to Sir Stuart." Catching the ball neatly, the official resumed his place at mid-court.

The battle began in earnest now. They darted after the ball like dragonflies chasing a meal, trying to outmaneuver one another without slamming into each other. The crowd gasped and clamored at near misses, thoroughly enjoying the show. In the end, it was the crowd that was Dizzy's undoing. When he should have been keeping an eye on Stuart, he was watching a pretty Wood Fairy lass.

"Point! And game, to Sir Stuart!"

The crowd erupted in cheers.

Stuart, realizing that he had won, dropped quickly to the floor, where he was promptly swamped by elated Wranglers and hoisted on their shoulders. Stuart, his wing muscles aching from the exertion, gladly relaxed where he was, waving occasionally at the crowd. When they finally brought him back to the sidelines, an apprentice was waiting with a tall glass of doctor's water.

"How badly did I beat him?" Stuart asked under his breath as he took the glass.

"You mean you…" The apprentice stifled his exclamation of surprise. "The score was fifteen to ten."

Chapter 12

Sitting quietly in her room, Cassidy was just finishing the Sky Fairy history of the pirate offensive. All four tribal histories—Sky Fairy, Plant Fairy, Wood Fairy, and Silver Fairy—were concise and to the point. While there was some variation in viewpoint, which was only natural under the circumstances, they all came to the same conclusion. Based on the evidence uncovered by the Sky Fairy Tribe and corroborated by the bits and pieces that the other tribes had simply never shared with each other before, the pirates were planning a massive attack on the Sky Fairy Tribe.

Cassidy knew from her childhood lessons that the Sky Fairy Tribe controlled the weather above the sea's surface. Enslaving that tribe would mean eventual domination over all four of Fairydom's surface tribes. Banding together against their common enemy, the surface tribes met the pirates in what they called the Mists—a section of the sea where a dormant volcano protruded just above the waves, the fumarole formed in its side spewing endless clouds of ash and foul-smelling, sulfurous smoke. The pirates must have mapped the area somehow, because the histories all agreed that, without the daring intervention of the Silver Fairies

Princess Rebecca, Hugh Lawson, and Rolf Warner, the Mists would have given the pirates shelter wherein to both hide from attack and launch attacks from.

Fascinating reading, really. Except that she knew something they did not. Pirates were even now in her tribal territories, having stumbled upon one of their surface access portals after a recent battle. Just a handful, to be sure, but how many seahorses did it take to strip a shrimp bed? And her tribe was laboring under what she now saw as deliberate misinformation—the lie that the surface tribes were attempting to rob the peaceable pirates of their rights in a clear cut abuse of power. With the pirates trying to convince her tribe to support them against their supposed oppressors, even intimating that the surface tribes were planning to attack the Water Fairies next.

Cassidy was actually frightened when she thought of the rest of the lie: that the surface tribes were planning to invade Water Fairy territories. When she first arrived at Weetu, she was half-convinced that there was evidence to support that theory. After all, the Sky Fairy Tribe had recently established new colonies closer to the sea than ever before. Now that she knew the truth of the pirate offensive—for she believed the four histories—she was reluctantly coming to a grim conclusion.

When the pirates failed to enslave the Sky Fairy Tribe, their wrecked and battered windships accidentally discovered the Water Fairy Tribe. Her tribe, which regulated the purity of the waters and controlled the levels of the rivers and streams. *Her tribe*, which could bring Fairydom to its knees without ever exposing itself to attack.

Setting the history down on her bed, Cassidy went over to the sink. For a moment she thought she was going to be sick, but after splashing some cold water on her face, she felt better. Irritated by the few drops that inevitably escaped under her collar, she dried her face, then hung the half towel back on the bar to dry. Facing her reflection in the mirror above the sink, she cocked her head to one side.

"Now that you know all of this, what can you do about it?" Her reflection watched her for several seconds before sighing and turning away.

"Doctor?" Daphne's voice called from the other side of the door.

"Yes, enter."

Daphne opened the door and poked her head inside. "You wanted to know as soon as he thought he was ready to leave?" She grinned at her witty phrasing.

"Yes." Cassidy did not even notice. "Thank you."

Daphne stepped aside with a puzzled frown. Something was bothering Cassidy, that much was obvious. A quick peek around Cassidy's bedroom showed only a sheaf of papers on her bed as being obviously out of place. Daphne probably would have slipped in for a little friendly snooping if Agnes had not called for her.

"Coming," Daphne called back, closing Cassidy's door with a guilty jerk.

Cassidy was about to start checking Isaac for release when Daphne hurried past her and into the surgery.

Isaac, who had spent the last few hours debating with himself the merits of not becoming too attached to Cassidy, saw at once how distracted she was. Oh, her manner was right enough, the cool, reassuring touch of a medical professional as she listened to his lungs, tested his temperature, and checked his surgery site for signs of infection. Isaac still had the terrible taste of Rosie's healing potion in his mouth.

"You," she announced, setting aside her instruments, "are in excellent health. It is about time we got you out of here so that Rosie and I can make a final selection from the others."

Isaac watched her as she shook out his shirt. He had never believed in love at first sight. Nor did he now. It was his continued attraction to her that told him this was different from anything he had before encountered. Perhaps he had been unfortunate up until now. Perhaps he had been too demanding of the women he met, expecting them to be as feminine as his mother, as adventurous as he was, and as wise as his grandmother. Either that, or he was finally ready to pursue someone who had two out of those three qualities. Marriage would be an adventure in its own right, truth be told.

He finally admitted to himself what he had decided. Repeatedly they told him it would take the better part of the winter season for him to walk freely. Alright. He was going to do everything in his power to make Cassidy an integral part of his therapy. He was going to spend as much time with her as he could. He just needed to be patient while he figured this out. If he fell further in love with her as time passed, he would even persuade her to remain with his tribe. Somehow.

Cassidy did her best to avoid making eye contact with Isaac while she eased his shirt on helping his wings find the appropriate slits in the back. She had felt his gaze on her while she moved about the room and was worried about what she might see in his eyes if she looked in them.

While she buttoned his shirt for him, she asked, "Do you remember your instructions?"

"Take it even easier than usual," Isaac grinned. "No bending or twisting or anything besides breathing." His nostrils flared slightly as he enjoyed the light scent of her perfume. It was a pleasant change from the women at court. He sometimes thought they were trying to outdo each other, foolish as that sounded. Whatever their reasoning, he blamed more than one sick headache on their excessive use of perfumes. Winter was the worst because there was rarely a good reason to excuse himself.

"Very good." Cassidy was about to button his top button but he reached up and caught her right hand.

"Not that one, please." Isaac was pleased that she did not immediately withdraw her hand. "I have a difficult time breathing when it is buttoned." Noticing that she was staring at their hands, he looked down as well, puzzled. It took few moments for him to realize he had used his *right* hand.

"Well." Cassidy swallowed hard and rotated her hand so that they were palm to palm. "What a pleasant side-effect." As far as she knew, no one had ever told Isaac the theory that his crippled hand was primarily the result of his feeling guilty for not being able to do more during the pirate offensive. After reading the histories, she was not sure what he had expected of himself. His windship squadron was credited with the destruction and capture of more than the average pirate windships.

"Side-effect?" Isaac repeated, looking at her sharply. His hand was sending rapid-fire distress signals to his brain, upset at being moved after months of inactivity.

"Of course," she fibbed. "What else could it be?" Tugging his right arm towards her, she used her left hand to 'examine' the bones of his wrist and forearm. "Can you feel that?" His pulse was racing and her attempt at standard doctor conversation was barely a whisper.

"Yes." Isaac moved towards her, but she instantly pressed him back against the pillows. Not the least bit deterred, he caught her by the shoulders and drew her to him. He watched her eyes widen as their faces came a breath apart. His right hand was still tingling most uncomfortably, but he ignored it and kissed her anyway. He never had been very patient.

She was stiff at first, so much so that he almost released her. Then her hands slowly moved up from where they were resting against his chest to his face. She kissed him back, lightly, before straightening away.

"Doctor?" Agnes' voice queried from the surgery where she and Daphne were just about done reorganizing the surgical instruments. "Is that someone knocking?"

Cassidy kissed Isaac once more. "Probably. It is about lunch time, after all." Turning away from Isaac, she went into the office. The knock sounded—again, apparently—and she opened the door to admit Stuart.

"You gave me a scare," Stuart grinned as he closed the door behind himself. "I thought I had the wrong door or something."

Cassidy did her best to laugh with him. "We might be persuaded to do just that," she joked back, "if you could help us find rooms with a view of the coral and seaweed glades."

Stuart frowned thoughtfully before shaking his head. "Sorry." He wheeled the cart into the recovery room. "I just rented the last place I had like that this morning."

"Really?" Cassidy's eyes narrowed as she noticed him wincing while he transferred items from the cart to the desk they were using as a table. "Your customers must have put up quite a fight." She touched him lightly on the back of his shoulder, just above his left wing.

Stuart pulled away at once. "Careful," he warned. "I think I pulled something in an airball game."

"I am sure you did," Cassidy agreed. "Daphne, Agnes. Lunch is here." Pointing at the packing crate Stuart customarily used, she ordered, "Sit down."

"But I," Stuart began to protest.

"Stuart." Isaac spoke from where he was still leaning against the pillows. "You might as well make it easy on yourself and sit the first time she asks." He winked.

Stuart chuckled and gave in. "Just like Rosie, eh?" The answering light in Isaac's eyes made Stuart stop to reassess the situation.

"Would you open your collar, please?" Cassidy opened a jar of anodyne preparation while he obliged her, then handed it to him. "Hold this." She expertly tested and treated his wing muscles, never making him wince more than once per trouble spot. "There." Wiping her hands on a convenient towel, she took the jar back and screwed the lid on.

As Isaac watched her treat his friend, he wondered if he should be jealous. When it was over, he decided, her manner with Stuart was strictly professional.

"What is air-ball?" Daphne asked curiously.

Stuart helpfully launched into a basic description of the game. Egged on by their questions, he was engaged in relating his latest victory by the time Cassidy took a tray over to Isaac. Not so engaged, however, that he failed to notice the way his best friend was looking at the doctor while she tucked the napkin into Isaac's collar and spread it across his chest. Ironically enough, he got so busy juggling the airball story and trying to decide how he felt about the romance obviously developing between them that he completely overlooked the fact that Isaac was eating with his right hand!

"Take your time," Cassidy murmured, reaching out to steady Isaac's hand when it seemed his latest forkful of stew was about to be shaken loose. "Here." She appropriated the fork after that bite. The others were completely engrossed in Stuart's story, so there was no fear of embarrassing him. "Your hand is still healing," she told him, scooping up about half as much stew as he had for his next bite. That made it easier to control while they negotiated getting it safely into his mouth. "Be patient with it," she advised, offering him another bite. "Use Rosie's therapy ball, but do not overexert it." She dabbed at a drop of stew that escaped despite their best efforts. "Sometimes, the most important part of healing is not reinjuring yourself."

Isaac smiled. "You really do sound like Rosie." He set his still-trembling right hand on top of her idle left hand.

"Did you ever kiss Rosie?" Cassidy teased softly enough that only he could hear, having come to the conclusion that her participation in this flirtation would be good for her patient.

"Never."

Cassidy dropped her eyes. His tone of voice did not sound at all like a flirtation.

"Isaac!" Stuart interrupted from his seat at the desk. "Is it true? Are you being released today?"

Isaac smiled at him around Cassidy's shoulder. "I tried to talk them into keeping me," he squeezed Cassidy's left hand lightly, "but they say they need the bed for their next patient."

Stuart's grin threatened to split his face. "All the work we did to make it so you could come in for an operation and here you are getting tossed out." His laugh was so contagious that everyone joined in; even Cassidy and Isaac. "Why, I almost forgot." He sobered abruptly. "Who is the next patient?"

Agnes shook her head. "No use asking," she informed him. "That sort of thing is strictly confidential."

"Ordinarily, yes." Cassidy handed Isaac his glass; he could easily handle that with his left hand. "In this case, however, we will need their help just to make it happen."

Recognizing the slight pinch of Agnes' mouth as a sign of disapproval, Stuart tried to soothe her by explaining, "As soon as they find out, they will tell everyone anyway."

"They certainly will," Isaac agreed. "It will be kind of nice," he chuckled, "having someone else to share the notoriety with."

Agnes took another bite of her meal. It all

seemed peculiar to her, but she had to agree with Cassidy's assessment of the situation.

"Stuart, do you think you could ask Rosie to come see me before supper?" Cassidy asked without turning away from where she was feeding Isaac his last bite of stew. "Can you reach everything alright?" she asked Isaac quietly, referring to the remaining roll and half a glass of nectar. When he nodded, she patted his arm, carefully withdrew her left hand, and flew over to the others. "I have narrowed it down to two patients, but I would like Rosie's opinion before I make a final selection."

"I would be glad to," Stuart answered honestly. "No one knows the patients as well as Rosie does."

Cassidy smiled. "Exactly what I thought." Daphne, as the junior member of her team, had set a place for Cassidy and lidded her plate to keep the food warm. Flashing Daphne a 'well done' smile, Cassidy took her seat. "How does your back feel?"

Stuart stretched his wings tentatively. "Much better, thank you."

"Try to get to bed early tonight," Cassidy suggested absent-mindedly. "The ache will return once the anodyne preparation wears off."

"Yes, ma'am," Stuart grinned. He assumed she was talking about what she rubbed on his back earlier. Rising, he began collecting the dirty dishes and utensils that Agnes and Daphne were through with. "By the way," he looked up from where he was staking them, "I have been wondering if you would like me to bring you a few books."

"Books?" Cassidy hid a smile behind her napkin.

"We brought an en-tire crate of books with us," Daphne answered with a chuckle.

"Really?" Stuart whistled softly. Her pronunciation was really improving. "That must have been a heavy crate. How…" He stopped himself before he could finish asking how they had transported such a thing from under the sea. That might be seen as too inquisitive, given that their tribe still protected their privacy so fiercely. "How about letting me borrow a few from you, then?"

Agnes very nearly snorted. "They are medical texts," she informed him patiently.

"Oh!" Stuart, perfectly comfortable with his level of education and role in his tribe, was not at all offended. "Yes, I see. I was offering you recreational books…adventures, mysteries, that sort of thing." He shrugged apologetically. "But those probably wouldn't interest you."

Cassidy, noticing how Daphne lit up, took the offer seriously. Months of the same seven faces could be a lot more pleasant with books to entertain and divert them.

"I suppose we could try them," Cassidy hedged, watching Agnes from the corner of her eye. As long as Cassidy had known her, Agnes had remained aloof from such entertainment, regarding it as a complete waste of time.

"Yes, may we?" Daphne pounced eagerly. "Think of it! Lib-rar-ies full of stories we have *never* read!" In her excitement, she nearly upset her glass and had to move quickly to steady it.

Cassidy set her fork down and reached for her glass. "If you would be so kind, Stuart, as to bring us a few books, we would very much appreciate it."

"My pleasure." Stuart bowed at the waist. He made a mental note to get Gallica to recommend some titles to him. "Now, by your leave," he bowed again. "I should get Isaac back in his chair."

"Let me help," Daphne volunteered, rising quickly. "It will take two," she pointed out unnecessarily.

"Thank you." Stuart retrieved Isaac's chair, which had been parked by the wall in the surgery. Once he had it in what he believed was the best position by the bed, he put the brakes on.

"Mind his back now," Daphne warned. They each put an arm under Isaac's legs and a shoulder under Isaac's arm. Together, they somewhat clumsily transferred Isaac from the bed to his chair.

"Here," Cassidy appeared behind the chair. "Lean him forward. Gently!" She slid one of the flatter pillows between Isaac's back and his chair. "Alright," she nodded at Stuart, who had been supporting Isaac. "How is that?" Cassidy asked.

"Better," Isaac answered tersely. The pain potion was not quite strong enough to protect him yet. "I will be back in time for supper and my evening injection," he tried to smile. "See you in a few hours."

Chapter 13

"Are you certain?" Stuart asked the caretaker.

"Oh yes, Sir Stuart." Her hands never stopped moving over the painting she was wiping down. It was her job to tend all of the paintings in this branch of the south corridors and she was proud of it. "I saw Princess Gallica go that way," the maid nodded down the corridor to her right, "less than half an hour ago."

Stuart was about to thank her and go on his way when a thought struck him.

"Less than half an hour?" He glanced up and down the corridor to be sure. Not a water clock or sandglass in sight. "How can you be so precise?"

The maid laughed pleasantly. "There are ninety-six paintings in this corridor. I dust them once a day."

"I see." Stuart watched in awe as she gave the frame a final swipe with her dust cloth and moved on to the next painting.

"It measures out to exactly five minutes per painting, though the little ones really don't take so long and the bigger ones sometimes take longer!" She beamed at him.

"So when you say you saw Ga…, um,

Princess Gallica less than half an hour ago, you really mean less than six paintings ago." He smiled. "You are quite amazing."

"Why thank you!"

His curiousity satisfied, Stuart left her humming busily. After delivering Cassidy's message to Rosie, Stuart had taken Isaac back to his quarters, where he helped Noland settle him comfortably. Reminding Isaac that he, Stuart, had promised some recreational reading to their guests, Stuart then excused himself to go in search of Gallica. What a search! And it led him to the south corridors, of all places.

"There you are."

Stuart whirled to confront his attacker. But she was not attacking.

"Lady Lorna?" If the mahogany statue of King Michael III beside her had begun to recite poetry, Stuart would not have been more startled.

"I thought you would never get here, silly boy." Lady Lorna fluttered her eyelashes at him.

Stuart blocked her attempt to take him by the arm. Holding her by the wrist, he frowned and looked around the small circular viewing area where they were standing. They were apparently alone. Odd. He would have expected her to plan a witness or two to their apparent tryst. But that made no sense. How could she have known he was coming here? He had not known that himself until… *Gallica.*

"You are hurting me," Lorna complained, trying vainly to free herself.

"I doubt it," Stuart muttered. Releasing her unexpectedly, he watched coldly as she threw out her wings to keep herself from falling backwards. "I am also not looking for you, nor planning to meet you at any time or any place. I would have thought by now that was plain enough, even to someone like you."

Lorna's eyes narrowed to slits. "Someone like me?" she hissed. "Are you maligning a lady of the court?"

"Lady?" Princess Gallica landed lightly beside Stuart. "You wear the title badly." Gallica casually took two steps to her right, putting a little distance between herself and Stuart in case Lorna rushed her. "And by no stretch of the imagination would you be considered a lady by the definition of the word."

Stuart watched, tensed for action, as Lorna stretched herself taller and taller, her wings opening to their fullest extent. He fully expected her to shriek like the chicken hawk she was beginning to resemble. Then her look changed. She shrank back to her normal size and smoothed her cape, taking on the look of a weasel instead.

"I wonder what your father will think when

I tell him I found your secret meeting place." Lorna snarled.

"I can tell him now that he thinks of you as little as possible," Gallica retorted, aware that the statement could be taken at least two ways and neither of them complimentary to Lorna.

Stuart briefly considered announcing the king's probable approval, but a glance at Gallica made him think again. Much to his relief, Lorna refrained from counter-attacking and flounced off down the hall in the direction he had just come from. He kept one eye on her retreat while he held out his near hand to Gallica, drawing her into a shadow with him.

"What are you doing here?" he whispered.

"Not now." Gallica whispered back, shaking her head slightly. She pressed a finger against his lips before he could speak again, leaving them standing there in silence.

Stuart counted his heartbeats to measure the time they waited. He might have tried stealing a kiss, but he sensed that Gallica was deadly serious about keeping quiet. Then something— not a sound, exactly, more of an instinctive perception of motion—stood the hairs on the back of his neck on end.

Someone slipped past them, moving from shadow to shadow without making a sound. Fortunately for them, whoever it was chose the shadow by King Brian III's statue on the far side of the viewing area from them. *So Lorna had not been alone after all!*

As a precaution, Gallica put the rest of her hand over Stuart's mouth. She knew who the shadow was, had gotten a good look at his face when she first saw him entering the south corridors. More important to her was what he had been doing between the moment where she lost sight of him a few minutes ago and when she heard Lady Lorna try to corner Stuart. At last the corridor was truly empty; except for them.

Stuart moved her hand and put his mouth by her ear. "Alone at last."

She almost laughed. Rather than giving their presence away, she caught hold of his hand and led him down the hallway, backtracking the prowler.

"I followed him as far as this painting," she indicated the self-portrait of Sir Alfonse the Great. "But I think he knew I was following him, because he stopped here and pretended he was interested in it."

"He must be a good actor," Stuart grinned. He easily deflected the elbow she playfully threw at his stomach and pulled her close. "I had to write an essay on this painting as an apprentice." He grimaced at the memory. Wranglers were expected to be literate and capable of doing more than writing basic skirmish reports. "Believe me when I say I am much more interested in you."

Gallica rolled her eyes at him and pushed him away. "That may be," she moved to examine the painting more closely. "But try to be serious, please." They both knew that the paintings in the corridor were too easily recognizable to be stolen and easily sold. There was a small treasure room further down the corridor, yet as far as she knew, the prowler had not bothered to go past this painting.

"If I am remembering correctly..." She fluttered backwards to the middle of the corridor, then looked up at the ceiling. "Of all the bizarre coincidences."

"Bizarre indeed," Stuart quipped, baffled by her behavior.

"Look." She pointed at the ceiling.

"A ventilation port. So?" He folded his arms across his chest. "There are ventilation ports all..." He frowned and stopped midsentence.

"All over the city," she finished for him. "The ventilation system is the perfect way to move through Weetu without being seen."

"To what purpose?" Stuart could tell she had given this a great deal of thought. He was just sorry that he could not say the same. Wandering troupers did not overly concern him, providing they were not wandering in the medical maze.

"I am not sure." Gallica looked sideways at him, disappointed with herself for not having an answer.

"Neither am I," he smiled. "But I think you are on to something. Here," he took her by the hand. "Come with me."

Flying swiftly, yet cautiously, down the corridor, they reached an intersection of main tunnels without further incident. Stuart waved to the guard at the main entrance and led Gallica along so rapidly that she would have gotten lost if she had not been born and raised in Weetu.

"Why are we going to the craftsfairy quarter?" she asked eventually. She knew about it mostly because she had never been there.

"To see Old Pete." Stuart kept going.

"Old Pete?" she queried. The name meant nothing to her.

"That is what everyone calls him. Not too long ago one of his relatives tried to prove he was the oldest fairy in Weetu." They entered the craftsfairy quarter just then, and Stuart slowed down a little to avoid calling attention to their passage.

"Is he?" Gallica played along, trusting more than understanding.

"Nobody knows." Stuart landed near the

section where most of the retired craftsfairies chose to live. "He refused to tell them how old he really was!" Stuart studied the honeycomb-like housing that lined the opposite wall for several seconds before lifting off again. "It has been a while, but I think he lives up there."

For the most part, Weetu occupied the tunnels bored long ago by the parasites that attacked sugar maple trees. This section was the one exception. With special permission from the king at the time it as built, the craftsfairies excavated a small portion of one of the soft tree rings and made their home there. During most of the year, the hundreds of houses stood empty on the face of the remaining soft ring, their occupants preferring to live on the old sugar maples' ample branches. Since it was winter now, everyone had returned home. The individual and family living quarters alike had cold fire mushrooms, which were sending streams of soft green light through every front window.

"It looks so magical," Gallica breathed. It looked to her as if the sky had fallen to one side, each doorway and window taking the place of a star.

"Have you never been here before?" Stuart asked, genuinely surprised.

"No," Gallica shook her head. "I have never ventured beyond the classrooms." Her training in the area of crafts was relatively broad, since she never sought an apprenticeship. She did pretty well at wood carving, was better than fair at sewing, and could even hammer out basic necessities like pots or pans.

"I used to come here all the time." Stuart looked around the area where they were flying. "There." He pointed at one of the windows. "The couple that lives there makes the best boots in all of Weetu. Maybe even in the whole tribe." He indicated another window. "And that family. They run long on leather workers, but their oldest daughter makes candy. I used to hang around there quite a bit."

"Oh, really." Gallica was not quite sure how it had happened, but they were facing each other as they ascended. And ascending much more slowly than at first. "I suppose you two were friends."

"Naturally." Stuart smiled down at his intended. "In fact, I introduced her to her husband."

"Hmm." Gallica allowed him to narrow the distance between them, her hands coming to rest on his arms. "How can you be remember where they lived? All of them look the same to me."

"No, not really." Stuart leaned closer, brushing his lips against her cheek. "Leather workers make their name signs of leather."

"Oh."   Gallica turned as if to look at the houses they were passing, incidentally offering him her other cheek.

"Wood carvers make theirs of wood."   He willing accepted her offer.   "And metal workers…"

"Make their name signs out of metal?"   She finished for him, giggling softly.

"It is amazing how quickly you grasp these things."   Stuart stole a quick kiss, then slowed to a hover.   "Which means that this house belongs to a…?"

"I cannot tell," Gallica admitted after studying the hodgepodge of materials used to make the name sign. It read simply 'Pete."

"It belongs," a thin, reedy voice announced, "to a Master of all crafts."

"Hello, Pete."   Stuart squeezed Gallica's waist reassuringly, for she had started a little when the voice came out of the relative darkness of Pete's porch. "I suppose you were sitting there the whole time?"   His effort at a mock-accusing tone failed miserably.

"Course I was."   Pete cackled a little. "Some folks say spring is the best time fer love. Me, I figger it blooms the whole year 'round."

"You always were smarter than most." Stuart and Gallica landed on his porch.

"You must be," Gallica inserted, duly impressed with his claim. "I have never heard of a Master of all crafts before."

Pete considered her briefly, then shrugged. "Most folks is happy with one occupation. Me, I never was. Got bored too easy."

"Pete has lived in every tribal territory on the map," Stuart added. "He even held the place of royal metalsmith a few Plant Fairy kings ago."

Pete cackled again and scratched at a bothersome spot on his chest. "This feller of your'n oughta know. He used ta come by most ever' night, beggin' a story." He poked harmlessly at Stuart with his cane. "Had to settle down to one spot after I married, though. Wife refused to be hauled all over. Truth be told, with all the blamed things she insisted on keepin' 'round, movin' would have been an awful chore." Pete's wife had died years ago, and he still missed her. Too stubborn to admit that to most folks, he complained about her so-called faults instead. Eyeing Stuart, Pete commented, "Ain't seen you fer quite a spell, though."

Before either of them could think of a response, Pete continued philosophically, "Figgered you was finally out livin' yer own stories."

"I was, Pete." Stuart was a little ashamed at the thought of just how long it *had* been since his last visit. "But we came tonight to hear one of yours, if you will humor us."

Pete considered. "I think mebbe you heard all o' mine."

Stuart laughed and pulled up the other porch chair for Gallica. "Tell it this time for my friend, here," he coaxed. "Tell her about the self-portrait of Sir Alfonse the Great."

Pete began to cackle again, only this time it seemed like he was not going to stop. Eventually he ran out of breath and started to wheeze.

"Here." Stuart picked up the heavy water pot from the table behind Pete's chair and poured Pete a dram of its contents. "Pete uses hot water to keep his lungs warm," he explained to Gallica as he replaced the pot.

"Thankee," Pete managed after a few sips of the water. "Sir Alfonse the Great, eh? The great what, I wanna know," he snorted. "Vainest Wrangler I ever saw. In or outta uniform."

"He did lead the attack against the serpents of Copper Valley," Gallica pointed out a bit timidly. Alfonse the Great was accredited with a great many more daring feats, but the one she mentioned was thoroughly documented.

"Sure did," Pete agreed. "Sure did. Oh, he was'nae a bad feller. He just, well, he was always spouting poetry and such." As best as he could, Pete contorted his frail body into an imitation of the pose Alfonse had painted

himself in. "Loved him a good riddle, he did."
Pete scratched his chest thoughtfully. "Mind,
now, I like a good riddle myself," he allowed.
"But that last riddle of his'n. Made no sense,
none at all."

"Do you mean the riddle about his
dragonfly?" Gallica asked, confused. As far as
she knew, the answer to that had been found
written on a paper hidden in Alfonse's saddle.

"No, not that one," Pete answered a bit
crossly. "The other one."

Gallica exchanged glances with Stuart.

"The one he writ on the back of his port-
rate."

"Yes, that story," Stuart encouraged.
Something about that story was bothering him,
but he could not put his finger on it.

"Ain't much of a story, but," Pete shrugged,
"if you wanta hear it?" When Gallica and
Stuart both nodded, Pete took another sip to wet
his whistle. "He come to me first, wanted I
should make him a leather back fer it. He was
kinder old by then, mebbe nine, mebbe ten
thousand year old." Pete ignored the amused
look exchanged by his young visitors. "I reckon
I was flattered, seein' as how I was jest gettin'
started at leather workin'."

"Was he interested in your suggestion of the
backgrounds he might use for his portrait?"
Stuart prodded.

"Not at all," Pete answered indignantly. "Told him I knew lots of purty places right nearby. Offered to guide him, no extra charge. And he turned me down flat. He was polite 'nuff about it, but he was dead set on a spot he already picked out."

"I always wondered why he spoiled a nice painting by putting the bramble bushes behind him," Gallica admitted.

"Bah, it was part of the riddle!" Pete shuffled his feet a little. "D'ya know what I hate most about that riddle of his'n?"

"What?" Gallica asked when Stuart did not.

"I still remember it." Pete thumped his port with his cane. "Remember it like he told it to me yestiday."

"That must be terrible," Gallica offered. "I guess we should be careful not to read the back of his portrait."

"Funny thing about that." Pete took another sip of his drink, enjoying the attention. "The riddle he told me and the riddle he writ there, they ain't word fer word the same."

Stuart crouched down by Pete's chair. "But you say you remember the riddle he told you exactly as he told it? Every word?"

"Course I do." Pete sniffed. "My mem'ry is better'n most folks half my age."

"I believe you!" Gallica promptly assured him. "I just wish I was not so curious."

"Eh?"   Pete looked over at her, not understanding.

"Well, now that you have told me about the riddles, why, I just will not be able to rest until I have solved them."   Gallica was only half-padding her part of Stuart's interested friend. She probably would lose a lot of sleep over this.

"That do beat all," Pete exclaimed in surprise. "You sure you ain't funnin' with Old Pete?"

"We both want to hear it," Stuart answered for her.

"How come?" Pete looked back and forth between them, unable to stifle the feeling that he was missing something important.

"Winter just hit," Stuart pointed out. "A long, hard winter by the looks of things."

"I ain't sure but what you is both holdin' out on me," Pete mused aloud. "If I could figger what it was you were holdin' out, I might want in."

Gallica laughed at that, an open, honest laugh that made Old Pete's lips twitch themselves into a smile.

"I give you my word of honor, Pete," Gallica told him. "If we find a treasure at the end of this riddle, I will make sure you get a fair share of it."

Chapter 14

Rosie leaned back in her chair across the desk from Cassidy. "I cannot decide between them," she declared. "The cases are so similar!" Gesturing at the two medical files spread out before her, Rosie began citing the things they had in common. "The patients are nearly the same age. They both suffered traumatic spinal injury due to being literally stabbed in the back by pirates. The wounds are in essentially the same section of the spine."

"One of them is male and one is female," Cassidy pointed out. She would like to have been amused, but the sad truth was, that was the primary difference in the two wounds. She chose them specifically because there was a very real chance that they would both need the gold strand treatment. They would never again walk without it. And also because she knew that, risky as the procedure was, time was a major factor in how well it worked.

"And both of them in peak condition for their age and gender. If only you could treat them both." Dejected, Rosie folded her arms across her chest.

Cassidy shrugged. "But I could."

Rosie perked up visibly, straightening in her chair. "Then why not do it?"

"Why not?" Cassidy paused to wonder why that had never occurred to her. "I would rather have treated them separately," she confessed. "We naturally will want to keep detailed records of their progress, and things will get rather involved, complicated even."   Of course, she did have Agnes and Daphne with her. It was a little unusual, but they were just as qualified for observations as Cassidy.

"That seems a relatively small problem," Rosie chuckled, "compared to keeping that hair of yours out of sight during their recoveries." For once in her long life, Rosie was grateful for her straight-as-a-stick hair. Brush it out, tie it up, and she was ready to go. Cassidy's curls, on the other hand, each seemed to have a mind of its own.

"Oh, yes." Cassidy tucked an errant curl back behind her ear. "If you sedate the patients in the regular surgery area, before you bring them here, we could at least get off to a good start."

"I am not sure how well that will work," Rosie admitted. "During the summer season, I might have arranged the surgeries for during the night, while everyone else was asleep. But during the winter, Weetu never really sleeps. Restaurants and shops are open around the clock, offering their services. Then, too, there are the performances. A troupe of traveling performers has agreed to winter here, and they put on two shows a day, plus smaller diversions." She shook her head. "There is no time of day that we could avoid having a hopeful audience hanging around outside the surgery waiting for news."

"Weetu must be a very rich city," Daphne exclaimed, having just entered the room. Rosie had brought with her a vial of the healing potion Isaac took after his operation and Daphne had just finished some preliminary tests on it.

"How do you mean?" Rosie asked, puzzled.

Daphne looked sheepishly at Cassidy for approval—a second nurse was not supposed to engage in social conversation with a chief nurse unless invited!—before answering.

"If I ate out every day at home, I would soon be very poor."

"Oh." Rosie laughed aloud. "Yes, how silly of me. I keep forgetting that you have no idea of how things are run in Weetu." Shifting so that she was able to see Daphne without craning her neck, Rosie explained, "Weetu is an exchange city. Here, let me try to illustrate. The restaurants need supplies and labor." She held out one hand, palm up. "The residents need food and diversion." She raised her other hand, palm down. Clasping her hands together she continued, "In exchange for washing dishes, for example, one might procure a fine meal of beef stew.   In exchange for a musical performance, one can expect at least a sandwich.   Then there are those who transported and stored the supplies for the restaurants this past fall. Having rendered such an important service guarantees them excellent food and service throughout the winter." She shrugged slightly with her hands. "We learned generations ago that it is too much work to exchange money all winter just to hand it back in the spring.   So, the greater the service rendered, or anticipated, the better the meal."

"How charming!"   Daphne was truly astounded.   She looked hesitantly at Cassidy, who nodded slightly. "And you said something about a troupe of trav-ell-ing performers?"

"Oh, yes. It is a common practice for them to find a city to entertain during the winter season. They get food, drink, shelter, and when they keep folks sufficiently entertained, whatever tips the spectators give them."

"They must be very tal-en-ted," Daphne observed in the hopes of coaxing more information from Rosie. How Daphne wished she could meet a *travelling* performer.   They must have seen and done so many things she never dreamed of!

"I cannot deny that," Rosie hedged.   "But you have to be careful of them, just the same. They are generally fine folks," she added hastily, remembering that King Hugh of the Silver Fairies had been raised amongst troupers. "Some of them, though, well, they give the others a bad name." Since Daphne was wearing her curiousity plain on her face, Rosie continued. "Most are true performers, dedicated to their art and their public. Others are greedy ne'er-do-wells, driven out of their own home towns by the fairies that knew them best. They cause plenty of trouble, in one way or another." Rosie shook her head slowly. "Mighty hard to tell which kind of troupe fairy is which, until they try to steal you blind."

Cassidy, deciding that they had taken up enough of Rosie's time for now, caught Daphne's attention.

"How are the tests coming?" Cassidy asked, smiling so that Daphne would not worry about a hidden reproof. Daphne was a brilliant scientist, but still a bit young and impetuous.

"I am almost done." Daphne tapped her finger against her chin. "I came in here because I need something…oh!" She spotted it on the shelf to her left. "I just need this microscope."

"Very well." Cassidy nodded her dismissal and leaned forward on the desk, folding her hands together. "I gather from all that you have said that if you tried to bring the patients here," Cassidy summarized aloud, "an 'audience' would follow?"

"Undoubtedly. This is of major importance to our tribe. A guaranteed treatment for spinal injuries was unheard of until Isaac announced his operation. Since then, no one has spoken of anything else."

Cassidy sighed unhappily. "I suppose he had to do it."

"Isaac?" Rosie clarified. When Cassidy nodded, Rosie nodded back. "If he had vanished from court right after winter hit, there would have been a lot of curious folks snooping around in places where they ought not to."

Cassidy accepted the statement as fact. In short, they ran the chance of being discovered either way. That thought made her uneasy. What if she had been too hasty in agreeing with Kuntza's request to come here? What if the tribal council, which she supposed was meeting and discussing the facts that it had, decided the treaty was already—irreparably—broken? No one above the surface would survive. Sick or injured, they would all be condemned together. It galled her terribly that she had no way to send them word of all that she had learned!

"Why did no one follow Prince Isaac?" Agnes asked from where she sat, writing a letter to her husband. She knew there was no way to post it, but had promised him to write at least a few lines everyday. In a way, that was the hardest part of being away for so long.   The Water Fairy Tribe had sophisticated means of communication thanks to their understanding of lightning and its properties. Here they could not even send or receive the most vital of communications, let alone personal missives.

"I suppose because they felt it was a matter for the royal family. Queen Fiona did visit me in my office twice, where I passed along updates."

Cassidy could not help being relieved, both by the change from the direction of her gloomy thoughts and by the news. "Did she? I am glad. I thought it was a little curious that only Gallica and Stuart have been coming by."

"Oh, the queen explained that to me." Rosie began gathering up one of the medical files. She was a firm believer in a tidy desk. "King Walter has assigned them to take turns bringing your meals and whatever else you might need. They are a little less in the public eye than other members of the royal family."

Cassidy disciplined a smile when she heard Rosie refer to Stuart as being part of the royal family. However, since Gallica and Stuart seemed to have made no announcement, she said nothing. Hmm, that was an idea. If they made such an announcement, it would redirect—or at least, divide—public scrutiny, would it not?

"Yes, I thought it might be something like that. I do think Isaac was disappointed, though."

"You mean she has not come by at all?" Rosie stopped organizing the papers to frown. "How odd. I know she told me she was going to try to visit Isaac this morning."

Cassidy dismissed the matter with a wave of her fingers. "Any of a dozen things could have prevented that. Anyway," she started collecting papers from the other file, "Isaac is out of recovery and easily accessible now." She was still marveling at his rapid healing. She had briefly considered objecting to the use of the Wood Fairy healing potions, since it and the regenerative decoction she was injecting Isaac with might have interacted badly. After a short discussion with Rosie, though, she agreed to allow it.

"Yes, that is true." Rosie tapped the file papers together and settled them in their folder. "About Isaac's therapy. You mentioned earlier that you would like him to continue in the pump rooms?" Rosie asked, rising.

Cassidy smiled, still rather impressed with the Wood Fairy Tribe's ingenious solution in combining necessities. The pump rooms provided the injured Wranglers with much-needed physical therapy but also satisfied their need to feel useful, for their efforts brought a critical supply of fresh water and air into Weetu.

"Yes, for now. In another week or so, though, I will need him to return here for a new kind of therapy."

"I look forward to learning more about that." Rosie accepted the second file folder from Cassidy.

"We will need some equipment made. See? Something like this." Cassidy took up a pencil and described it as she sketched out the apparatus she was referring to. "Two railings, tall enough and near enough together for Isaac to put a hand on each for support." She demonstrated with her own hands the approximate position Isaac's arms would be in, bent slightly at the elbows.

"I will have a Master Craftsfairy start work on it as soon as I get some measurements from Isaac," Rosie promised, accepting the picture. It was really quite good, down to the figure of a man standing between the railings and leaning on them.

"Wonderful, thank you. He will need them while he practices walking."

"You truly believe he will be able to start using them in the next ten days?" Rosie averaged out the 'week or so' Cassidy spoke of a moment before.

"It is difficult to be sure," Cassidy acknowledged. "I have never administered the decoction to anyone who was also using a healing potion like the one Isaac is taking." She chewed on her lower lip while she thought it over. Again. "Ten days may be a little optimistic, but it is the best estimate I can make under the circumstances."

"I understand," Rosie smiled. Tapping the file folders she was holding, she asked. "Which of them shall I offer the surgery to?"

Cassidy made up her mind. "Both of them. One may decline, given the awful risk, but either way, we will be ready." She slipped her hands into her jacket pockets, frowning. "I just wish I knew how we were going to get them here without inviting trouble."

"I was thinking about that." Rosie cleared her throat. "It might be simpler to bring you to them."

"What? But that is impossible!" Cassidy was not sure whether Rosie was joking or not.

"I think it could be arranged," Rosie asserted. "You wore a disguise while you were travelling here, did you not? No one recognized you then," she pointed out without waiting for a response to her question.

"Well, yes, we did," Cassidy could not deny that. "But part of our disguise was poor lighting." Impatiently, she reached up and pulled her hair back. "Even with our hair completely wrapped, what do you still see?"

Rosie sighed. "Your eyebrows." She saw Cassidy's vividly pink eyebrows, standing out against her pale skin like an invitation for trouble. "Unless…" She grinned, knowing how her next suggestion was going to sound. "We could color them brown."

Chapter 15

"No, no jacket," Isaac told Noland, who was helping him dress. "It just gets in the way."

"Of course." Noland hung the jacket back in Isaac's closet. "Have you decided which cravat you will be wearing?"

Isaac looked up from where he was finishing buttoning his shirt front. The muscles of his right hand still gave him a twinge occasionally, but it already felt much improved.

"Do you think the burnt orange would be too much?" Isaac asked.

Surprised, Noland took his time shutting the closet door before he responded. It was not like Isaac to worry about being flashy. Everyone knew Isaac's outgoing personality and most agreed that his wardrobe matched it perfectly. Besides, the burnt orange cravat was one of Isaac's favorites; he claimed it made him look more tan.

"Ordinarily I would say no," Noland answered. "But since the winter season is upon us," he produced a hanger with several suitable options, ranging in color from a cheerfully loud red cravat with white polka dots to a more conservative yellow silk one, "brighter colors are the order of the day."

Isaac chuckled. He could just imagine

Cassidy's response to him showing up in the cobalt blue cravat shot through with pink and gold polka dots. After all, she had no way of knowing that everyone wore bright colors during the winter season to help combat the monotonous sameness of life in the tunnels. Some even had separate bed clothes for this season, sheets and blankets of startling shades. Isaac, on the other hand, liked to keep his bedroom furnished more simply: white sheets with military corners; orderly closets that were closed when not in use; his shoes lined neatly against the wall. Even his regular sitting room sported just one love seat and three comfortable chairs arranged around the window. Well, usually arranged around the window. The sitting room was closed for the duration of the winter; it was just too cold in there, even with a fire.

"Here, let me have the goldenrod cravat." Isaac suddenly felt the need for the splash of color to contrast with his otherwise stark outfit of black pants and white shirt. He began chuckling again as he lifted his collar to set the silk cravat under it. "What an impression I am going to make!"

Noland promptly leapt to a conclusion. It all fit together in his mind. Not only had Isaac returned from his surgery with a more-or-less functioning right hand, he brought a faint scent with him. A woman's scent. Noland had dismissed the fact upon noticing it, naturally. It might have come from the queen, or Gallica, or Rosie for that matter. But Isaac's preoccupation with making a good impression—his own word—convinced Noland that Isaac had found a companion for the season. Part of Isaac's social duties lay in accompanying the unattached female guests at Weetu to the various entertainments and diversions offered, but Noland could not remember ever having seen Isaac more than politely interested in any of them. This was new. This, this air of barely suppressed excitement. The full and complete return of Isaac's good spirits, even before he was walking again. Noland suddenly felt better. That had to be why Isaac was being so secretive! A budding romance was something to keep close and cherish.

"Wait a moment." Isaac cocked an eyebrow at a dreamy-eyed Noland, who was about to kneel down and help him with his footwear. "Those are my dress boots."

"Yes, sir," Noland agreed.

"But I will only be gone an hour or so," Isaac protested.   "I told you, my father is meeting me here to discuss matters of state with me over supper."

"Oh."   Noland was understandably embarrassed. Isaac had told him exactly that.

"Of course." Returning the boots to their place, he retrieved a pair of more comfortable slippers. "Perhaps these?" Isaac's lady friend was no doubt discreet enough not to inquire as to his choice in footwear.

"Perfect," Isaac smiled. He might have asked Noland what was wrong, the poor fellow's mind seemed to be continually elsewhere of late, if Stuart had not let himself in just then. "Stuart!" Isaac fumbled a little with the cravat, his right hand declining to cooperate in the intricate process of tying a cravat. "Welcome and congratulations!"

"Why," Stuart looked blankly at Isaac. "Thank you."

"Come now," Isaac submitted to allowing Noland to tie his cravat for him. "Did you think I had not heard?" Isaac waited a beat, then said, "About your win against the trouper fairy?"

"Ah." Stuart smiled. "That."

As soon as Noland finished tying the cravat, Isaac dismissed him with a nod. When he and Stuart were alone in the bedroom, they both started to talk at once.

"Confound it, what is wrong with everyone?" Isaac began.

"Isaac, I need your help with something…" Stuart stopped, realizing he was talking over Isaac, who had also stopped.

Isaac sighed, his frustration vanquished by

Stuart's asking for help.

"Help with what?"

Stuart looked over at the water clock. "If we hurry, I have time to show you before your appointment."

"All right then," Isaac beckoned to him. "This chair is not going to drive itself!"

Stuart grinned and hurried over. He preferred an impatient Isaac to a sulky one, no doubt about it! Seizing the chair's handles, he expertly maneuvered it between the bed and the dresser, and through the doors into the corridor.

"Where are we going?" Isaac finally thought to ask.

"It is a surprise," Stuart decided aloud. His grin widened when he heard Isaac's snort. Since roughly one-third of Weetu's population was getting ready for dinner, the traffic in the corridors was very light, allowing Stuart to make good time getting from Isaac's quarters to the south corridors. Stuart waved at the same guard he and Gallica had seen earlier.

"You must be joking." Isaac looked over his shoulder at Stuart and came to the conclusion that this was no laughing matter. In addition to Stuart's grim expression, there was the speed with which he was propelling the chair along. Isaac faced forward again. "Can you tell me now?"

"Do you remember the hours we spent writing essays on these art pieces?" Stuart asked, his tone casual.

"How could I forget?" Isaac stiffened slightly. Was it his imagination, or was the tapestry depiction of the Triumph at Morning Meadow shifting—and *not* with the air currents? "We tried turning in accounts of the events they depict, the first time. We thought they were much more exciting than the pieces themselves."

Stuart chuckled. "Then we spent hours more trying to find words that might somehow make the art pieces sound exciting." He drew up in front of Alfonse's self-portrait. "This was the worst assignment of all."

Isaac glanced casually at their back trail. "I think we are alone."

"Probably," Stuart agreed. Setting the brakes on Isaac's chair, he moved forward to examine the painting once more before he made a crazy-sounding statement.

"Well?" Isaac was back to being impatient. "Are you going to tell me what this is about or are you going to stand there stroking that painting?"

Stuart lowered his hand. After their interview with Old Pete, he had kissed Gallica and sent her on her way with a copy of Pete's version of the riddle while he, Stuart, came back here to get the one from the painting. Except that he had found no riddle or markings of any kind of the back of the painting. A closer look convinced him that the painting he was examining was not the genuine portrait. But now…

"I do not understand."

Isaac glared at him. "Neither do I."

"This is not the painting that was hanging here earlier," Stuart clarified. Quickly, he moved to take it down off the wall. His time with Isaac was short—Stuart, for one, was expected to sit at the king's table, along with the queen and a few hand-picked guests, the kind who would not ask too many questions about why King Walter and Princess Gallica were not joining them for supper. That was why he was so flamboyantly dressed. The only thing more futile than trying to remain inconspicuous at the king's table was trying not to feel out of place when one's manner of dress was inconsistent with that of the other guests.

"What are you doing?" Isaac asked. He promptly got a face full of portrait.

"Hold this," Stuart ordered. Taking out a stub of pencil and a pocket-sized pad of paper, he rapidly wrote what he saw on the back of the painting.

"What are you doing?" Isaac repeated more loudly.

"Tell you in a minute," Stuart promised, returning the paper and pencil to an inner jacket pocket. "Thanks." Taking the painting from Isaac, he hung it on the wall in its original spot. "Here we go." Releasing the brake on Isaac's chair, Stuart turned it around.

"Stop." Isaac did not raise his voice, but it was obviously a command. "Tell me what just happened."

Stuart tugged on his ear, decided it would probably take less time to explain it all right then and there, and put the brake back on. Coming around so that he was facing Isaac, Stuart took a deep breath.

"While Gallica was following up on the reports of trespassers in this area, she saw someone inspecting that painting." He pointed at the portrait. "We did a little investigating and came to the conclusion that there is something odd about the painting."

"There is something odd about this entire affair. Why would anyone bother to steal that thing? The only reason it is hanging here is because after Alfonse died nobody in his whole family would…" Isaac stopped himself. "You *are* saying it was stolen?"

"I already checked with the curator," Stuart informed him. "Neither she nor the cleaning staff were aware that the original portrait was missing." Running his fingers through his hair, he added, "I fully expected to bring you back here and prove it to you by showing you the fake."

"But now you are saying that is the original," Isaac asked pointedly.

"Yes, exactly," Stuart agreed.

"And what did you want with the back of it?" Isaac pressed.

Stuart looked up and down the corridor uneasily. "You will not believe me."

Isaac put his head in his hand. "I cannot believe any of this."

"You are meeting the king for supper, are you not?"

"Yes, yes." Isaac sat back in his chair. "You know that I am."

"Then I will come as soon as I can to your chambers and tell you everything that I know there," Stuart promised.

"Very well." Isaac made a forward motion with one hand. "But now, please take me to my appointment. I am going to be late."

"Not if I can help it." Relieved, Stuart whisked him along the corridors towards Rosie's office. When they reached the turnoff, he stopped as if to ask Isaac a question, double-checked that they were alone, then hurried down the final leg of the trip.

Daphne answered at the first knock. "Come in," she giggled, delighted to see Stuart. "Did you bring the books?" She whispered as she closed the door, not wanting the others to overhear.

Stuart mentally kicked himself. "Not yet," he apologized. "I was going to ask Gallica for some title suggestions, but something came up."

"Oh?" Daphne seized on the idea of consulting Gallica. "Yes! She will be here in just a few more minutes and we can both talk to her about it!"

Isaac cocked an eyebrow at Stuart. "Now it is you who are going to be late."

"Maybe. But I would not count on it." Stuart was still grinning as he darted out the door.

"What was that all about?" Cassidy asked, wide-eyed.

"Stuart is escorting my mother to supper this evening," Isaac smiled ruefully at the crestfallen Daphne. "He insisted there was something I needed to see over on the other side of Weetu," Isaac shrugged. "But if he is late reaching my mother, then the whole meal will be delayed. Lord Dean, one of our nobles, would be very put out about that," he laughed.

"Is the court dining here very grand?" Daphne asked longingly.

"No, not very." Isaac caught a signal from Cassidy and began casting about in his mind for something more interesting to say on the subject. "The Silver Fairy Tribe, though. They have fancy state dinners all the time." Encouraged by Cassidy's slight nod and the way Daphne leaned towards him, Isaac related his recent visit to the Silver Fairy Tribe. "It was their summer tourney," remembering belatedly that they would have no idea what that meant he spelled it out, "a gathering of some of the finest athletes in their tribe."

Cassidy listened, unaware of the way her smile was wreaking havoc on Isaac's attention span, while he told them in glittering detail about the engraved silver utensils, the patterned tablecloths, the delectable dishes. Cassidy was grateful to him for Daphne's sake; the dear woman was positively captivated!

"What has always amazed me the most," Isaac had been keeping an eye on the water clock and hoped Gallica would arrive within the next sixty seconds, "is that they entice the lightning bugs to perch on the ceiling of the dining room. The subsequent display of natural lighting is positively breathtaking."

Daphne sighed with sheer joy at his account.

Isaac sighed—quietly—with relief when he heard Gallica's knock at the door.

"Here, Your Highness." Cassidy released the brake on his chair and took hold of the handles. "While they get the supper things laid out, you and I can take care of your injection, shall we?"

"Capital idea," Isaac agreed.

Cassidy kept a firm grip on herself until they were safely inside the surgery. When she bent to put his brake on, her shoulders were shaking with suppressed laughter.

"What, may I ask, is so funny?" Isaac asked dubiously. He would not have told them about all of that if Cassidy had not urged him to do so.

"Her face." Cassidy barely managed not to let the laughter escape. "The look on Daphne's face! She was so…enthralled!"

Isaac allowed himself a small smile. "I am a very good storyteller, if I do say so myself." He sniffed for effect.

Cassidy wiped at her eyes and clapped one hand over her mouth to keep the laughter in. The last thing she wanted was to hurt Daphne's feelings.

"Shall I, um, get ready?" Isaac asked, grinning at her. When she nodded, still laughing silently, he undid the bottom few buttons of his shirt and slid himself forward.

Cassidy stopped laughing. Wiping her eyes once more, she stepped forward and put her hand on Isaac's shoulder.

"Do you realize what you just did?" she asked.

Isaac blinked at her. "I was just trying to get my shirt out of the way," he began to say.

"No, not that." She looked down at his legs, back up into his eyes. "You moved yourself." She felt his shoulder straighten under her hand and almost did not recognize his intent in time. "Remember," she warned, putting her free hand on his where he placed it on the arm of his chair. "The most important part of healing is not reinjuring yourself."

"But I can do it," he insisted, looking up into her eyes. "I want to do it."

"I know you want to," she put her hands on either side of his face. "Please believe me. It is too soon for you to try standing by yourself."

Isaac pulled impatiently away from her. A moment later, he began pounding his fist against the arm of his chair in frustration.

Distressed, Cassidy watched while he worked through the emotions assailing him. She had known from the first that he was a man of strong feeling. It was good that he listened to her instead of stubbornly trying to stand, but now she found herself caught between conflicting emotions of her own about how to help him work through this. Her doctor's instincts told her to calmly inform him that everything took time. Her womanly instincts made her want to find some way to hold him, comfort him.

"What is it?" Gallica appeared in the doorway. "Isaac!" She grabbed the hand that he was beating against his chair arm. "Isaac, you stop it this instant!"

Cassidy felt her knees go weak with the release of tension. The moment for action was past. Her indecision was inexcusable.

"What happened?" Gallica dropped to her knees beside Isaac. It was like old times, looking up at her big brother. Only this time she was the one doing the comforting. "Hey," she waited until he looked at her. "What happened?"

"I..." Isaac took a deep, shuddering breath. "I guess I got excited."

"Tell me what you were excited about," Gallica coaxed.

Isaac took another deep breath and forcibly exerted control over himself.

"I moved forward in the chair," he told her. "Without any help."

"Oh, that is wonderful!" Gallica smiled at him, smiled at Cassidy. Their lack of responding smiles brought her back to the trouble. "Why were you so upset?"

Isaac ran his fingers through his hair and tried to find the words.

"He wanted to stand." Cassidy let the sentence hang in the air.

"Can he do that?" Gallica asked, her eyes as

wide as saucers.

"I would rather he waited."

"I see." Gallica *did* see. When a fairy was injured to the point that they would never regain certain abilities, they adapted. That was why they referred to the first few months after a decisive injury as the 'adaptation period.' In Isaac's case, his prognosis changed drastically with Cassidy's arrival. How could he help but be impatient? "May I have a moment with my brother, Doctor Cassidy?" she asked.

"Of course." Cassidy went into the other room, closing the door behind her.

"Are you going to be all right?" Gallica asked Isaac once they were alone.

"According to the doctors? Yes. Eventually."

"That is not what I meant." Gallica squeezed his hand and released it. "You are my big brother, remember? I have seen you face disappointment and frustration before. You overcame them then. Will you do it now?"

Isaac looked into the face of his beloved younger sister, unable to answer around the lump in his throat. The expression in her eyes made him feel as though he had been thrown back five hundred years to the time a rainstorm caught their family unawares while on a picnic. He and Gallica were playing off to one side of the clearing and got separated from the others when everyone dove for cover. She had been frightened, cowering against him with each drop that hit that ground outside. If not for her need, he would have been overpowered by his own fear.

He put his hand on hers. "I will," he promised.

Chapter 16

Later that evening, Gallica took a very subdued Isaac back to his quarters.

"Just park me in front of the fire, please," Isaac instructed.

"Where is Noland?" she asked, looking around the dark apartment.

"I gave him some time off," Isaac answered. "Dad will be by to talk to me shortly and I thought it might be something he would rather discuss in private."

"Alright." Gallica kissed his forehead, put on the chair brake, and let herself out.

Alone with himself for what he thought was the first time since his injury, Isaac stared into the fire. What had happened to him? Had he lost his courage, his sense of perspective with the use of his legs? Idly, he rubbed the arm chair he had been beating on less than an hour ago. Temper tantrums yet.

He scoffed at himself. What must Cassidy think of him? She had not returned to give him the injection. She sent Agnes instead. Agnes, who never said a word either way about his behavior, just efficiently administered the injection and told him he could go. He had not even regretted leaving his supper behind when he went. A twig in the fireplace popped a

broke in half, eaten in two by the flames. Isaac watched the flames around it shift and swirl before settling back to their work of consuming the twig.

"Never mind what others think," he said aloud. "I have to live with myself." Setting his chin, he forced himself to relive the last few months, to reevaluate his behavior from his new vantage point. Even his behavior in the pump rooms, with his comrades at arms, had been false, an act he subconsciously put on because he felt that it was expected of him, their prince, to set a good example. Several vivid memories of his behavior in private made him wince and want to shy away, but he summoned the courage to continue his self-examination.

He was a much humbler, more serene young man by the time his father's hand came to rest on his shoulder.

"Isaac?" Walter shook his son's shoulder gently. "Wake up, son."

Isaac reached up to put his hand over his father's. "I am awake, Dad."

Sensing that something important had happened to Isaac, Walter put his other hand on top of Isaac's and waited.

"I feel like I just woke up for the first time since the pirate offensive."

"You sound as though you have come to a decision," Walter observed.

"I have." Isaac withdrew his hand and gestured to one of his guest chairs. "Please sit down."

Walter did so, after pulling the chair closer to Isaac.

"I have decided that I am not going to behave like a child any longer," Isaac informed his father. "Whether I walk again or not, I will be myself, prince of the realm and grateful member of your gracious family."

Walter swallowed hard. Watching his son struggle with the adaptation period was the hardest thing Walter had done since waiting to welcome him into Fairydom when he was born.

"I am glad, son." It was so wonderful to see the confidence radiating from Isaac's eyes that Walter would have liked to just sit there and look at him for a very long time.

Stuart, who had entered the room unheard and unseen—and just in time to hear Isaac's last statement—remained uncomfortably by the door. *Now I know they taught me to knock first,* he thought sardonically. That gave him an idea. Slowly reaching behind himself, he knocked on the door from the inside.

"That must be Stuart," Isaac said.

"Ah, good. I was hoping to find him here with you." Walter started to rise. "Shall I let him in?"

"Dad," Isaac chuckled. "I know Stuart knows how to open a door."

Hearing that made Stuart smile sardonically.

"Come in, Stuart," Isaac called.

Stuart, his hand already on the door knob, opened the door a bit and flew past the gap as if he was just entering the room.

"Took you long enough to answer," Stuart complained, crossing the room towards Isaac's chair. "Oh." He half-bowed to King Walter. "Good evening, sir."

Walter waved the formalities away. "Take a seat, Stuart. You are just in time."

"For what?" Stuart asked, seating himself.

"It has come to my attention," Walter began, "that Lord Dean Boyer is in Weetu."

Isaac and Stuart exchanged glances. Lord Dean was a famous—almost infamous—collector. Art, manuscripts, jewelry, weapons from historic encounters, anything that was hard to come by, Lord Dean collected. Weetu's south corridors were full of items that might interest him, assuming he did not care how he got them.

"That should make for an interesting," Isaac was being diplomatic, "winter season."

"Indeed," Walter agreed. "This is a major deviation from his routine."

Stuart's mind was whirling with possibilities. On his way to Isaac's quarters from supper, Stuart had bumped into Gallica, when they exchanged duplicates of the riddle versions that they each possessed.

Isaac looked closely at Stuart. "You think his being here has something to do with that portrait," Isaac guessed.

"Indirectly, yes." Taking the copies of the two riddle versions from his jacket pocket, Stuart offered one to Walter and one to Isaac. "Gallica and I discovered these today."

Walter, shifting so that he was not blocking the light from the cold fire, read his aloud.

"Behind the great fairy's ego hides something of great worth."

"I found that written on the back of Alfonse the Great's self-portrait," Stuart explained.

"This is not quite the same," Isaac frowned at his note.

"Read it," instructed Walter.

"*Under* the great fairy's ego hides something of great worth." Isaac emphasized the one different word.

Stuart had only been puzzling over the riddles a few minutes longer than they had, so he held up both hands in self-defense as they looked quizzically at him.

"I have no idea what it, that is, they mean."

"Where did you get the second version?" Walter inquired.

"From Old Pete," Stuart answered, "a retired

Master Craftsfairy who knew Alfonse."

Walter's eyebrows went up. Alfonse had lived quite a while ago, so long that Walter found it remarkable that anyone still lived from that time.

"Where did he get it?" Walter inquired next.

"He says that it was the original riddle," Stuart replied. "The one Alfonse first planned to write on the back of his self-portrait."

Isaac's eyebrows went up this time. "Alfonse the Great." The others looked at him. "Behind the *great* fairy's ego…" He shrugged. "Do you suppose it is possible?"

"The riddle was behind the painting," Stuart pointed out, not sure he was following where Isaac was trying to lead.

"Yes," Isaac nodded. "And I am sorry for doubting you earlier. Dad, Stuart was just showing me that painting before supper."

"Oh?" Walter looked at Stuart.

"Yes, sir." Stuart, reassured by Isaac's apology, began at the beginning. "Gallica followed someone into the south corridors after lunch. When I found her there, she told me that whoever it was spent a considerable amount of time inspecting the portrait." He dropped his eyes sheepishly. "I did not take a good look at it then, because I remember a story that Old Pete used to tell. So I took her to Old Pete, who told us the story and the original version of the riddle. Then I went back to get the riddle from the painting…"

"Go on," Walter prodded him when he paused.

"But it was not there."

Isaac jumped in as soon as Stuart paused again. "He tried to tell me about it before supper, but I thought it was too incredible. Dad. The painting he found hanging there was a fake."

Walter shot to his feet. "Do you mean it has been stolen?"

Isaac hastily began trying to flag his father down. "It was returned," he told him.

Astonished, Walter dropped back into his chair.

"Between the time that Stuart found the fake and the time he tried to show it to me, the original was returned." Isaac turned his hands palms up, indicating that he had no explanation.

"Oh." Walter said uncertainly.

"We agree, sir. It makes no sense," Stuart informed him.

They sat in silence for several minutes, just watching the fire burn.

"Then, to sum up," Walter looked at them. "One or more troupers have been seen in the general vicinity of Alfonse the Great's now-mysterious self-portrait. Said painting was temporarily removed today. We have two variations of one riddle, which may or may not be significant. And Lord Dean is in town." More silence followed his observations.

"I would assume Lord Dean wants the painting, but since it has already been stolen once and returned, I find that highly unlikely," Stuart admitted.

"What if he did not want the painting?" Isaac suggested. "What if he was after the riddle?"

"I suppose it is possible," Walter conceded. "But why?"

"I would like to study the painting again," Isaac announced. "It might help me answer that question."

"What do you have in mind?" Walter asked.

"I have a hunch. The first riddle gave it to me." Isaac looked at his hands. "And I am not sure that you will like it." They just looked at him. "I think the riddle means that there is something important under the paint."

"What are you suggesting?" spluttered Walter, aghast. "That self-portrait was painted by one of our greatest heroes! It has been in the south corridors since my great-grandfather had it hung there!"

"Dad." Isaac's quiet tone got Walter's attention. "I do not make the suggestion lightly. That is why I wanted to study it first. The paint always seemed a little thick to me."

"Of course," Stuart agreed. "You are right!
I always thought Alfonse went back over it to
cover a mistake, but what if he was covering a
secret?"

Walter was not pleased. "The curator. I
will have her examine it, first thing in the
morning." He rose.

"That might be too late," Isaac cautioned.

"Too late?" Walter echoed unhappily.

"As long as we are supposing," Stuart
interjected, "should we not suppose that the
troupers will come to the same conclusion that
we have?"

"They already have a very convincing fake,"
Isaac reminded his father. "Take a few
moments to exchange them, and voila. We
missed our chance."

"Our chance to risk ruining one of our tribal
treasures," Walter grumbled.

"The curator will surely take better care of it
than they would," Stuart reasoned.

Walter closed his eyes in defeat.

"Come with me."

Isaac was so focused on convincing his
father to test his theory that he forgot himself
and stood up.

"Isaac!" Stuart was at his side immediately,
helping him sit back down.

Walter stared at his son, mouth slightly
open in shock.

"Forgive me," Isaac apologized. "I forgot myself."

"Forgive you?" Walter murmured, still dazed at the sight of his erstwhile paralyzed son standing on his own two feet.

"Cassidy warned me not to be overeager," Isaac explained. "My spine is just beginning to really heal since she removed the bone slivers, and the risk of my reinjuring myself is still quite high."

"Oh," Walter said, speechless for the second time that evening. Fiona had advised him of the results of the operation, naturally. But either she had no idea how rapidly Isaac was progressing or this was a *very* new development.

"After you, Father." Isaac deferred, nodding at the door.

Stuart took the cue and moved to open the door for Walter. Going back to Isaac, Stuart took the handles of his chair and followed Walter into the hallway, nodding his thanks when Walter shut the door to Isaac's quarters behind them.

"To the curator first," Walter decided aloud. "I hope she can tell us something useful."

The curator was having a late supper with a friend, according to the secretary on duty. When they assured him it could not wait, he dispatched a page to fetch her.

"Carry on," Walter told the secretary, realizing the fellow was waiting to be dismissed.

"Thank you, Your Majesty." Bowing, the secretary returned to working on the catalogue he was updating.

The others were not so fortunate. Having nothing with which to occupy themselves, they pretended to study the art objects in the office. Some were marked for cleaning. Others had tags indicating where repairs would need to be made. Stuart spent quite a little time staring down into a large, lidless crate labeled 'Sky Fairy Exhibit.' However, he could not have said if it was being packed or unpacked, just that he was glad to see the curator arrive.

"Your Majesty." Tammy curtsied, acutely conscious of her casual manner of dress. She and her friend had planned to go wall climbing after supper, so her outfit consisted of a pair of light slacks and a short-sleeved shirt with a collar. "Is anything wrong?"

"No, nothing." King Walter was adamant. "Everything is fine."

Isaac hid a smile behind his hand and coughed. Everyone looked at him.

"My father and I were discussing the art exhibits after supper," he smiled at her. "And when a certain painting came up, we found we could not agree about it." He was intentionally vague.   "Eventually, we realized there was nothing for it but to come seeking your professional opinion."

Tammy looked at the three men standing before her and came to the conclusion that this was not as simple as they were trying to make it sound.

"I would be happy to help any way I can."

"Marvelous."   Walter offered her his arm. "Please."

Tammy was surprised enough to accept, placing her hand lightly on his forearm. Whatever this was really about, it was going to make a fabulous story!

The four of them marched along the corridor until they reached the painting in question. Clasping his hands behind his back, Walter eyed it suspiciously. The longer he thought about it, the more he felt that Isaac was right about how easily the original could be replaced by a well-done fake. Especially if the fake's artist had added the riddle in the meantime. By now, he was anxious to have her start off by confirming that it was the original.

"What can you tell us about this painting?" Isaac asked her.

Tammy looked at the painting and back at Isaac.

"I mean, besides its unique history," Isaac expounded smoothly.

"Please tell us about the materials he used," suggested Stuart.

Tammy raised the pair of noseglasses she had hurriedly scooped up as they were leaving her office and turned to scrutinize the painting. Finding nothing out of the ordinary, she lowered the glasses.

"As you can see, Alfonse the Great used leather instead of the traditional canvas or wood surfaces."   Seeing the king frown, she hastily continued, "But the paint is quite ordinary for the period. It was colored with…"

"Pardon me," Walter interrupted her. They were getting nowhere fast. "Are you positive that this is the original painting?"

Tammy stood stock-still for several heartbeats, wondering if she had heard him correctly.

"There is no doubt in my mind," she stated. Her curiosity only increased when all three of them visibly relaxed.

"Getting back to the paint that he used." Isaac brought one elbow up onto the arm of his chair and turned his hand palm up inquisitively. "Would you say he used more of it than the average painter? That it is thicker than you would expect?"

Tammy turned back to the painting, noseglasses in position. She had not really given that sort of thing much thought, being a curator, not an artist, but, given her vast experience, she was able to quickly come to a conclusion.

"Yes. Especially here," she indicated the section of the portrait where Alfonse's slightly disproportionate head was featured. That was something she had never liked about the painting, especially given that, by all accounts, Alfonse's head was no larger than anybody else's. "This was his first painting, of course." That was part of what made it so valuable, the fact that Alfonse's first work had turned out so well. "He probably had to try more than once to get his features the way he wanted them."

She looked behind her in time to spot the triumphant look the king was giving his son, who simply leaned forward to put his chin in his hand. Even Sir Stuart, whom she recognized from seeing him around in Weetu, looked unconvinced about something.

"I could probably be of more assistance if you told me exactly what it is that you are looking for," she hazarded.

Walter considered her logic and had to agree with it.

"We have an idea that there might be something hidden under the thicker paint," he informed her

Tammy narrowly resisted the urge to ask where they got such a crazy notion from. "I see." Slowly their reason for coming to her sank in. "And you would like me to investigate?"

"Yes," Isaac said.

"If it can be done without damaging the portrait," Walter said at the same time.

Tammy shook her head slowly. "I cannot guarantee the portrait's preservation if I try to remove some of the paint."

Walter grappled with himself. What made the decision more difficult was that they were not certain of anything. The whole reason they came down there was because they actually knew nothing.

"Can we put the portrait away somewhere?" Walter asked heavily. "I need some time to think about this."

"Certainly, Your Majesty." Tammy smiled. "I will have my secretary bring it to my office, where I can secure it for the night."

"Allow me." Stuart flew lightly forward. Having handled both the original and the fake that day, he took his time getting the painting down. The riddle was there. "Not a speck of dust," he smiled at the curator.

"Our staff takes a great deal of pride in their work," she smiled back.

"Yes, of course." Stuart glanced casually at the wall where it had hung. Something had occurred to him. With the riddle written plainly on the back of the painting, how could it have remained a secret for so long? "When do you suppose was the last time this was taken down?"

Tammy helpfully supplied, "Not since it was hung there by the decree of King Brian."

Chapter 17

They all congregated at the curator's office the next morning: King Walter, Isaac, and Stuart. Even Gallica was there. She dropped breakfast—and some books for a very enthusiastic Daphne—off at the surgery early just so she could attend.

Tammy watched the somber group for a few minutes before clearing her throat.

"I have given the matter some thought," she began. "And I now believe I was wrong last night when I told you that the paint could not be removed without ruining the portrait." All four pairs of eyes were on her now. "As I said, the paint itself is quite ordinary for the period. However, under these circumstances, it has one rather special quality." Turning to face the painting, which had only one set of eyes, she folded her arms across her chest. "In order to render the substance liquid, so that it may be applied as paint, it must be heated."

Gallica snapped her fingers. "Of course! I remember hearing about that in one of my craft classes. It was," she frowned in concentration while she dug into her memories. "It was a story about Anaba, the famous painter. In the early days of her career, if a painting did not sell, Anaba would reclaim and recolor the paints, then use the canvas to paint a whole new picture!

"So," Isaac steepled his fingers. "Am I correct in deducing that, if Alfonse had made mistakes, he could simply have warmed the paint and removed them?"

"Precisely," Tammy agreed.

King Walter flew over to study the painting. He was no art expert, it was true, but even he could see that, artistically speaking, it probably lacked quite a bit. Shading, composition, subject matter—all the little whatnots that distinguished the works of a gifted painter from those of a rank beginner. Nevertheless, Walter felt a great responsibility not to destroy a tribal treasure if he could help it.

"This painting is very old," he reminded Tammy softly. "Can you guarantee that the leather can withstand the process of warming?"

"Your Majesty, there would be no need to warm the painting itself," she assured him. "I have tools here that I can use to heat and remove just the paint."

"Which begs the question," Stuart observed gravely, "of what the message underneath is made of."

King Walter's frown deepened. He was accustomed to deciding which animal wrangling contracts to accept, what changes should be made to the standard-issue weaponry, even to writing diplomatic letters of state. The facts that he needed to use to make those decisions leapt easily to mind, ready and waiting to be added to either the positive or negative side of the mental balance he utilized. This decision was well outside of his area of comfort.

"It seems to me," Gallica offered, thinking back to what Stuart had told her after leaving her father the night before, "that Alfonse the Great knew what he was doing." Encouraged by Stuart's half-nod, she continued, "He chose the materials. He wrote the riddle. He knew that the best way to get at the riddle's answer was to heat and remove the paint."

"Therefore," Stuart finished for her, "he would have found a way to leave that answer that would not be damaged by the process of removing the paint."

Walter hoped he did not look as relieved as he felt. Their reasoning seemed sound to him. And he wanted the whole thing over with, anyway.

"Please proceed," he told Tammy.

"At once." She was as good as her word. In fact, after an all but sleepless night, she had come in early, started a fire in the small stove that they used regularly for art restoration projects, and set two of her favorite knives inside to heat. Donning insulated gloves, she now went to retrieve those knives. "Please set the painting flat on my desk," she instructed Stuart. Opening the door to the stove, she was pleased to see that the knives were glowing with heat.

"Princess, could you bring that tray over as well?" she asked, taking the knives by the handles. Further anticipating this decision, Tammy had prepared the tray for use by applying a thin coat of paraffin wax, which could easily be scraped off the back of the paint after it had cooled and hardened again. With the ease of long practice, she closed the stove door with one foot and bumped the security latch into place.

Isaac thought she looked like an insane fairy bent on doing bodily harm as she approached her desk, a red-hot knife in each hand and an intense expression on her face.

"Will you hold the frame, Sir Stuart?" Once he nodded that he had a good grip on said frame, Tammy went to work. With infinite care, she pressed her knives into the paint on either side of Alfonse's face. Slowly, precisely, she heated the paint in a circle around his face, watching as the material between the knives absorbed the heat as well. Now came the tricky part.

Holding the knife in her left hand over the center of his face, she positioned the knife in her right hand back at its starting point. Tammy was sweating, but not from the heat. If she succeeded, she might become famous. If she failed, she was just as likely to be discharged. At the very least, a tribal treasure would have joined the ranks of those lost to history.

Gallica held her breath without realizing it, completely absorbed in the drama unfolding before her. She could sense the moment of truth coming in the way Tammy's shoulder tensed, then relaxed inch by inch, a tactic Gallica recognized from her experiences in the field as a Wrangler. Tensing up just made things more difficult when it came to executing rapid, smooth movements.

Tammy's left hand swung down into the paint and she brought both knives together in a quick, fluid motion. Alfonse's face lifted cleanly off the leather surface and she deposited it on the tray Gallica was still holding.

Gallica, finding herself staring into Alfonse's body-less head, hastily set the tray down on the desk.

They gathered round in a hushed silence to inspect the results. In the center of the lopsided circle where Alfonse's face had spent the last fifteen thousand or so years, ten words were written.

"It looks like some kind of ink," Isaac remarked, having pushed himself up to a half-standing position, using the arms of his chair.

"With her amulet of power, she commands the lightning carriers." Gallica read the inscription aloud. Moving abruptly away from the others, she closed her eyes in deep thought.

"Another riddle." Walter sighed.

"Yes, but at least this proves the first riddle meant something," Stuart half-protested.

"How thrilling." King Walter's flat tone belied his choice of words. Checking the water clock to see what time it was, he sighed. "Let me know what you figure out. I have my annual appointment with the Minister of Finance to keep." It always took a few days after winter set in for the minister to finish reviewing his ledgers. The end result was that Walter had a stimulating few hours of reviewing tribal net expenditures and profits ahead of him. They would argue a little over the value of the Plant Fairy Tribe's payments, which were always made in foodstuffs, then try to agree on whether or not it had been a successful year overall. Walter had to stifle a yawn just thinking about it.

"Good luck, Dad." Isaac, who had once foolishly accepted an invitation to join them, was smiling slightly.

"And to you, son." Walter managed to smile back, then took himself off to his offices.

Isaac looked over at Tammy. "Do you see

that scorch mark there?" he asked, indicating a blemish inside the circle she removed.

"Yes. I was just wondering how it got there," she admitted.

"You are certain it did not come from one of your knives?" he inquired pointedly.

"Perfectly certain." She did not hesitate. "I can see flecks of the paint inside the raised fibers."

"What does that mean?" Stuart wanted to know.

"It means," Tammy glared at the painting, "that someone else has already tried this."

Shocked, Stuart exclaimed, "Impossible! It was only gone for a few hours today."

Isaac raked his fingers through his hair. "Gone? Gone where?" He jabbed a finger in the direction of the riddle. "This only took a few minutes." Since he was looking at the painting, not at Gallica, he completely missed the thoughtful expression that flitted across her face.

"Removing the paint did," Tammy countered. She refrained from pursuing the subject of the self-portrait's removal from the corridors. For now. "Replacing the paint, without damaging the work itself, will take longer. Not to mention the time required for the paint to cool and harden again." Picking up a magnifying glass from her desk, she leaned over the painting. "I can tell you that the scorch is a recent addition. Very recent."

"How can you tell that?" Stuart leaned closer, too. Since he had no magnifying glass to help him, it was a useless effort.

"The scorch tells me that," Tammy answered. Watching carefully with her magnifying glass, she ran the pad of her forefinger ever so lightly across the top of the mark. "Just as I thought." She straightened. "If the scorch mark had been there at the time the paint was originally applied, the paint would have set deep into its raised fibers. Then, when I removed the paint just now, most of the fibers would have lifted off with it." She offered her magnifying glass to Stuart. "As you can see, most of the fibers here are intact. Whoever beat us to this did it so recently that paint never had a chance to fully harden again."

Dismayed, Stuart leaned over the painting, glass in hand. All he saw was what Tammy had told him he would find, so he abandoned the search.

"It would seem," Isaac ground out, "that our opponent has at least a one point advantage."

"Hopefully just the one." Stuart set the magnifying glass aside. "We ought to go to the library," he suggested. "We might find some reference to this amulet in the histories."

"I suppose so." Isaac remembered to smile at Tammy. "We thank you for your assistance in this matter. Without your help, we would never have gotten this far." He was confident his father would never have allowed them to just scrape the paint off on the far-fetched chance that what was behind the portrait was more valuable. "Can we help you with returning, um…" His voice trailed off. It was a bit unsettling to look over at the tray and see just Alfonse's face smiling triumphantly at him; after all, Isaac was accustomed to seeing the head attached to the body in the painting.

"I can manage," Tammy assured him.

As Stuart reached for the chair brake, Isaac had another thought.

"We are also relying on your discretion," he told Tammy. "The time will come, I imagine, when this will all be shared with the tribe; but that time is not now."

"I understand." Tammy was disappointed, it was true. On the other hand, it looked like her part in this story was just the beginning. How much more exciting to be part of this larger story, with riddles and intrigue galore!

Gallica held open the door while Stuart slowly drove Isaac's chair out of Tammy's office.

"We have to go to," Isaac glanced around, remembering that they were traversing a main tunnel. "To see Rosie before we can even think about going to the library." They had taken to calling visiting the surgery as 'going to see Rosie' as a way to prevent those around them from overhearing something they should not.

"We do not have to go to the library," Gallica asserted, surprising them both. "Truly. I know what the riddle means."

"Not here." Isaac glanced around again. "Can you come with us to Rosie's?"

"Yes," Gallica nodded. "I am free until half past nine."

"Good." Isaac settled back in his chair. "Stuart, you can stop dawdling now."

They made good time the rest of the way to the surgery, each of them keeping their eyes and ears open for unwelcome attention, like followers.

Agnes opened the door when they knocked and hastily stepped aside to let them in.

"Well." She hid her hands behind her back. "This is a surprise."

"How so?" Isaac, preoccupied with the riddle, was not inclined to mince words. "I usually do come by in the morning for my injection."

"Of course." Agnes started to gesture towards the surgery, then remembered why she had her hands behind her back. That only added to her irritation with what Cassidy had asked her to do that morning. "Go right in," she instructed. "I will be with you in a minute."

Gallica, who liked all three of the Water Fairy visitors, even the occasionally grouchy Agnes, could tell that something was up.

"Sorry if we interrupted something." Gallica gave Agnes her best, most friendly smile. "And forgive me for running off earlier. I would have loved to have stayed."

"Not at all." Agnes, taken off guard by Gallica's charm, brought one hand up to smooth her hair. "The morning has just been a little hectic for us."

Stuart started to say something and Gallica took him firmly by the arm.

"Take your time," she smiled at Agnes. "We will wait."

Stuart responded to Gallica's tug on his arm by driving Isaac's chair through the recovery room and into the surgery.

"Did you see her hand?" Isaac murmured as soon they were all safely inside.

"Her fingers were brown," Stuart recalled. "What in Fairydom is going on here?"

Gallica had a faint idea, given something Rosie had let slip to her.

"Never mind about that," she ordered. "Let me tell you about the riddle."

Isaac conceded the point with a nod. One mystery at a time was sufficient for him.

"Isaac, do you remember the nanny we had before you began school?" Gallica asked.

Confused, Isaac shook his head. "Not really."

"She was a wiry little old lady named," Gallica shifted gears when Stuart coughed politely. "She used to tell us the most spellbinding bedtime stories."

"Yes." Isaac's eyes narrowed thoughtfully. "That much I do remember."

"When you moved into your own room, I asked Mother if she could stay with me, and she agreed." Gallica put her hand on her chest to indicate herself. "But what makes her so important is that she told me the story of Lady Edith and her victory over the fire ants."

"Lady Edith?" Stuart frowned, trying to remember. "Was she a Sky Fairy?"

"Yes!" Gallica was all but jumping up and down with excitement. "I must have heard the story a thousand times, but only from a child's perspective!"

Thoroughly lost, Isaac and Stuart stared blankly at her.

"Here, look." Gallica snatched up a blank piece of paper and a pencil. "This is the Sky Fairy capital, Regalis." She drew a clumsy mountain and marked it with an x. "The ants attacked from below." She added arrows pointing up towards the x. "Lady Edith drove them back with lightning from the sky!"

"Yes, I remember the story now," Isaac agreed. "I just do not see how you are relating it to the riddle."

"With her amulet of power, she commands the lightning carriers," Gallica recited the riddle.

"As in, actual lightning. Not messengers who could travel as swiftly as lightning," Stuart was understandably incredulous. "Not..." His imagination failed him. "You think she could actually control lightning."

Agnes, who had just entered the room, turned as white as the bedsheets. "Who can control lightning?" Her voice quavered when she spoke.

"Nobody," Isaac asserted. "Lightning is as wild and dangerous as the boars that haunt the marshes. No one can control it."

"But what if Lady Edith could?" Gallica protested.

Isaac reached up to rub the bridge of his nose. His head was beginning to ache and he almost wished he *had* joined his father for the meeting with the Minister of Finance.

"How?" Stuart asked. "How could any fairy control lightning?"

"With her amulet of power!" Gallica declared staunchly.

Agnes, whom they had forgotten, looked up

sharply. "Whose amulet of power?"

"Lady Edith's!" They chorused.

Agnes thought she was going to faint. "The missing dial," she murmured. And then she did faint.

Stuart caught Agnes in time to keep her from hitting the floor.

"What did she say?" Isaac asked sharply, coming to his feet while Stuart carried Agnes over to the operating table. "The missing dial?"

"Yes, I heard her say that, too," Gallica concurred. "Though it means nothing to me."

"What is going on here?" Cassidy's voice startled them, making Isaac and Gallica both jump. "You should not be standing!"

Isaac guiltily resumed his chair. When he looked over to apologize, he found himself facing a stranger. Brown curls, still a little damp, framed the stranger's face. Her face with lovely, dazzling hazel eyes under convincingly brown eyebrows.

"Cassidy?" Gallica squeaked. She had guessed that Agnes' brown fingers and guilty expression might have something to do with coloring Cassidy's hair, yet it was still something of a jolt to see the final result.

Isaac's mouth opened and closed a few times, but nothing came out.

Cassidy, trying to find somewhere to look besides at Isaac's stunned face, spotted Agnes.

"What happened?" Cassidy hurried over, her fingers automatically seeking her friend's pulse.

"She is fine," Stuart assured her. When she turned on him, eyes faintly accusing, he tried again. "I mean, she just fainted. I caught her and…I am sure she is alright other than that."

"One does not 'just faint,'" Cassidy reproved. "That requires a stressor of some sort, like a great shock."

Isaac muttered something under his breath about being glad he was not the fainting type and Gallica smothered a hysterical laugh. Isaac took a deep breath.

"We were discussing a riddle while we waited for Agnes or someone," Isaac's eyes strayed to Cassidy's hair, "to come give me my injection. Agnes came in, heard what we were saying, and crumpled to the floor."

"Wait, you are forgetting something," Gallica interjected. "Before she fainted, she said, 'The missing dial.'" Looking eagerly at Cassidy, Gallica asked, "Do you know what she meant?"

"Not at the moment." Intent on her friend, Cassidy pointed at a container of small vials. "Bring me that one with the green cap and line across the top, please." All of the medicines in the room were color-coded, and where the medicinal properties overlapped, simple marks clearly indicated which like-colored medicine was which. "Thank you." She accepted the vial from Stuart. Unscrewing the lid a little, she passed the vial under Agnes' nose.

Agnes stirred, then groaned. "Missing," she murmured cryptically. Her eyes fluttered open and she looked up at Cassidy.

Chapter 18

"Easy." Cassidy patted Agnes' shoulder. Taking the vial away from her friend's nose, Cassidy shut it tightly and handed it back to Stuart. "Give me a couple of deep breaths, please."

Agnes swallowed, then complied.

"Good." Smoothing Agnes' hair back out of her face, Cassidy smiled down at her. "Feel better?"

Agnes smiled back, more embarrassed than anything else. Casting diplomacy aside, she spoke to Cassidy in Margua, their native tongue.

"I overheard them speaking of the missing dial."

"Yes, they told me you said something about that before you fainted," Cassidy nodded.

"It is impossible." Agnes tried to sit up, her voice rising as though someone had contradicted her. "It is impossible for them to know of the dial!"

"Yes, of course," Cassidy restrained Agnes gently. "I will investigate this if you will promise to rest." She held Agnes' gaze for a handful of heartbeats. "Agreed?"

Agnes sank back onto the bed. "Agreed."

"Daphne," Cassidy called, stepping back

from the bed. Still in Margua, Cassidy ordered Daphne, "Stay with Agnes. Keep her calm and remind her that she promised to let me do the worrying." Then, in the common surface tongue, she addressed the others. "Come with me, please."

Gallica, Stuart, and Isaac dutifully followed her from the surgery to the outer office. They watched, unsure of what was going on, as she closed the door between the office and the recovery room.

"Is she alright?" Gallica was the first to speak.

"Yes, I think so." Cassidy slipped her hands into her pockets and looked from one face to the other. "Please tell me exactly what you were saying when she entered the room." Cassidy was hoping against hope that Agnes had misunderstood them somehow.

Stuart and Gallica looked uncomfortably at Isaac, who grimly accepted the fact that he had just been nominated spokesfairy.

"We were discussing a new riddle. It goes like this, 'With her amulet of power, she commands the lightning carriers.'" He was watching Cassidy closely, but she did not bat an eyelash.

"Go on." Cassidy directed flatly.

"That was all." Isaac ran his fingers through his own hair since he could not reach Cassidy's.

Blasted distracting curls! "Oh. Gallica said she thought the riddle meant there was a way to control lightning; that it was referring to a Sky Fairy legend by the name of Lady Edith."

Cassidy blinked. Now she understood why Agnes fainted. But how could she explain it without revealing secrets that were not hers to share? Secrets vital to the Water Fairy Tribe's security. Walking over to the desk, she eased herself into her chair.

"We...have a legend also," she began tentative. "My grandmother used to tell it to me when I was very young. It all happened a long, long time ago, before..." She stopped. She was so rattled that she had been about to tell them that her tribe used to treat the advena differently. Before the events of the story occurred, those advena who swore never to tell of the Water Fairy Tribe's existence were released to return to their lives above the sea's surface.

Gallica was about to urge her on when Isaac caught her eye and shook his head. They were just going to have to be patient.

"A woman called Edith came to live among us. She was very smart, but treacherous. After we took her in and," Cassidy neatly glossed over the details of how they taught Edith what they knew about lightning, "taught her our ways. Years passed and she seemed happy.

Then news came from our outposts that made her very sad. She stole a precious item before she returned to the surface."

"Would that precious item," Isaac leaned his elbows on the arms of his chair and rested his chin on intertwined fists, "be called a dial?" Cassidy's nod left him looking at Stuart, then Gallica. Neither of them appeared to comprehend it any more than he did. The surface tribes had dials: sun dials; pressure dials; other kinds of dials. Just no 'precious' dials.

"I do not think you have a word in your language that means to you what 'dial' means to us." Cassidy told them after observing their exchange of glances.

"We have amulets." Gallica shrugged back at Isaac's frown. "The riddle says 'amulet of power.'"

Cassidy nodded slowly. "The stolen item could have been disguised as an amulet." Especially since there was nobody around who could possibly have identified it for what it really was—an experimental device designed to help test the peculiar phenomenon of earth-based lightning. One of their scientists accidentally discovered that it was possible to create weak lightning arcs between two electrodes by placing them in wet earth. The experiment for which the dial had been created was arranged without the approval of the local scientific body, and shut down immediately after they realized what Edith had done, thus rendering the dial useless. So…so why not turn the dial into a piece of jewelry?

"Uh-oh." Stuart looked up from where he was leaning against the wall. "I just thought of something."

"What?" Isaac and Cassidy demanded at the same time.

"I saw a crate in the curator's office. It was labeled 'Sky Fairy Exhibit.'"

Isaac sat back in his chair, his mind churning. "The curator must have arranged to trade one of our exhibits with one of theirs. Something new for Weetu to look at during the winter season"

"Isaac." Stuart raised his eyebrows. "Weetu *and* her titled guests."

"Lord Dean," Isaac breathed. It all made sense now. Lord Dean had broken his tradition of retiring to his private estate for the winter in order to have the time necessary to track down and interpret the riddles. How he got wind of them was anybody's guess; likewise, he would have had no way of knowing how difficult the riddles would be to interpret. A week, a season, a lifetime?

"Who?" Gallica asked after trying to remember where she had heard the name before.

"Lord Dean Boyer," Stuart answered. "He is wintering here." Looking over at Isaac, Stuart reminded him that, "We have no actual proof of his intentions. This could all be some bizarre coincidence."

"If this is a coincidence, then I am Alfonse the Great." Isaac motioned for Stuart to come drive him. "We have to see what is inside that crate."

"Wait!" Rising, Cassidy held out her hand to stop them. "I am coming with you."

"That is absurd," Isaac protested.

"Why not let her come?" Gallica interrupted. "I grant that she is a little pale, but otherwise I think she could pass for a Wood Fairy now that her hair is colored."

"In those clothes?" Isaac pointed out. "The cut is all wrong." The buttons on her blouse were made of mother-of-pearls, too, a very unusual material in the fashion of the day. Wood Fairy clothes were made mostly of barkcloth or cotton, simply cut and designed for comfort as well as fashion. Well, with the exception of the cravat. "She would stand out like a yodeler at a poetry reading."

"I must insist." Cassidy drew herself up to her full height. "You call me Doctor Cassidy, but among my own tribesfairies I am known as Lady Cassidy Clark, daughter of the Botere clan, and a zaldun of the Water Fairy Tribe by rite of passage."

Isaac was again glad that he was not the fainting type. Served him right for falling in love with someone he barely knew.

"Your pardon, Lady Cassidy." Isaac did, vaguely, remember his mother calling her by that title when they were first introduced. "Of course a representative of the Water Fairy Tribe should be present to identify the stolen item." He gestured in her general direction. "Gallica, surely you have some clothes that would fit her?"

"It would be my pleasure," Gallica smiled. She understood Isaac's retreat into formality, but she wanted Cassidy to know she was still among friends. "Please excuse me. I shall be right back." The door clicked shut behind her almost before she was done speaking.

"While she is gone," Stuart spoke into the subsequent silence, "perhaps you could give Isaac his injection?"

"Right this way." Cassidy flew over to the closed recovery room door and let herself through it."

Stuart, who had gotten halfway across the room to Isaac before Cassidy stopped him, now went the rest of the way.

"Stuart?" Isaac asked as his friend bent to release the chair brake. "Do you know what a zal…zaldoon is?"

"Of course not." Stuart shook his head for the hundredth time in the last three days. He had been shaking it so much, in fact, that he was beginning to worry it would unscrew itself and fall off his shoulders.

Cassidy was waiting for them in the recovery room, syringe in hand. Stuart helped Isaac remove his jacket, then discreetly retired to the office, shutting the door behind him.

"I am going to stand up now," Isaac informed her. When she made no protest, he rose. Untucking his shirt, he began to roll it up in the back.

"I need you to sit over here, please." Cassidy indicated the bed. "So I can see the injection site better."

Isaac obliged without arguing, excited to walk again even though he had to lean a little on her arm for support. "Is Agnes alright?" he asked as Cassidy daubed the numbing salve on his back.

"She will be." Cassidy set the used applicator aside. It was strange, talking to Isaac's back. "I did not tell Agnes or Daphne about the amulet."

"Probably a good idea," Isaac agreed. "That way, if it is not among the items of the Sky Fairy Exhibit, they will not be disappointed."

"As disappointed as I will be, you mean?" she asked, picking up the syringe. "Ready?"

"Ready."   Isaac considered her other question in silence. "Those things you said out there, the titles. What do they mean? Are you a princess?"

Cassidy looked at the back of his head. "No, not a princess. The Water Fairy Tribe has no royal family."

Isaac almost turned to face her, but thought better of it at the last second.

"None at all?"

"Naturally that seems strange to you," she acknowledged for them both. "I understand that all of the surface tribes are governed by royalty." She touched his back with the tip of the needle to check the numbing, then inserted it slowly into his muscle.

"That is right." Keeping his torso facing forward, Isaac tried to look over his shoulder at her. "How is your tribe ruled?"

"Face forward," she admonished with a faint smile. "I am nearly done." Closing tired eyes, she sought for the right words. "I said I was a daughter of the Botere clan. That means I belong to one of the most powerful families in my tribe. We are responsible for making sure that our cities are clean and safe. We help to regulate trade. We also help govern the sundry scientific bodies and their research."

"Science is very important to your tribe, I gather."

"Yes," Cassidy agreed as she removed the needle. "There. You can put your shirt down now." Turning away to give him a modicum of privacy, she unscrewed the needle from the barrel and set them back on the tray to be cleaned later by Daphne. "We study everything. Plants, animals, rocks." She chuckled.

"Have you studied love?" Isaac asked from directly behind her. When she did not respond, he finally allowed himself to reach out and touch her hair. It was as soft as he imagined. His hand dropped to her shoulder.

"I am also a zaldun," she reminded, even as she allowed herself to be turned towards him.

"Which is?" Isaac slipped his arms about her waist

"A guardian. Protector."

"Warrior?" he suggested.

"Yes, even a little of that." Cassidy, zaldun of the Water Fairy Tribe, rested her forehead against his chin. "Are you tired yet?" He had been standing for some time now. The recovery of his spinal column was unbelievably rapid, but that did not mean his leg muscles were ready to support him the way they used to.

"Hmm?"

"I asked if you were tired yet." Cassidy leaned back and looked up at him. "You are still standing."

"Oh." Isaac looked down at his legs. Shrugged. "I am alright for now." He stroked her hair. "I like it this color."

She laughed. "Agnes was horrified when I proposed doing this."

He laughed with her. "Did Rosie give you the coloring?"

She nodded. "I only agreed because there seemed to be no other way for me to operate without risking exposure."

"I see." He kissed her forehead and cradled her close. "So you did it because you are wise and kind and wonderful."

Cassidy could feel the blush rising in her cheeks. "Stop."

"Stop what?" Isaac kissed her cheek. "Falling in love with you?"

"No, please." She pulled away, walked over to the door that led into the surgery.

"Cassidy." Something in his voice made her look over her shoulder at him. "Please understand me. Whatever your rank or position or occupation may be, I am in love with you. I did not know it could happen this quickly. Or this completely. However," he held up his hand to forestall the protest she seemed about to make. "I realize that I can speak only for myself. And even if you told me, in no uncertain terms, that there is not a chance in a million that you could love me or stay with me,

I would want to spend every available second with you. Right up until the second where I have to let you go."

Cassidy looked away again. It was the best way to hide the tears streaming down her cheeks. And how could she not weep at his devotion to her?

"Isaac?" Gallica's voice preceded her knock. "May I come in?"

Isaac walked slowly over to his chair and seated himself. "Come in," he called. "Bring Stuart with you." Isaac grinned at Stuart as though his heart was not beating in Cassidy's hands. "There you are. How about helping a fellow give the ladies some privacy?"

"Stuart's transportation, at your service." Stuart pretended that he could not tell something significant had happened in his absence and grinned all the way into the office, shutting the door firmly behind him.

"Cassidy?" Gallica took a handkerchief from her pocket and offered it to her.

"Thank you." Cassidy tried to smile as she mopped her face. "May I explain this later? I am not quite up to it right now."

"No explanation is necessary," Gallica assured her, placing a hand on Cassidy's arm.

Cassidy clasped her hand over Gallica's gratefully. The shared moment of friendly, almost sisterly, understanding cemented their friendship forever.

"Now." Gallica held up the bag of clothes she brought. "You better rinse your face with some cold water before we get started?"

Between the two of them, they got Cassidy out of her Water Fairy garb and into a Wood Fairy outfit in a matter of minutes.

"Wait," Gallica stopped Cassidy when she started to put her hair up. "Women are wearing their hair down this year."

"Then why do you wear your hair up?" Cassidy asked, perplexed.

Gallica grinned. "Because I cannot stand to wear it down. It gets in my way and tickles my neck."

Laughing, Cassidy dropped her hair tie on top of her folded Water Fairy clothes.

"Let me just tell them that I am going," Cassidy told Gallica. With that, she disappeared into the surgery.

Gallica decided to rejoin the fellows in the office.

"Ready so soon?" Isaac asked, looking up in surprise. "Where is Cassidy?"

"She will be right out," Gallica answered. Catching Stuart's eye to give him fair warning, she flew over to him and slid her arms around his waist. She just needed a hug after seeing Cassidy in tears.

Stuart looked quickly over at Isaac even as

he wrapped his arms around Gallica's shoulders and hugged her back.

Isaac's eyebrows went up at the display of affection, but he wisely made no comment. Apparently Stuart had made some progress since the last time they'd talked! The sound of wings told him Cassidy was coming out from the surgery and he signaled Stuart, who gave Gallica a squeeze before releasing her.

"Shall we?" Cassidy asked from the doorway.

"By all means." Isaac and Stuart led the way through the medical maze out to the main tunnels.

As Cassidy stepped out into the brightly lit area, she was amazed by what she saw. Dozens of colorful pushcarts were crowded in the center of it all, their owners shouting over each other that their merchandise was the biggest, the best, the tastiest. Fairies streamed around them, some walking, some flying…which drew her attention to a second, upper level of vendors, their wares spread on platforms suspended from the cavern's ceiling.

Gallica slipped one arm through Cassidy's and gently tugged her along with them.

Cassidy came at once, embarrassed to have been caught staring. She even tried to control her facial features as she flew through the foreign city. As they moved away from the tunnel intersection, the noise level dropped considerably, but the smells increased. Delicious, tantalizing smells.

"We will be passing some restaurants shortly," Gallica told her. "Someone is bound to recognize Isaac, Stuart, or myself, and will probably call out to us. We may even have to stop to talk to them for a few minutes. Just keep us in sight and keep moving, alright?" Releasing Cassidy's arm, Gallica walked a little faster until she was abreast of Stuart.

Cassidy slowed her wingbeats, dropping back enough that a few fairies were between herself and the others. Gallica was right. They were no sooner in sight of the restaurants than fairies began to notice them. It was a revelation to Cassidy to watch their carefree interactions. It was all so terribly informal. No titles, minimal bowing or salutations. One burly fellow, who was in a uniform of some kind, even punched Stuart on the shoulder before letting him resume his way. Cassidy smiled wryly when she saw Stuart, who took the punch without flinching, shrug that shoulder a few times once they were out of the ruffian's sight.

Eventually the restaurants thinned out, the tunnel narrowing until they were back among fairies that were busily trying to get to their destinations. That was when Cassidy saw the guard. His uniform was different from the brown and tan garb of the fellow who accosted Stuart; it was designed to help him stand out, not blend in.

Gallica motioned for Cassidy to rejoin them as they neared the entrance to the south corridors. Linking arms with her again, Gallica pasted on a cheery smile.

"Good evening, Your Highnesses." Steve, the guard bowed. "Sir Stuart." He looked expectantly at Cassidy.

"Good evening, Steve." Isaac was smiling as well. He and Stuart stopped while Gallica and Cassidy, apparently deep in conversation, walked into the corridor beyond the guard. "Has it been busy today?"

"My, yes." Steve smiled back, pleased at the attention. "They are getting ready to open a new exhibit and all sorts of folks have come by to try to get a peek at it."

"Tsk, tsk." Isaac shook his head in mock disapproval.

"You will have to forgive us," Stuart flashed a winning smile at Steve. "Our friends are waiting."

Steve gave them a knowing wink. "Nice looking pair of friends they are, too." And a nice bite of new gossip, come to think of it. What with Princess Gallica being Prince Isaac's sister, it stood to reason that she was seeing Stuart. That left Prince Isaac with the pretty, mysterious stranger. Whistling, he hooked his thumbs in his belt and walked away.

"Good thing Gallica was out of earshot when he said that," Isaac muttered as Stuart drove his chair into the corridor.

The four of them moved swiftly towards the curator's office now, their goal nearly in sight. But when they got there, the door was closed and locked.

Isaac snapped his fingers. "The new play. It opens tonight." In all the excitement, he had forgotten.

"So they left everything to go see it?" Cassidy asked in disbelief.

"Looks that way." Stuart scratched his cheek. "Shall we let ourselves in?"

"Not yet. Remember what Steve said about the new exhibit?" Isaac returned.

"Yes, but he did not say where it was," Stuart objected. "It would take hours to search all of these corridors."

"Time that I doubt we have." Gallica asserted. When they looked at her, she shrugged. "I have a funny feeling."

Isaac and Stuart frowned simultaneously. Gallica's 'funny feelings' were famous for keeping her Wrangler squad out of harm's way.

"Over here!" Cassidy was at the office window, her hands cupped around her eyes as she looked inside.

"What is it?" They asked in unison.

"It looks like a model of the exhibit."

"How can you tell?" Gallica queried, fluttering over.

"The banner across the top says 'Sky Fairy Exhibit,'" Cassidy grinned at her.

Gallica rolled her eyes and began peering inside as well. "I recognize that alcove!"

"Where is it?" Isaac could hardly contain himself. Granted, there was no guarantee that the amulet was not locked up in the office. But if it was, then why was Gallica so worried?

"Come on!" Gallica took off, zipping away and around a corner.

Stuart, taken completely by surprise, looked down at Isaac and his chair.

"Go on," Isaac urged him without looking round. "We can manage."

When Cassidy made a shooing motion at him, Stuart took off after Gallica. She was a qualified Wrangler, no argument there. She just also happened to be the woman he loved!

"How do you propose we find this alcove?" Cassidy inquired as she came over to drive Isaac's chair.

"Luckily for us, that corridor," Isaac pointed at the one they were heading towards, "has only two branches. A dozen or more alcoves, but only two branches."

Cassidy laughed softly. "Let me see if I can

narrow it down for you. The model showed a round room with several display stands."

"Mmm, sorry. All the alcoves in this section are round, and the display stands are mobile. Do you remember how large the alcove was?"

"Sorry," Cassidy mimicked his tone teasingly. "Since there were no other models to compare it to, I have no way of knowing how large it actually is."

"Of course." Isaac clenched his teeth. "What else did you see?"

"I saw an odd marking on the ceiling. It looked like an x inside a square."

Frowning, Isaac tried to remember which alcoves had ventilation fans. It was the sort of thing one hardly noticed, unfortunately.

"Go straight," he instructed when they reached the first branch. "I think it is an alcove off this main corridor."

Obediently, Cassidy went past that branch and the next, too.

"Do you hear that?" Isaac asked abruptly.

"I hear something," she confirmed. Sound travelled differently here inside the solid-walled passageways of Weetu, she had found, than it did in the tunnels of her youth.

"It sounds like a fight." Isaac's fist came down on the arm of his chair. Just once.

"Should we go get help?" Cassidy asked,

certain that she could not trust Isaac to remain safely in his chair when his sister and best friend were in jeopardy.

"No, we are almost there. By the time we found someone and got back, it would be over."

"Alright." Cassidy stopped and put on the chair brake. "*Please* wait here." And she, too, was gone.

Isaac, finding himself suddenly alone, got at once to his feet. The entire lower half of his body protested when he took a step forward. He had been feeling so well at lunch that he opted to forego his pain relieving potion and now he was paying for it. Grumbling, he returned to his chair, released the brake, and stepped around behind it. Leaning on the chair handles for support, he started walking. The chair nearly ran away from him at first. With no one inside it to weight it down and Noland's superb care, there was almost no resistance when he leaned on it. After three or four more attempts, he finally set the brake to half, jammed his cravat in the gap so it could not jiggle free, and tried again. It was slow going. Agonizingly slow. And the sounds of fighting had already stopped.

Isaac was exhausted by the time he finally reached the alcove. Collapsing into his chair, he surveyed the damage from there. Cassidy was tending a cut on Stuart's cheek, but thankfully seemed unharmed herself. Gallica was on the far side of the alcove from them, busily engaged in trussing up a pair of fairies that Isaac did not recognize. Isaac managed a smile when he saw that she was using their own sashes to restrain them.

The alcove itself was a disaster. Four of the five display stands had been knocked over, spilling their contents randomly across the floor. A shield, which bore the Sky Fairy royal crest of crossed quill and sword, had been skewered with what was probably its companion weapon. The last objet d'art that Isaac could see was a painting hanging to his right, which had apparently come through the fighting intact.

"Isaac!" Cassidy rushed to his side. "Are you alright?"

Isaac, having regained his wind, just looked up at her. Then, taking her hand in his, he kissed it. If anything, he knew he loved her more than ever.

Cassidy smoothed his hair with her free hand and used the cuff of her sleeve to dab at the drying sweat on his forehead. She doubted Gallica would mind.

"You should have waited for me," Cassidy began to say, then dropped her eyes. How was she supposed to handle such stark admiration? "But I understand why you could not."

"Shhh." Gallica was staring up at the ventilation shaft. The fan had been removed somehow, and the grate was hanging down from the ceiling as if the room was yawning in boredom. "They might hear us."

While Isaac and the others wanted to ask her *who* might hear them, that would have been a direct violation of her order to be still.

Motioning for Stuart to follow her, Gallica headed for the ventilation shaft. This time, however, he was expecting the move and caught her before she reached it.

Lowering his mouth almost to her ear he stated firmly, "My turn to go first." He was not quite recovered from entering the alcove to find her battling Dizzy from before while Phil Girard—of all fairies!—strained to free the sword from the artifact set behind her.

Gallica blushed and nodded.

Cassidy watched with more than a little trepidation as they entered the shaft. "Suppose," she whispered to Isaac, "they actually find someone at the other end?"

"A ventilation shaft only has no real end," Isaac murmured back. "Only a beginning. And that is the pump room. I think Gallica has somewhere else in mind."

"Oh." Cassidy eyed their prisoners. "What do we do now?"

"Did you see the amulet?" he asked.

She shook her head. "Stuart searched them, too. It is not here."

"Then you go for help." He smiled at her surprised expression. "Gallica tied them up, remember? They are not going to get loose, I promise."

"Alright," she agreed reluctantly. "But where do I go? I thought everyone was at opening night."

"Not everyone. Do you remember that restaurant with all of the fairies wearing brown and tan?"

"How could I forget?" Cassidy grinned despite herself.

Isaac cocked an amused eyebrow and continued, "That was the Eagle and the Serpent, where the Wranglers like to go when they are off duty. Take this." He handed her his signet ring. "Tell Sugar I need him here quickly."

Cassidy's mouth opened slightly in shock at the name he gave her.

"Are you sure you can find your way there and back?" Isaac double-checked before letting her go.

"Yes." Impetuously, she stole a quick kiss and flew away. Going straight down the corridor was the easy part. As soon as she exited, she bore right. Following her nose, she retraced their steps back to the restaurant section of the tunnel. At last she saw a restaurant sign with—she hoped—an eagle and a serpent.

"Excuse me." She approached the group in brown and tan seated at the window. "Is Sugar here?"

"Oi, he has all the luck, blast him," she heard one of them remark.

"He just left," another fellow rose and grinned at her. "Maybe you should have dinner with me, instead."

Cassidy almost laughed in his face. Of all the nerve!

"No, thank you. Prince Isaac asked me to find Sugar for him, and I would hate to keep the prince waiting."

"What did I just hear?" a voice boomed from deeper inside the restaurant. "Prince Isaac sent you?"

Cassidy suddenly understood why Isaac had only asked for Sugar. Assuming that the giant approaching her was Sugar, of course. At a quick guess, she would estimate that he could wrap his arms all the way around the two full-sized water barrels in front of the restaurant. She noted that the barrels looked to be mostly full and decided he could probably lift them regardless.

"Yes, he did." She opened her hand to show him Isaac's signet ring. She had been holding it so tightly that his seal was impressed upon her palm.   "He asked me to bring you to him, quickly."

"Is he in some kind of trouble?" frowned the fellow who had tried to get her to dine with him.

The others perked up at the mention of trouble and Cassidy scrambled to put them off.

"He is waiting for us in the south corridors."

The others slumped back into their seats. Excitement was instantly replaced with intense boredom.

"Nothin' ever happens around here," one of them complained.

Sugar winked at Cassidy in a conspiratorial fashion and offered her his crooked elbow.

"Enjoy your meals," he tossed off a wave as he and Cassidy left together. Once they were away, he asked seriously, "This is important, yeah?"

"Very."

"Right, then."   He wrapped his near arm around her and spread his wings. "Off we go."

Cassidy clung to him for dear life as they swooped through the tunnels towards the south corridors. By the time they reached them, though, she was starting to enjoy it. There was a tense moment when Sugar tucked his wings and barreled through the entrance without slowing down, but he handled it so smoothly that she quickly forgot about it.

"That way!" She pointed at the corridor she wanted. "Just…keep going straight."

"What took you so long?" Isaac laughed when they landed beside him. "Hi, Sugar."

"Isaac." The massive Wrangler clearly did not feel the need to bother with titles. "What have we 'ere?" He scanned the alcove quickly, but his gaze stopped on the prisoners. They cringed when he frowned at them. "Trespassers?"

"Thieves," Isaac corrected. "Or at least, that was what we think they had in mind."

"Shall I escort them to the jail, then?"

"That would be immensely helpful, thank you, Sugar."

Sugar cracked his knuckles. "My pleasure."

Cassidy watched in awe as Sugar picked Phil and Dizzy up by the sashes that bound them together and slung them over his shoulder, one before and one behind. He had to shift them a little to get his wings comfortably extended, but otherwise he did not even seem to know they were there.

"She yours?" Sugar asked Isaac, jerking his chin in Cassidy's direction.

"I…am working on it." Isaac gave him the short version.

"Good. I like her. She has a nice accent, too." Tossing a casual salute at Isaac, and with another wink for Cassidy, Sugar vanished down the corridor.

Cassidy abruptly sat on the arm of Isaac's chair.

"So. What did you think of Sugar?" Isaac was enjoying himself. It helped him to not worry about Gallica and Stuart.

"I think he is two fairies stuffed inside a costume," Cassidy retorted.

Isaac rocked with suppressed laughter.

"He seems to like you," Isaac commented after he caught his breath.

Cassidy shrugged. "I like him, too, for the sixty seconds that I have known him." Her brow creased and she twisted around to face Isaac. "Sugar?" She inquired.

Isaac chuckled. "His real name is Qaletaqa Campbell. We were apprentices together, he, Stuart, and I. He got tagged with the nickname of 'Sugar' because he likes it so much. Pies, cakes, candy, whatever he could get his hands on."

Cassidy smiled at the mental image of Sugar trying to find a single pie large enough to satisfy his over-sized stomach. She considered saying something about the dangers of eating too many sweets; however, since it was unlikely that Sugar could get his hands on a sufficient quantity to really damage someone his size, she refrained. Instead, she looked down to see what was jammed against her calf. It was the chair brake.

"What is this?" She showed him a greasy, shredded bit of cobalt blue cloth.

"That was," Isaac stressed the past tense, "my cravat. I needed something to jam the brake into position with."

"Oh." Cassidy noted that he was indeed missing the garish cravat from earlier. Without further ado, she reset the chair brake and hoped it would hold. Especially since she was sitting there, too. "You probably want your ring back." She had forgotten about that for a moment.

Isaac smiled a little wistfully as he slid it back onto his finger, but said nothing.

"What do we do now?" Cassidy folded her arms across her chest. "Find the curator?"

"Not yet." Isaac lifted something from its hiding place under his jacket. "Recognize this?"

"The dial!" She snatched it away from him. "Where did you find it?"

"One of the prisoners kept looking at that section of wall there." Isaac indicated the spot he meant. He left the door open behind him, so it was much easier to see now. "I eventually got curious enough to investigate and found that utility closet…" His voice trailed off when he saw the way she was turning the amulet over and over, inspecting it from different angles. "What is it?"

"This is a fake." She looked over at him. "It looks exactly like it should, but the materials are all wrong."

Isaac scowled. He might have been able to argue with her about what it looked like, since she could never have seen a 'missing' dial. However, her next statement, about it being made from the wrong materials, convinced him that she knew what she was talking about.

"It should come apart, too. See these?" She showed him the back of the item, touching what looked like nail heads.

"May I?" Isaac held out his hand. Accepting it from her, he drew his small boot knife with the other hand.

"What is that?" Cassidy was not sure whether to laugh or cry.

"This," Isaac showed her the knife, "is a relic in its own right." He carefully explored one of the nail head's with the thin edge of the blade. "A few seasons ago, boot knives came back in style. Fashion does seem to cycle around every generation or two," he rationalized the foolishness. While he himself made no effort to stay on the cusp of the ever-changing fashion trends, Noland kept him informed as part of his job. He tried to remove another of the nails to no avail. "Eventually everyone came to the conclusion that these blades are inadequate for routine chores, and belt knives came back in," he went on absent-mindedly while he tested a third nail. "No use. These nail heads are just for decoration, no doubt to make it look like the real thing," he declared, returning the knife to his boot.

"You kept your boots." Cassidy waited, expecting him to respond. His statement about the nail heads was no surprise to her, she already knew the item was a fake. "Everyone else got rid of theirs and you kept yours?"

Isaac grinned sheepishly. "They are my most comfortable pair."

"What in tarnation is going on here?" Steve, the guard who was meant to be monitoring the main entrance, landed beside them with a thump. "I saw that Sugar fella leaving with two more slung across his shoulder and…" He gulped in horror as his attention finally got as far as the exhibit. "Who wrecked the display?!" He glared at the two of them without regard for title. "Hey…where are the other two that were with you earlier? Princess Gallica and Sir Stuart."

"They left that way." Isaac calmly indicated the still-open ventilation shaft.

Chapter 20

They all rendezvoused at the curator's office. Gallica and Stuart returned unharmed, much to Isaac and Cassidy's relief. They were talking quietly when King Walter, Queen Fiona, and the curator, Tammy, arrived a little later, having come directly from the play together at the request of an anxious page. Steve lounged in one corner of the office, hoping to go unnoticed. He reasoned that his relief would be there in just a few minutes, plus he could see the main entrance to the corridors through the office window. Anyway, this was too good to miss if he could help it.

"Father. Mother." Isaac greeted his parents. "Curator. Please accept our profound apologies for interrupting your evening again."

"Not at all," Tammy smiled. The play would be performed again. This drama, on the other hand, was a once in a lifetime show.

Isaac thanked her with a nod and got right to the point.

"Father, you wanted us to let you know if we ever solved the second riddle."

"Yes?" King Walter crammed a lot of curiosity into that single word.

"Gallica solved most of it. It reminded her of a bedtime story our nanny used to tell us."

Isaac kept a perfectly straight face. "Stuart and I were pretty hard to convince until," he hesitated, "something else was brought to our attention." He could hardly explain about the Water Fairy involvement with an audience present.

"We came here to investigate," Gallica picked up the narrative. "On the chance that the answer to the solution was part of the Sky Fairy exhibit. The office was locked, but we could see a model of the alcove where it was being displayed, so we went to take a look at it."

"Gallica recognized the alcove," Stuart announced proudly, one arm about her waist as if it belonged there. She certainly seemed to think so.

"Someone else got there first. They entered through the ventilation shaft and were preparing to leave the same way when Gallica and Stuart found them. As you might expect, they resisted all efforts to detain them." Once again, Isaac looked apologetically at Tammy. "I am sorry to have to tell you this, but the display is a shambles."

Tammy sucked in her breath. "Was anything damaged?"

"I am no antiquities expert," Isaac evaded. "I did, however, notice that the sword from the sword and shield set was, um, embedded in the shield." From the corner of his eye he thought he saw Stuart's grip on Gallica tighten a little.

Tammy's stomach dropped. The estimated value of that set was…no, she would worry about that later. For now, at least, the display could be rearranged. They had only put out a handful of the items on loan, intending to trade them out periodically to give their visitors something to look forward to. She glanced protectively over at the half-full box of Sky Fairy artifacts that Cassidy was admiring. And maybe things were not as bad as Isaac said?

"I see," she said at last.

"Did you find what you were looking for in the display?" Queen Fiona asked. Walter had filled her in on the riddles and the terrible risk they took with Alfonse the Great's self-portrait.

"No," Isaac responded dejectedly. "It looks like a dead end."

"Not exactly," Gallica interrupted. "We caught three trouper's," she instantly regretted specifying their demographic when she remembered that Steve was in the room with them. "I mean, three fairies dressed as troupers," she hastily amended, "who were involved in the attempted theft."

"One of them was anxious to cooperate," Stuart added. He thought that was perfectly understandable, given the way Gallica had slipped up behind Lady Lorna, the poor lookout, who thought she was alone in the abandoned section of the medical maze, and scared the living daylights out of her. They practically had to gag her to shut her up, but not before she babbled most of the plan and how she snuck Dizzy into the south corridors for a final look at the painting before the theft. "Lady Lorna told us who hired them."

King Walter's face twisted in a most unbecoming scowl. "Who?"

"We arranged to have the accused party meet us," Isaac opted for discretion, "elsewhere." Turning back to Tammy, he flashed an apologetic smile at her. He made eye contact with Cassidy, who was standing a short distance behind Tammy. Cassidy nodded slightly and Isaac wrapped things up. "We could hardly continue to impose on the curator when she has so much to do."

"Thank you so much," Gallica gushed, finally leaving her place at Stuart's side. She hugged Tammy while Cassidy slipped out the office door. "You have been so very helpful."

Stuart was likewise occupied with distracting Steve. "Who is on guard?" he asked sternly.

Steve twitched. "Martin." Without looking away from Stuart, Steve pointed with his thumb towards the office window. "He just came on. I was only away for a few minutes," he continued comfortably.

"A few minutes is much too long," Stuart reprimanded him. "I can see we are going to have to completely rethink the security of this area. Guards leaving their posts. Intruders entering through ventilation shafts. Displays nearly robbed."

"Yessir." Steve began nodding and could not seem to stop. "Very good points, sir." He began backing towards the door. "Thank you, sir!"

Stuart watched through the window as Steve beat a hasty retreat as far as Martin, the other guard. A small smile played across Stuart's face when he saw the animated conversation they were having. Steve left a moment later and Martin remained, shoulders squared and walking briskly, a distinct contrast to his casual, stationary slouch of a few minutes before.

"We will leave you to it," Isaac told Tammy. He was not surprised to find Stuart instantly at his side, releasing the chair brake. There was still a lot to be done. "Mother, Father. If you will bear with us a little longer?"

They left the office en masse, and at a sedate pace. Cassidy filtered out of the shadows just before they reached the restaurant sector, nonchalantly joining the procession. By now things had quieted down considerably. Most of the fairies they saw there were restaurant staff, efficiently clearing tables and preparing for the next shift of customers.

"Where are we going?" Walter asked Isaac.

"To your offices." Isaac answered.

They went the rest of the way in relative silence, unconsciously picking up speed until they were all moving at a fast walk. It would have been faster to fly, but nobody wanted to leave Isaac and Stuart behind.

"How are you feeling?" Cassidy asked Isaac, slipping her hand into his.

"Hungry," he joked. They had all missed their supper this time.

"Me, too," she smiled. "But how are you really feeling?" He was paler than she ever remembered seeing him. She wished they could stop somewhere so she could examine him, or at least find something to ease his pain.

Isaac squeezed her hand. "I am alright for now."

Fiona almost sighed with relief when the office doors came in view. The suspense was really getting to her! Who was waiting inside? Had the often-maligned Lord Dean been apprehended at last?

King Walter was similarly beset with questions, but waved for the guard to open the doors for them as nonchalantly as if he was not. The others came in behind him and the doors closed again.

A red-faced older man sat in a chair by Walter's desk. The guard beside him saluted when the king entered the room.

Walter returned the salutation and instructed, "Please wait outside." After the cagey way Isaac and the others related the events of the evening, Walter felt it was best to keep this first interview with Lord Dean as private as possible.

"I presume you can explain this outrage." Lord Dean ground out between clenched teeth.

"I presume you can explain why a fairy caught in the act of attempting to rob the Wood Fairy Tribe would claim you masterminded the theft," Walter fired back, having put two and two together.

"Balderdash," Dean snarled. Jumping to a conclusion, he reminded himself that he had warned Phil against bringing that fool of a woman in on such an important task. Handled precisely as he, Boyer, had laid it out, this should have been just one more chore for Phil and Dizzy. "She just said that because, well, because everyone has heard of me."

"She just mentioned you—specifically— because she knew your name?" Walter pressed.

"My name and my completely unfounded reputation!" Dean's bushed eyebrows rushed together like a thundercloud. "I know what everyone says about me." He fully intended to talk his way out of this.

"Lord Dean." Isaac leaned forward in his chair. "My father did not say the fairy we caught was female."

Dean harrumphed. "I assumed it. Not many female thieves, are there?" He rejoined defensively.

"I would not know. But I am surprised to hear you claim you had nothing to do with the attempted theft of Queen Eliza's emerald broach." Isaac snapped.

"Are you mad?" Dean sneered at him. "That broach is not even part of the exhibit."

"How could you know that?" Walter pounced. "The display is not even open."

"Why," Dean floundered briefly. "That confounded broach was stolen years ago. I thought everybody knew that." He glared at Isaac. "And I had nothing to do with it!"

Isaac had known about the theft. The broach in question was 'lifted' from a similar display some years ago. Nobody was certain when, because the theft went unnoticed until an expert came to clean them and decried the item for the fake that it was. It seemed to indicate a pattern that matched tonight's events beautifully.

"But why did you hire these troupers to steal the medallion?" Isaac persisted, hoping to goad him into making a mistake.

"The amulet." Dean froze.

"What was that?" Walter asked sharply.

"I called the item a medallion," Isaac supplied helpfully. "He correctly termed it an amulet."

"With her amulet of power, she commands the lightning carriers." Gallica quoted the riddle. Nobody looked at her, though. They were all watching Lord Dean sweat.

"Stop spouting nonsense."

"It is not nonsense," Gallica retorted. "We found that riddle the same way you did, hidden behind Alfonse the Great's self-portrait." She began slowly closing the gap between herself and Lord Dean. "But we did it in the curator's office and with the approval of our king. Your hired thugs found it in an abandoned chamber at the edge of the medical maze. They were in such a hurry," she leaned down so that her eyes were level with his, "that they damaged the leather backing."

Lord Dean wanted desperately to reach for a handkerchief with which to mop his brow, but he was still trying to bluff his way out of the mess he was in. Confound that double-crossing trouper!

"Which am I being accused of?" He snorted in her face. "Vandalizing a miserable painting or attempting to steal a Sky Fairy artifact?"

"Both." Cassidy was done with the subtle

approach. "We found an exact copy of the amulet hidden in a utility closet near the display." She produced something from her pocket, let it dangle from her fingers on the cheap, gilded chain they found with the copy. "I cannot imagine why you wanted this old thing." And it was obvious that he wanted it. A positively greedy glow lit up Lord Dean's face as he devoured the amulet with his eyes. "It is not even that pretty."

"Pretty!" Dean cried, coming to his feet. That was more than he could take. "You think I wanted it for its looks? You clowns. All of you!" He glared around the room, fearlessly making eye contact with each of them. "I have been hunting for that for half of my life! I followed clue after clue. I solved all of the riddles that led me here. And now you have robbed me of my prize!" His fingers reached for it, but he remained where he was. "You call that item an amulet. You treat it like a bauble, ignorant of its true purpose. Of the power it contains!"

"Power? What power?" Walter's tone was appropriately disdainful. It worked.

"The power to control lightning!" Dean roared. He was in a frenzy now. "The power to call it forth the way it did when Lady Edith used it to vanquish the ants attacking her tribe. It is the ultimate weapon!"

Cassidy thought she was going to be physically ill. What a fool he was. What an ignorant, power-hungry fool.

"And you, Lord Dean Boyer," Walter folded his arms across his chest, "wanted to have that weapon. Why? Against whom were you going to wield it?"

Dean came back to himself then. Dazed, he stared at King Walter without answering. As the full realization of what he had just done sank in, he shrank back, finally collapsing into his chair, where he sat moaning pitifully.

"Lord Dean Boyer, I declare you an enemy of Fairydom." Walter ignored the gasps of the others in the room. This went beyond the theft of valuable artifacts, though they would probably find quite a few when they searched Boyer's estate in the coming spring. "You are hereby stripped of your title. You will live out the remainder of your days in seclusion and within the confines of your estate—after we have removed any and all items you cannot prove you have legally acquired." The moans of the now frail-looking man before him increased. "And upon your death, your estate will be given to your nearest relative upon swearing an oath of fealty to the tribe." Walter hoped that, someday, Dean would take comfort in knowing that his family was not to be punished as well. At the moment, he seemed wholly engaged in bewailing his failure.

"Stuart." Walter turned away from the pitiful scene before him. "Instruct the guard to return Boyer to his chambers and to keep him there the rest of the season."

"Yes, sir."

Walter next looked at Cassidy. He had not recognized her at first. The brown hair was a little easier for him to look at, though. As soon as the guard had escorted Boyer from the room, Walter spoke to her.

"May I see it, please?"

Cassidy hesitated.

"I assume you have the real amulet." Walter smiled tiredly. "That is what you were doing while Isaac distracted the curator, is it not? Exchanging the fake for the genuine article?"

Cassidy blushed and nodded. She had also switched the chains, thinking that it might delay the discovery of the substitution.

"The item is Water Fairy in origin," Isaac stated simply. "And *Lady* Cassidy is an officer of her tribe." His eyes told his father that he would have more to say on that later.

"I see." Walter shamelessly scrubbed one hand over his tired eyes. "So Boyer was right."

Cassidy understood the assumption King Walter had to make. The Water Fairy Tribe now not only possessed the ability to exterminate the surface tribes by withholding water from them, they could also obliterate them at will by throwing lightning bolts at them. Except he was not in possession of all the facts. Nor was Cassidy at liberty to explain. Lightning was the most closely guarded of all Water Fairy secrets.

With all of her might, Cassidy threw the amulet against the closest wall. Old and relatively fragile, it broke on impact. Dozens of pieces went their dozen ways, ultimately landing on the floor.

"You could always make another one." Walter hated what he was doing, but what choice did he have?

"The scientist who designed that dial was experimenting without the knowledge or approval of the governing bodies," Cassidy informed them. "When they discovered it, after Edith stole the dial and used it to destroy the invading ants," she felt quite charitable for remembering that Edith at least had used the dial for defensive purposes, "the experiment, along with all of the papers and research connected with it, was destroyed." She shrugged. "No one now lives who could have used that dial."

They all waited expectantly while Walter looked back and forth between Cassidy and the shattered artifact.

"Very well." Walter nodded. "But I want those remnants burned."

Cassidy promptly flew to the fireplace, took up the ash broom and pan, and swept up the remnants. She poured the pan's contents into the briskly burning fire herself.

"Thank you."

There was a collective resumption of breathing after Walter spoke those words.

Suddenly Fiona laughed. "Well, that was exciting."

Walter slipped his arm about her waist. "Still sorry we had to leave the play early?"

"No, and I was not really sorry when we left," she told him, smiling conspiratorially. "I just put up a fuss so that everyone would know we were not just walking out."

They all laughed then, the tension rolling off them and leaving them feeling refreshed.

"I am starving!" Gallica announced.

"Did you miss supper, too?" Fiona asked, eyes wide.

"Yes! We got started talking about that riddle while we were at the surgery for Isaac's injection and have not stopped for love nor money since."

They laughed again at her colorful phrasing and pained expression.

"I wish that all problems were this easily resolved," Walter said. Offering his arm to his wife, he smiled a smile that took them all in. "Follow me to the kitchens!"

"Last one is a rotten egg!" Gallica declared and zipped out the door.

Stuart, caught again by surprise, grinned and took off after her. "Obsessed with food, I see!" he called after her.

Fiona gently propelled Walter through the door as well and closed it behind them.

Cassidy, still standing by the fire, leaned against the warm bricks. When Isaac's arms slipped about her waist, she stayed where she was.

"You handled that beautifully," he complimented her. The seconds passed in silence until he decided to try again. "Cassidy?" He stepped around in front of her. "Thank you for what you did."

She looked up from where she had been watching the fire devour the last of the dial.

"You should not have fallen in love with me." Her tone was as flat as her mood. "We can no more be together, you and I, than I could have let that dial fall into the wrong hands."

"But I thought you said no one could use that dial anymore."

"I did. And I told the truth." She pulled away from him, walked to the far side of his father's desk. She was letting her emotions get the better of her again. "It was all of the things that I *cannot* tell you that made up my mind for me."

Of a necessity, she avoided any declarations regarding her feelings for him. Telling him she loved him would only make things worse. And she did love him. That was what made this conversation so vital. How could she love someone she was unable to speak freely with? That she had to be constantly on guard with, lest she reveal something she should not? The penalty for revealing the secrets she carried were too severe to risk. The life of every fairy on the surface could be said to lie in her hands. She simply could not put herself before them. Perhaps someday, if her tribe agreed to restore communications…

Angrily, she pushed a brown curl out of her face. "I will operate on your tribesfairies. I will repair wings and heal what I can. But you should know right now that I will be leaving in the spring."

Her ultimatum delivered, she spun on her heel and rushed out into the corridor. She stopped when she saw the guard.

"Please send for Rosie, the nurse," she ordered. "Prince Isaac is in pain and needs her at once." *Do the surface tribes have a pain-relieving potion for a broken heart?* she wondered. If they did, she wanted some, too. Somehow, she made it from the king's offices back to the medical maze, retracing her steps back to the chamber of vendors and then finding her way through the tunnels to the closed door. She went in without knocking.

"About time you got back," Agnes declared. "Your food is probably cold by now."

"I am not hungry, thank you." Brushing past her, Cassidy was on her way to her bedroom when Daphne popped out of the surgery.

"What do you think?" Daphne asked eagerly, spinning around so her shoulder-length *brown* hair was easily visible.

Cassidy gaped at her, truly stunned. She had not given Daphne approval to color her hair. Agnes had been adamant that she was happy with her hair the way it was, but Cassidy specifically told Daphne to wait until…

Cassidy began to laugh. "You," she gasped at Daphne. "Your hair looks fine." Wiping away the tears, Cassidy leaned against the wall behind her. "But your eyebrows are still pink!"

"Oh, yes." Daphne turned and wiggled her eyebrows at her reflection in one of the mirrored cupboards. The books Gallica had been providing her with only made her more anxious to venture beyond their assigned rooms and this was the only way she knew how to do it. "I ran out of coloring!"

That did it. They were all laughing now. Cassidy, her appetite restored through humor, sat down to eat supper with Agnes and Daphne.

"We will have to ask Rosie to bring more coloring as soon as she possibly can," Cassidy smiled as she helped herself to the mashed potatoes. Her mind promptly detoured back to the king's office. Had Rosie reached there yet?

Unbeknownst to Cassidy, the guard she sent for Rosie knew Weetu in and out, so his trip took far less time than Cassidy's wandering route. Rosie was not only with Isaac by then, she was scolding him.

"As if I had nothing better to do than rush the length of Weetu because someone," Rosie glared at him over the top of the mug of plain water she was busily stirring a vial of potion concentrate into, "chose to skip his afternoon dose. My word, what do you think I am?"

Isaac listened to her fussing without attempting to interrupt. His heart was badly wrenched from what Cassidy said, and that hurt far worse than any overexertion.

"You have to work up to walking again." Rosie banged the spoon down, denting the silver serving tray. "Your muscles have had months to atrophy and if you wear yourself out, you could fall or trip and undo all of the good Cassidy's decoction has done." He finally looked up and she stopped talking. Offering the mug to him, she watched as he took a sip, grimaced, and drank it down.

"Delicious." He handed the mug back to her. "Thank you so much for coming." After a heartbeat passed, he added gently, "I hope you know we do not take you, or any of your excellent medical staff, for granted."

Rosie, sensing that she was no longer needed—or wanted—bobbed an ungraceful curtsy and took herself off, closing the door behind her.

Settling back in his wheelchair, Isaac considered the fire that was still burning briskly in the office fireplace, providing warmth and cheer. Outside, he knew, the ice lay thick on the bark of the old sugar maple; last spring's leaves lay moldering under snowdrifts that would last well past the first spring venture; and somewhere beneath the glassy sea lay the source of Cassidy's unease. She had not rejected him; he vividly recalled her every word and she never once implied that her decision was due to any defect on his part. So. Resting his elbows on the arms of his chair, he folded his hands and rested them against his chin. There were months between now and spring, months that he planned to spend befriending with Cassidy. Then, when the ice melted and the skies opened again for travel, they would see who would go—and who would stay.

Chapter 1

Cassidy hissed in pain and snatched a tissue off her desk. Deftly, she wrapped it around her papercut before she got blood on Bert's medical file.

"Will you need stitches for that?" Agnes asked teasingly from where she was mending a tear in the sleeve of her nightgown.

"Probably not." Cassidy smiled at her old friend. "Just needs some pressure to stop the bleeding."

"You'd better let me take a look," Agnes insisted, weaving her needle partway into the fabric and setting the garment aside. A quick flit of her wings brought her to Cassidy's side, where she gently appropriated the damaged hand. Peeking under the tissue, she nodded. "Oh, that's not too bad."

"See?" Cassidy didn't really mind Agnes' fussing. Her assisting nurses, Agnes and Daphne, were the only other Water Fairies in the whole city of Weetu, the Wood Fairy capitol. It hadn't seemed important while they packed to leave their home in Noddfa, but now she could honestly say that the prospect of spending the entire winter 'safely' inside this maple tree without them was dreadful.

"Still, you might want to wrap it while you're changing for this evening," Agnes suggested, setting the hand on the desk. "And you should probably do that soon."

"Change?" Her finger forgotten, Cassidy looked down at her outfit. While the matching gray waistcoat and skirt weren't glamorous or anything, at least they toned down her shrieking yellow long-sleeved shirt a little bit. She ought to be wearing a minimum of three vibrant colors at all times according to Wood Fairy winter custom, but that gave her a headache. "I was planning to wear this outfit."

"To a dress rehearsal? Are you sure?" Agnes frowned. "You don't want to stand out." They'd gone to great lengths to avoid that, even coloring their pink hair and wing points in an effort to blend in. Daphne, the youngest member of the Water Fairy medical party, saw the whole thing as an adventure. Thankfully by now no one in Weetu was as tan as they would have liked, so Cassidy and her nurses, fair-skinned from lifetimes beyond the reach of the sun, were able to blend in much better than they had at first.

Of course, it really wasn't much of a sacrifice compared to what would happen should the treaty between their underwater tribe and the surface tribes be broken. If the secret of her tribe's existence became common knowledge, everyone on the surface would be fatally affected. Not for the first time, Cassidy questioned her choice to come to Weetu and operate on Prince

Isaac, who'd been partially paralyzed in a battle with some pirates.

"I don't think that's what *dress rehearsal* means," she mused aloud, remembering that Agnes was waiting for her to respond. "Just in case, though, I'll wear my toffee-colored gown with the crimson sash," she compromised.

"You wore that four days ago at the banquet." Agnes calmly resumed her mending.

"My other gowns are out being laundered." Cassidy frowned, annoyed. Her borrowed wardrobe only had so many choices and she'd been avoiding some of them for good reason.

"Not all of them." Agnes continued innocently sewing up the tear with precision stitches.

Cassidy folded her arms across her chest. "I am not wearing that dress." She tossed her hair, irritated further when her *brown* curls bounced around her face. "I refuse to go around Weetu looking like a coral reef."

Agnes bit her lips to keep from laughing. "Don't be ridiculous," Agnes scoffed when she'd gotten hold of herself. "Anyway," she nodded at the water clock resting on the shelf behind Cassidy. "You'll barely have time to change as it is."

Cassidy twisted in her chair to look at the primitive time-keeping device. Less ornate than most, it consisted simply of two reservoirs and a float. One reservoir emptied into the other at a carefully calibrated rate, causing the float in the second reservoir to rise. She had to squint a little to make out the times marked on the float.

"Oh no!" Springing to her feet, Cassidy flew into her bedroom, closing the door behind her. Laughing at her situation, she unfastened her skirt and let it drop to the floor while she unbuttoned her waistcoat on her way to the closet. One outfit lay strategically strewn about the room by the time she'd finished changing into the other, which was how it was going to have to stay until she got back.

"Don't forget your case!" Agnes flagged her down as she zipped towards the outer door of their quarters.

"I'm not expecting a medical emergency..." Cassidy started to protest, then shook her head. By definition, one never expected an *emergency*. Returning to her room, she took the slim leather pouch from her top drawer and tucked it into her waistband under her left arm. "Don't wait supper for me. I promised to eat with Isaac after the rehearsal."

"Again?" Agnes frowned as the outer door closed behind Cassidy. They'd talked a little about the futility of the romance begging to happen between Cassidy and the prince. Cassidy could no more stay on the surface than Isaac could join her beneath it. But they were both young and Cassidy in particular was inexperienced in such matters. A brilliant scientist and dedicated doctor, she'd followed in her widowed father's footsteps, to and from the laboratory, until his path had nearly become her own.   Shaking her head doubtfully, Agnes finished the last couple of stitches and tied of her thread.

Cassidy, meanwhile, was winging her way towards the main theater.   Two amateur productions were taking place in the other performance halls, which were kept nearly constantly in use by Weetu's captive population, but tonight's dress rehearsal was open to invited guests only.   She smiled and did her best to ignore the looks she was attracting in the awful gown.   Fortunately for her, she happened to know the playwright personally.

"There you are!" Prince Isaac stopped pacing in front of the theater entrance and stared, transfixed.   Her cherry-pink gown accentuated the lovely color in her cheeks.   She shook her head to clear the curls out of her face and he noted the graceful curve of her neck, as white as a swan feather. He couldn't imagine a life beyond the reach of the sun, yet as he looked at her, he found himself tempted. "I," he swallowed, "was starting to think you weren't going to make it." Thank goodness she was wearing her glasses or he might never have recovered. Her spectacles served only one purpose—that of hiding her mesmerizing hazel-green eyes, the likes of which could not be found among any of the four surface tribes.

"I almost didn't," she admitted with a laugh. "If Agnes hadn't reminded me to change, I would probably still be at my desk, studying Bert's file." Silently, she marveled at how easily he'd been moving only moments before. Thanks to sophisticated Water Fairy medical equipment, and the astonishing healing powers of the local potions, Isaac had recovered in record time. His severed right forewing was another matter entirely.

He laughed with her, then cleared his throat. "Where would you like to sit?" Leading her inside, he surveyed the rows of empty seats as if it was a packed opening night.

"Over there, perhaps?" Cassidy played along, indicating the row nearest their friend and burgeoning playwright, Bert. She'd grown accustomed to Isaac's dry humor by now, but she still felt sorry for Bert, who was signaling frantically at them. Like Isaac, he'd been wounded during the battle against the pirates that recently plagued Fairydom's four surface tribes. The amputation of Bert's leg, however, was something she could not repair.

"Hmm. Do you really think that would be wise?" Isaac frowned mischievously. His heart twisted painfully when he saw Cassidy smile at Bert—or any other man, for that matter—even though he knew she was just being friendly. Winter was half over and she would be returning to the Water Fairy Tribe in the spring. Which was why he was spending every available moment with her. "He looks quite the type to talk through the entire play," he joked. Two short months ago, when Isaac first met Cassidy, he, like Bert, was dependent upon a wheeled chair.

"No more dawdling," Cassidy admonished him, brushing a brown curl back out of her face. "You know how much this dress rehearsal means to him." She still wasn't quite sure what a 'dress rehearsal' was, just that Bert was fidgety with nerves when he asked them to attend.

Neatly cornered by her compassionate logic, Isaac dropped all pretenses. "Shall we?" He gestured towards Bert.

Bert almost relaxed his ramrod straight posture when he saw that they were finally coming over, but four hundred years of military service made that his natural bearing.

"You cut it awfully close," Bert informed them sternly as they slipped past him to their seats. "Everyone else is already here." By 'everyone else,' he meant Isaac's parents, King Walter and Queen Fiona of the Wood Fairy Tribe. They'd arrived early and their presence was doing nothing to settle Bert's nerves.

"You must forgive me." Cassidy made a point of taking the blame—and the seat nearest Bert, in the hopes of keeping them from spending the entire play swapping friendly insults. Wood Fairy etiquette, such as it was, was very different from the more formal atmosphere that prevailed in the Water Fairy tribe, but she flattered herself that she was getting the hang of it. "I have an important surgery tomorrow and I quite lost track of time when I sat down to review the files after lunch."

Bert smiled sheepishly at her. The reconstructive surgery she spoke of was for his lower left wing, which was shredded by the vile brass needles worn by a pirate who attacked him from behind.

"I can forgive that," Bert agreed. He nodded to the pair of young troupe fairies blowing out the candles that lined the walls of the theater seating area. "I just hope they can." He grinned. "They might even be as nervous as I am!"

The troupers backstage would have laughed if they'd heard him say that. Performing was the lifeblood of their group, one of the primary reasons the king's steward engaged them for a winter of distractions and amusements in the city of Weetu. Sure, things went a little sideways with the discovery that the troupe master, Phil Girard, and his flunky, Dizzy, were involved in a series of jewelry and antiquity thefts. Harry, their new leader, figured the troupe was better off without them. Sure, he had to pull double duty now, playing the tragically sensitive Prince Cambrian of the Sky Fairies as well as keeping track of the props, but things could be worse. And often had been.

Harry, who was busy applying the final touches of makeup to his costume, sensed the eager mood of what he now thought of as his troupe and smiled. This new play, *Winter Delayed*, was not a comedy like their last play, *What's for Supper?*, but he felt it had a lot of potential. The mystery of this winter's late arrival was still a topic of discussion in the restaurants around Weetu, so the audience was guaranteed to be engaged. For a basically true story, it had it all, too. Danger, adventure, romance, combat, and a victorious ending. He shivered. It had taken some serious guts for the Sky Fairies to challenge not only enemy windships but a monster snow cloud, too!

Rising, Harry tugged at the front of his doublet until it was smooth. "Can I have your attention, everyone?" He extended his lightly-tinted wings enough to lift himself to where he could be easily seen. "We all know who's out there, so I'll keep it simple. Remember your lines. Hang onto your wigs." Like most of the rest of them, Harry wore a blue wig that covered his painfully close-cut hair. "And remember that we are not just acting out scenes from an untried playwright. We are spinning dreams of grandeur. We are sharing hopes of feeling the sun's rays again." Making fists of his hands, he held them up, one above another, miming his next words, "We will *wring* tears of envy from the Wranglers that they were not present at this glorious battle with Dame Nature." His voice swelled with excitement.

"Curtain?" called a roustabout anxiously. The theater manager looked like she was about to come raise it herself!

"Curtain!" Harry agreed, back to his normal voice. Looking at the eager group about him, he instructed, "Places everyone!"

Bert almost sighed with relief when the curtain finally began to rise. This was his first dress rehearsal. Ever. He leaned forward to hear the opening line without realizing it.

"Father!" Harry-Prince Cambrian flew in through a 'window' and landed center stage. "The scouts are back. They report that there is not so much as a snowflake between here and the high peaks!"

Partway through the rehearsal, the cast 'took to the skies' aboard a thin windship shell that was supposed to represent the *Wind Sorter* (the now-fabled cloud chaser). A handful of stagehands were assigned to help create 'the illusion of savage winds raging about the windship' by shaking the sails vigorously. It was going well until one of them misjudged the distance between the end of a spar and an actor's head, knocking the poor fellow to his knees.

Bert dropped his face in his hands and muttered something unintelligible.

Cassidy would have rushed up to aid the injured actor if she had not seen someone slip out from the behind the backdrop to do just that.

Isaac was suffering, too, but for different reasons. This entire play was based on the letter of introduction Prince Cambrian sent with Doctor Cassidy. A few paragraphs, really, those deemed suitable for public knowledge. After praising Water Fairy medicine highly, Cambrian's mood had turned grave as he reflected on the dangerous mission other Sky Fairies were undertaking.

Isaac couldn't help spending most of the play gloomily pondering the fate of Fairydom—would there still be a Sky Fairy Tribe in the spring? And if there was, would all of the surface tribes live to see summer? He straightened in his chair in time to hear 'Prince Cambrian' deliver some very dramatic dialogue to the cheering crowd of extras gathered about the windship shell. Judging by the backdrop, which strongly resembled the docks at Regalis, they were returning triumphant and he'd missed most of what had to be a highly imaginative third act.

"Nay, save your praise." Harry flung up his hands and the cast obediently quieted so 'Prince Cambrian' could deliver his lines. "We had old Dame Nature on our side. How then could we fail to restore the balance of the seasons?" Majestically throwing back the protective hood of his weathersuit—almost completely dislodging his blue wig—he led the others from the windship shell to center stage, where they were greeted by a few more dutifully cheering extras from the wings.

Isaac began clapping politely as soon as he saw the curtain begin coming down. He did not have to look behind him to know that his parents were applauding as well. The play would serve its purpose, educating and entertaining the citizens of Weetu without revealing the hidden Water Fairy tribe.

"Well?" Bert asked Isaac eagerly. He fiddled with the brake on his wheeled chair to keep from giving way to anxious anticipation. After a rough and ready life on the wind, working his way up from able-bodied windfairy to captain, he found show business surprisingly terrifying. "Stop clapping and tell me what you really think of it!"

Isaac looked hopefully to Cassidy for an enthusiastic answer, but she was still staring at the curtain wide-eyed. This was only the second theatrical production she had ever attended above the surface of Fairydom's sea, and Isaac knew that she would have questions. They would discuss them later, away from prying ears and eyes, but with no hope of romance.

"I am no theater buff," Isaac complained to Bert. "What do you want me to say?" Waving one hand at the stage, he continued before Bert could respond. "The scenery is excellent. The casting is better than most winter dramas, which is astonishing given that this is the same set of trouper fairies that regaled us with their brilliant rendition of the comedy *What's for Supper?* less than a month ago." Isaac could not help grinning as he remembered the hilarious play; it featured everything from a disastrous mix-up in grocery deliveries to an unexpected supper guest.

"Isaac." After months of working with him in the water pump room, Bert had finally come to terms with addressing Prince Isaac by just his name. "The story. What did you think of the **story**?"

Isaac scratched his jaw contemplatively. "The story is fine," he proclaimed at long last. "I just do not see how you can be comfortable writing an entire play around so few concrete details!" He twisted around so he could look Bert in the face. "We cannot even be sure their plan worked."

Bert laughed aloud. "My friend, you have no understanding of storytelling. The story may be only one quarter truth and three quarters imagination. What matters is that the audience enjoys it!" He held up a finger to emphasize his next point. "And in mid-winter, the audience will enjoy almost anything." He waved away their chuckles. "You know that I am right. In two short months it will be spring and things will be different. When it is warm enough, the citizens of Weetu will pour out of this sugar maple's reopened doors and dare anybody to make them go back inside. For now, they are living from diversion to diversion. Why, I daresay that most of them have already lost a sense of which meal is which."

"Is that why you spent so much time portraying the dangers of the snowstorm?" Cassidy frowned, shivering in sympathy with the brave fairies who risked so much. Thoughts of the dangers of winter only added to her yearning to be back in her underwater city.

"Exactly!" Bert beamed at her. "Not even the Sky Fairies, with their skill for manipulating the weather, can tolerate the winter conditions that rage over the surface of Fairydom four months of the year. And building up the suspense will greatly increase the audience's delight when our heroes arrive safely at home."

Cassidy nodded and sat back. It was hard not to correct him, even though she barely knew more than he did. Her cousin, Kuntza, wrote a little of the situation above the surface in the same letter he sent asking her to leave her beloved home and spend the winter healing at Weetu. Those brave windfairies depicted in the play had not made it home; not *yet*. Each surviving storm chaser crew had scurried off to a separate village high in their mountains, where they hoped to find sanctuary for the deadly winter months. Then, if the *monster* snowstorm hadn't obliterated the Sky Fairy tribal territories as they knew them, destroying even their storied mountain fortresses, they would return home in the spring.

"Bert." Isaac folded his arms across his chest. "Why do they talk like that?"

"Like what?"

"Like…" Isaac nodded at the stage. "Like that last speech. 'We had old Dame Nature on our side.'" He cocked an eyebrow in Bert's direction. "I have never heard anybody talk like that."

"Not even in a play?" Bert grinned.

Isaac tried to keep a straight face, but in the end he yielded to the answering smile tugging at the corners of his mouth.

"It is an old artistic tradition," Bert explained, feigning loftiness. "Besides. Prince Cambrian is a poet and will not mind my taking a little artistic license with such a wonderful story."

Isaac certainly hoped someone else would have the dubious pleasure of informing Prince Cambrian that he was Fairydom's latest hero as far as Bert's play, *Winter Delayed*, was concerned.

"Thank you so much for inviting us." Cassidy, sensing a somber mood building in Isaac, smiled at Bert. "It really was a fascinating experience."

"You're not leaving?" Bert protested as they rose. "The evening has only just begun! I must go over costume details; remind half of the cast that they should never, ever get between the others and the audience… Not to mention what happened with that falling spar." His nose wrinkled in disgust. As if a Sky Fairy windship spar would just come loose like that!

"Bert, I promise." Isaac clapped his friend on the shoulder. "We will not mention it."

"No, not a word." Cassidy pressed a finger to her lips. "Of course, we probably will not be able to help discussing the play a little over supper." She nudged Isaac's arm with one elbow in Wood Fairy fashion and he naturally slipped that arm about her. Because they were in public, she permitted it as a friendly gesture. Since her blunt declaration that she would be returning home in the spring—whether he loved her or not—Isaac had graciously assumed the role of chum instead.

"But no details." Isaac put his free hand on his heart as if making a pledge. "They will just have to wait and watch *Winter Delayed* for themselves." He winked knowingly at Bert. The theater would be stuffed with eager fairies on opening night the way that a jar was stuffed with pickles, regardless of whether or not Isaac and Cassidy began a whisper campaign. Nevertheless, he could tell that it made Bert feel good to think of hundreds of fairies all around Weetu discussing his play.

"Alright, you two lovebirds." Bert did his best to hide his surprise at the way they hastily drew apart. He thought they were perfect for each other. "Just be sure he takes you home early." He grinned up at Cassidy from his wheeled chair.

Cassidy smiled warmly at him. "And you be sure that you arrive a little early tomorrow morning. Agnes will need some time to prepare you for the procedure."

Bert cheerfully saluted, then released his chair brake. "Now get lost, you two. This is my chance to talk to the king and queen!" Expertly he gripped the right wheel and forced the left forward, spinning his wheeled chair about in a perfect half circle.

Learn more about the author at
leacarterwrites.wixsite.com/wholesomefantasy